ALL
MY
BONES

Also by P. J. Nelson

Booked for Murder

ALL MY BONES

An Old Juniper Bookshop Mystery

P. J. NELSON

MINOTAUR BOOKS
NEW YORK

This is a work of fiction. All of the characters, organizations, and events portrayed in this novel are either products of the author's imagination or are used fictitiously.

First published in the United States by Minotaur Books, an imprint of St. Martin's Publishing Group

EU Representative: Macmillan Publishers Ireland Ltd, 1st Floor, The Liffey Trust Centre, 117–126 Sheriff Street Upper, Dublin 1, DO1 YC43

ALL MY BONES. Copyright © 2025 by P. J. Nelson. All rights reserved. Printed in the United States of America. For information, address St. Martin's Publishing Group, 120 Broadway, New York, NY 10271.

www.minotaurbooks.com

Designed by Meryl Sussman Levavi

The Library of Congress Cataloging-in-Publication Data is available upon request.

ISBN 978-1-250-90997-8 (hardcover)
ISBN 978-1-250-90998-5 (ebook)

The publisher of this book does not authorize the use or reproduction of any part of this book in any manner for the purpose of training artificial intelligence technologies or systems. The publisher of this book expressly reserves this book from the Text and Data Mining exception in accordance with Article 4(3) of the European Union Digital Single Market Directive 2019/790.

Our books may be purchased in bulk for specialty retail/wholesale, literacy, corporate/premium, educational, and subscription box use. Please contact MacmillanSpecialMarkets@macmillan.com.

First Edition: 2025

10 9 8 7 6 5 4 3 2 1

Always for LNN

My sister Marlene gathered all my bones,
tied them in a silken scarf,
laid them beneath the juniper tree.
—"The Juniper Tree," *Grimm's Fairy Tales* (1812)

ALL
MY
BONES

1

APRIL, DESPITE WHAT T. S. Eliot may have told you, is not the cruelest month, at least not in Enigma, Georgia. Azaleas are everywhere, evening skies are Parrish blue, and on the first day of that month in our little town, everyone is a fool.

I'd been back home in Enigma for nearly six months. Settled in nicely, running the Old Juniper Bookshop left to me by my aunt Rose, I was just beginning to feel at home. And why not? The shop was doing remarkably well for a place that sold books. A small group of students from the local college thought of me as some sort of weird guru. And a certain David Madison, gardener extraordinaire, had asked me to dinner a full seven times. Which was seven more times than anyone in Atlanta had asked me out during the last six months I'd lived there.

My aunt, who was not my aunt, Dr. Philomena Waldrop, head of the psychology department at the aforementioned Barnsley College, had, at last, gotten out of Whispering Pines, a very private psychiatric care facility hidden away on Sapelo Island. And while she understood what a cliché it was for a psychiatrist to need a stay in a looney bin—her phrase, not mine—she wore it well. She seemed to be on a much more even keel than she had been six months before when she'd set fire to the gazebo behind the bookshop.

In short, all was well in my blue heaven. Or so I thought.

It was Sunday morning, the quietest day of my week. I slept in, then I waded out of my dreams, down my stairs, and into my kitchen. I took my coffee, French press and all, to the lovely new gazebo that David Madison had rebuilt. I watched a rabbit nibble my parsley and was glad to share it with her. And by the time my cup was empty, there was Gloria Coleman, the feistiest Episcopal priest in the Southeast, rounding the corner of the house and headed my way.

"You can get yourself out of bed and into that gazebo but you can't make it to a ten o'clock Mass?" she called out.

"I can't come to your church in my pajamas," I said, "whereas the gazebo doesn't seem to care."

I lifted the French press in her direction, and she nodded. I poured her a cup.

"You missed a really, *really* good sermon," she told me, taking the cup and sitting right next to me.

Gloria was a surreal bit of adventure even when she was sitting still. She looked more like a stevedore than a priest; the purple shirt and clerical collar did nothing to belie that impression.

"It was my April Fools' sermon," she went on. "I read from the 1631 pressing of the King James in which the printer accidentally left out the word *not* in a certain commandment. It tells everyone, 'Thou *shalt* commit adultery.' Which was a big hit with the congregation in general."

I smiled and sat back. "I'll bet. Although most of the college boys who patronize my little shop don't really need that kind of encouragement."

She shrugged. "Small town. What else is there to do?"

"Drink cheap beer, watch high school football, shoot rats at the county dump." I refilled my cup.

"Those aren't really acceptable substitutes for sex, though, are they?" She sipped.

My eyebrows arched. "If memory serves."

She was not in a commiserating mood. "Cry me a river. I'm a *priest*."

"You're an *Episcopal* priest," I said. "You're *supposed* to have sex. It's in the Anglican rule book."

She set her cup down for emphasis. "Let me start over. I'm a *female* Episcopal priest in a small town in South Georgia. I couldn't get a date if I had a shotgun and an arrest warrant."

"Maybe you're looking for the wrong kind of dates," I said, "if you think you're going to need firearms and a legal paper."

"And besides," she went on, "you've got David. Everybody in town knows you went to dinner with him at that fancy place up in Tifton."

"Okay, yes, we've had a few dinners and some great . . . conversation."

"Ah." She picked up her cup again and drank. "Conversation."

"Still," I said with a sigh, "hope springs eternal."

"What about that tall fireman?" Gloria teased. "The one that put out the fire in your gazebo."

"Captain Jordon." I smiled. "He's called a couple of times. But David is so . . ."

"The thing you have to know about David is that he moves slowly and carefully," she said, and her voice was quieter than it had been. "He thinks in terms of growing seasons, not days or weeks. How long did it take for him to build this gazebo? Four months? But just look at it. Look how solid it is, right?"

I stared up at the exquisite ceiling, ornate without being precious, delicate and strong at the same time.

"Maybe that's the kind of relationship he's building with you," she continued, apparently reading my mind.

"Wouldn't that be nice," I mused, staring into my coffee.

She looked around the garden. It was something to see. The daffodils were nearly done, but the flowering quince and double-blooming azaleas around the borders of the garden were filled with pink and peach. The phlox carpet around the gazebo was rich purple, and the Johnny-jump-ups were still hanging on. Parsley and sage and tarragon filled the herb garden.

Between the hedge and the back door of the house, I would eventually plant the first of the kitchen garden, the three sisters: squash, corn, and beans. And too many tomato plants, not enough red peppers, and, later, way too much okra.

"I'm thinking of trying tomatillos this year," I said idly.

"You should do something about the front of the house," Gloria said instantly. "This looks great back here, but the front of the place looks abandoned."

She was right. I had neglected the front yard, as had my aunt Rose before me. Her idea was that people wouldn't take the bookshop seriously if it looked too nice, too *Better Homes & Gardens*. People would think, she'd told me long ago, that the house was some kind of frou-frou boutique instead of the serious literary institution that it actually was. And I had followed suit. Grass neglected, shrubbery dead, gravel from the driveway spewed everywhere, it did look a little like an abandoned house. Owned by the Addams Family.

The house itself was a proud Victorian remnant of the town's former glory as a leading producer of turpentine in Georgia. Turpentine money had built the town, and then abandoned it, leaving a few lonely, hulking houses like mine which the town regarded as embarrassing memories of its lost Eden. An Eden that never really existed. I'd managed to get it painted, restored to its former declaration of wealth and taste. But the yard was still a symbol of what had happened to the town after the Depression. Hobo weeds and rock-hard dirt, it was a perennially winter landscape refusing to ever acknowledge that Easter had happened, that spring was abroad in the land.

So I said to Gloria, "You're right."

And I stood up so suddenly that it startled her.

"I'm going to that big garden center in Tifton," I went on.

"Now?"

"No, not now," I admonished. "What kind of heathen business would be open on Sunday around here?"

"Well," she assured me, "*my* place of business was open . . ."

"Okay." I ignored her. "I'm going to buy a dozen red azaleas, four flats of impatiens, and some variegated monkey grass. At least."

She shook her head. "Isn't that a little pedestrian for a place as unusual as the Old Juniper Bookshop? Don't you need, like, lupins and climbing jasmine or . . . wait! Get roses."

"Well, of course."

Aunt Rose had actually bred her own hybrid when she'd first retired from New York theatre and moved back to Enigma. She called it "Ophelia's Last Laugh" and she was uncommonly proud of its unique regal color, which she insisted she'd taken from Gertrude's speech about Ophelia's drowning: the long purple of "dead men's fingers." But the small-minded American Society of We Get to Reject Your Rose's Name, or whatever it was called, wouldn't go for it, so she pulled them all up, cut them all down, and had rosewood footstools made for the various chairs and sofas in the shop. Seemed like an overreaction but Rose was nothing if not theatrical.

Still, a dozen or so Knock Out rosebushes along the front of the porch seemed like the perfect starting place for my new, improved front yard.

"You know you're going to need a backhoe or something on that ground out there," Gloria warned me. "Or a pile driver. Maybe a couple of sticks of dynamite."

"It's hard," I agreed, "but smashing into the stubborn clay of my homeland is a perfect way for me to get out my frustrations."

"What have you got to be frustrated about?" she asked me.

"Did I forget to mention that the only activity between David and me so far is *conversation*?"

She nodded. "Right. Hang on."

She took off her clerical collar and unbuttoned the top of her purple shirt.

"What are you doing?" I asked her as she stepped out of the gazebo.

"I'm helping you," she snapped. "Or did I forget to mention the whole priest-in-a-small-town motif running through my own personal frustration?"

"Got it," I affirmed. "I'll get you some gloves."

Not twenty minutes later we were both out in front of my house, I with my pickax, she wielding a shovel. I'd changed into my cute green overalls and given Gloria an extra-large denim work shirt to wear. She was standing on the footholds of the shovel, balanced perfectly, rocking, trying to coax it into the impenetrable ground. I bashed the pick down over and over again, screaming like a Viking, with no discernible effect. That went on for almost an hour.

"Why are we doing this, again?" Gloria asked, sweating.

"Because it's spring!" I said, pretending that anger was the same as determination.

She nodded. "Okay. Let's switch tools."

I took the shovel and began to skim across the surface of the land, shaving it one thin layer at a time rather than breaking it. After a while I stood back and Gloria smacked down the pick in the same place. The old shave-and-smack method.

Miraculously, or ridiculously, it began to work. Loose rocks and heavy clay gave way, eventually, to something like actual dirt.

Gloria stared down at it. "Now you need some peat moss and some compost. Mix it in with all this crap."

"Agreed." I knelt. "Let me just see a little bit more of what's under the surface. It gets better as you go down, doesn't it?"

I pulled my big trowel out of my back pocket and began to move things around right next to the front steps. Rocks and dirt and clay went flying.

Then I hit something severely hard a little deeper down. I figured it to be another rock, maybe a larger one. I could see that it was vaguely white and fairly round, and my trowel was no match for it.

I stood and held out my hand. "Shovel, please."

Gloria handed it over.

I wedged the pointy blade of the shovel between the rock and the loosened ground and leaned in with all my weight. The ground complained and the rock broke.

"Should I use the pickax?" I asked Gloria.

She stood over the spot and stared down. "You seem to be making headway here. I say keep going with the shovel. Try to pry that white rock out."

I nodded and stood down hard on the shovel with both

feet. The ground shifted, the rock moved, the shovel flew away, and I fell backward onto the ground.

Instead of the laughter I expected to hear from Gloria, she gasped—worse than gasped. It was a tearing noise, a warning from a horror film, a sound a priest shouldn't make.

"Gloria?" I asked, still on the ground.

She stared, wide-eyed. That was her only response.

I got to my feet and went to see what had caused such a garrulous woman to be struck so dumb. And there it was, from *Hamlet*, act 5, scene 1: Yorick. Not a rock at all.

It was a human skull.

IT took Billy Sanders exactly eleven minutes to get to the house, and when he did, it was with his siren screaming. He bolted out of the car, face red, eyes wide. He had decided last Christmastime that he was going to run for sheriff, so it was possible that he was trying to impress everyone. But it was more likely that a dead body buried in someone's front yard was impetus enough. Especially since my house had been the scene of a fairly gruesome murder only six months before.

The fact that I had been Billy's babysitter when he was eight and I was in high school only made the moment more surreal.

He moved quickly for a boy his size and came to a frozen halt at the front steps, staring down at the treasure Gloria and I had dug up.

"Well." He sniffed. "That's a human skull all right."

Gloria laughed. Partly because it was such an idiotic thing to say, partly because she was a little unhinged by the situation. As was I.

"Who is it?" Billy went on.

"Amelia Earhart," Gloria said instantly.

"Oh." Billy looked up, and said softly, with a straight face, "Another mystery solved, then."

Because, despite appearances, Billy Sanders wasn't a complete idiot.

Gloria was staring down at the skull. "This had to happen at night."

Billy looked at her, then at the ground. "Uh-huh."

"Because," Gloria went on, "it had to take a while to dig this ground and then to . . . I mean, wouldn't someone have noticed?"

"Well, we are at the end of the road," I said, "and the road mostly has abandoned buildings on it until you get into the center of town. And don't forget there was a period of time when the shop was closed. Rose was in the hospital and I wasn't in town yet."

Billy nodded. "At night, weeknight, shop closed—I believe you're right. Both of you. Who would have seen this?"

Further banter of that ilk was prevented by the arrival of a pickup truck from Weller's Funeral Parlor. Two men in denim jumpsuits got out, one with a pick, the other with a shovel, and lumbered over to where the rest of us were standing.

"Shouldn't we have some kind of crime scene team here?" I ventured.

"Tad and Allie are certified," Billy said absently. "And the guys from Tifton won't be here until later this afternoon."

"Guys from Tifton?" I asked.

"Crime scene investigators," he snapped. "Like you said. Damn."

It was the testiest reaction I'd ever heard from Billy. He was clearly more on edge than he looked.

Tad and Allie went to work, starting three feet away from the skull, breaking up the ground in a surprisingly careful, almost gentle way.

"More coffee," Gloria muttered, and headed into the house.

"Right, sorry," I agreed. "Billy? You want coffee?"

He blew out his breath. "Yeah."

I stepped up onto the porch. "You know, Philomena was supposed to come over here for lunch."

Billy nodded. "I knew she was getting out this weekend. You didn't go pick her up?"

"She didn't want me to."

"Embarrassed," he assumed.

"She said she didn't want to bother me," I told him, headed into the house.

"She's still not sure you forgive her for . . . you know."

Dr. Waldrop, my aunt Rose's closest friend and life companion, had been so upset that Rose's will left the bookshop to me that she'd burned down the gazebo behind the house moments after I'd arrived to claim my inheritance. It had taken me a while to forgive her, but I had, eventually, and it was a clue to her weather-beaten personality that she was still worried about my feelings. The incident had also convinced her that she needed to check herself into a care facility, as she had at other difficult moments in her life. And still, she was more concerned with my feelings than anything else. So how could I help loving her?

"I forgave her six months ago." I sighed. "When I made her an equal partner in this bookshop, I told her I did it because I was keeping it in the family."

"Because she *is* family," he said, following me into the house.

"My point is," I said, heading for the kitchen, "maybe I

should call her and tell her that now's not a good time for a visit."

"I understand what you mean," he said, "but maybe this is just the kind of thing she needs."

I stopped and turned. "What?"

"This gives her a chance to feel like she's helping you," he said softly. "Like she's comforting you or protecting you. She's that kind of person; it makes her feel better when she's helping somebody else. You know?"

I considered what he said. "You're wasted in the police department. You should be a therapist."

"Or a priest!" Gloria called from the kitchen.

Billy couldn't help smiling. "We already got a funny priest in town, and Dr. Waldrop is the best therapist in the state, but I'm not a bad policeman. I like to stay in my own lane."

"Well, this particular police matter," I began, glancing toward my front porch, "is going to take quite a bit of police work, don't you think? I mean, for one thing this is the second dead body we've had in this house—just in the past six months. There's got to be something to that, right?"

"Yeah," he said, looking around the bookshop. "What is this place, anyway? The kiss of death bookstore?"

"You should change the name to *that*!" Gloria shouted.

"We already attract enough of the ghoulish crowd as it is," I said, coming into the kitchen. "Some of the kids at the college refer to this place as 'the murder shop.'"

Billy sighed. "I love this place. Let's just keep the Old Juniper Bookshop the way your aunt Rose wanted, hear? This place is a sanctuary, not an *attraction*."

"Man, Billy," I said, catching his eye. "You really have grown up to be a remarkable person. What you just said . . . it's a very insightful observation. And subtle."

And I know this sounds ridiculous, but I could feel that the house agreed. Golden light streamed in through the wavy glass windows. The dust motes, lazy in the sun, moved by some unknown, unseen force, swirled around the bookshelves. Every downstairs room, except the kitchen, was filled with books and records and comfy chairs and antique sofas and for a moment, the briefest of moments, I could hear sentences from every single one of the volumes, like a kind of pale white noise that filled up the entire house. They were written in the alphabet of the air, an alphabet that has only two letters: the sound of all sounds at once—and silence.

2

BILLY AND GLORIA and I were still sitting at the kitchen table in the back of the house when one of the two "certified" front yard diggers came in and stood at the front door, calling out for Billy.

"Officer Sanders?"

"Allie?" Billy was up and out of the kitchen instantly.

Gloria and I followed. Allie's face was red and wet, and his coveralls were covered in white and red gunk.

"Okay, so, this is weird," Allie said. "That dirt out there, around them bones? It's got QUIKRETE mixed in with it. That instant concrete stuff."

"That's why it was so hard to get into," Gloria said, mostly to herself.

"Why would that be?" Billy asked.

"It wouldn't be no reason to do that," Allie said. "Not with all the red clay out there too—except to make it really hard to crack open the . . . you know, the grave, or whatever."

"That is weird," Billy agreed.

"Let me get this right," I said. "You think somebody mixed dry concrete with Georgia clay and buried that body in it?"

Allie nodded. "Yes, ma'am. That's what it looks like to me."

"Who would do that?" Gloria muttered.

"*Why* would you do that?" I asked.

"Yeah," Allie said. "It don't make no sense."

"Except that everybody in town knew how Rose felt about her front yard," Billy said slowly. "She deliberately wanted to keep it a little spooky. No plants and such, so it wouldn't be too fancy, or . . . however you'd say it."

"Gloria and I were just talking about that," I said. "She was afraid no one would take the shop seriously if it looked like a tourist attraction."

Allie grunted a laugh. "Well, it don't look like *that*."

"Anything else?" Billy asked.

"Come on," Allie said, and he was back outside.

Allie and Tad had made more headway than I might have expected. There was a large oval-shaped space around the bones, about three feet deep, beside a pile of dirt half the size of a Volkswagen. Most of the skeleton was exposed but not entirely unearthed.

"The thing is—" Allie began.

But he was interrupted by Billy's observation. "That neck's been broke."

It only took me a second longer to come to the same conclusion. The neck bones made a right angle and the skull lay flat on the shoulder bone.

"That's what I mean," Allie continued.

"Are we thinking that this person was murdered?" Gloria asked, coffee mug in hand.

"Not necessarily," Billy said.

"Okay, but this person didn't bury themselves in my front yard," I assured him. "So somebody—"

"Let's not jump to any conclusions," Billy told us all. "We

got the coroner and *that* crew coming from Tifton, and until that happens, I believe we ought not to speculate."

It was a reasonable, mature suggestion. Which I chose to ignore.

"I see mostly red clay in this pile of dirt, here, Allie," I observed, "so there couldn't have been a whole lot of QUIK-RETE involved."

"Well, the clay don't let the concrete dust get enough moisture to set it right," Allie explained.

Tad was staring at the pile of dirt.

"But she's right," he said without looking at me. "There's not enough of the stuff to make it as hard as you want concrete to be."

"It was done hastily," Gloria pronounced. "Someone was in a hurry to bury the body, not really thinking, maybe panicked, and somehow thought it would keep the body hidden."

"Could we *please* stop all this speculation!" Billy demanded, a little louder than he needed to. "It's more likely to lead a person to a wrong conclusion."

"Officer Sanders has a point," Tad agreed. "I mean, for one thing, it's perfectly legal in Georgia to bury a family member in your yard."

Allie nodded. "I don't believe you even need a permit in this county."

"Well, Rose would never have done anything like that," I assured everyone. "And all her relatives were dead before she came back to Enigma and started the bookshop."

"But her family goes a long way back in this house," Billy said. "This might be some long-lost relative of yours, Maddy."

It was a testament to Billy's distracted mind that he did not call me Miss Brimley as he usually did in front of other people, mostly because he thought it made him seem more professional.

We were still standing around outside watching Tad and Allie work when Philomena pulled up in her 1989 Buick LeSabre. It was the only car she had ever owned; she'd bought it new. It still ran perfectly, despite its antique status, for one reason, and that reason was Elbert. He was a genius. I would have stacked him up against any rocket scientist or nuclear physicist on the planet. Except that a world-class car mechanic was infinitely more valuable than any person of science—certainly in Enigma, Georgia. Elbert had taken Igor, my poor old Fiat—so named after a series of unfortunate accidents, none of which were my fault—and made it over in the image of a fire-engine-red angel. The fact that Elbert had done a little time for attempted murder did nothing to diminish my estimation of him.

And there was Philomena, bouncing out of that car like a woman half her age.

"Sugar!" she called out to me, beaming.

We were holding on to each other three seconds later.

I loved Phil. She was a troubled soul, but not without good reason. A bout of rheumatic fever as a child had left her with a panoply of health issues, chronic pain, and occasional doubts about the nature of reality. She had been my aunt Rose's closest friend for decades, and we treated each other like family. Because I guess that's what we were.

"I missed you," I whispered in her ear before letting go of her.

She was dressed in one of her many navy-blue dresses. She wore a silk Hermès scarf around her neck and black horse-bit 1953 loafers—a nearly one-thousand-dollar pair of Gucci shoes—on her feet.

"Your visits meant so much to me," she said, peering past me. "Hey, Gloria. What's all this?"

Gloria nodded. "Well, Maddy and I were thinking of planting some roses out here and instead we found a skeleton buried in the yard."

I instantly wished that Gloria hadn't blurted it out that way.

Philomena blinked once. "What?"

"Maybe you all could go on back inside," Billy suggested. "Let Tad and Allie work?"

"Hello, Billy," Phil said absently. "Is there really a skeleton in this yard?"

"Well," he began.

Phil craned her neck to see into the shallow pit, saw the bones, and immediately closed her eyes.

"Yes," she managed to say. "Let's do go inside. I would like to sit down, I think."

So with that, Gloria and I ushered Phil into the house, through the shop, and landed at the kitchen table. I could have kicked myself for not calling Phil and telling her not to come over. I would have had to explain things, but that clearly would have been better than letting someone in her condition see a skeleton in the yard of her home away from home.

Phil's life was, by her design, well-ordered. She had a full class load at the college, she kept generous office hours, she graded papers, and she spent most evenings and weekends with me at the bookshop. As she had with Rose when Rose was alive. Deviations from that order were at the very least disconcerting for her. Even the suggestion that someone had been buried in the yard could have, I thought, sent her into a spin.

"Who is it?" she whispered.

I turned on the electric kettle and started preparations for new French press coffee.

"No idea," I said. "We just discovered it."

She turned to Gloria, and her voice was hollow sounding. "You were going to plant roses?"

"That was the thought," Gloria confirmed. "Although mostly Madeline and I were just taking out some very specific frustrations on the dirt. We hadn't bought any roses yet."

"You know," Phil went on, her voice still ghostly, "Rose created her own hybrid. It was never officially sanctioned, but . . . I have some of them at the college. Or, actually, David has them in his greenhouse. You should plant those."

I sat down next to her. "Are you okay?"

"Hmm?" She looked into my eyes. "Oh. Yes. But I'll be better, I think, when I know who was buried in my yard."

My yard. Well, it was her yard. Half of it, at least.

Gloria broke the partially uncomfortable silence. "So, how was your stay in the looney bin?"

Before I could object, Phil laughed. "Aside from the fluorescent lighting and the medicinal smells, it was very relaxing. My medication was adjusted and I got a chance to really talk it out with my therapist."

"Talk *what* out, exactly?" Gloria pressed.

Then I understood what Gloria was trying to do. She wanted to distract Philomena, and maybe me too, from the business in the front yard.

It worked. The three of us spent an hour or more talking about tasteless institutional food, weird therapy jargon, and how full the wisteria in the garden had been that year.

"I thought the clusters of flowers smelled like grapes,"

Phil said, "but maybe I was influenced by the fact that they *looked* like grapes."

Which was when Billy came into the kitchen.

"Okay," he announced. "Coroner's here and says it looks like the victim's neck was broke, but she can't tell how long the bones have been in the ground."

And that provoked another moment of uncomfortable silence.

"It's a lady coroner?" Phil asked at length.

"What I mean is," Billy went on, "that your yard is now a crime scene."

"Are you saying that the lady coroner thinks the pile of bones was murdered?" Gloria asked.

"Suspicious circumstances," Billy mumbled, "but we'll all know more once they get everything back to the lab and do the . . . you know, the tests and . . . like that."

Billy was clearly disturbed by the situation.

"So it might not be just a case of some weird but permissible family burial." I stood up from the table.

Billy exhaled. "Might not be."

"Okay, so, I hate to sound callous or anything," I said, "but what does that mean in terms of my opening the shop tomorrow morning?"

He nodded. "They'll have collected everything they need pretty soon, they said. I don't see why you couldn't open as usual, but I'll ask."

He turned and was gone.

"You could tell just by looking at it," Gloria said, "that the neck was broken."

"Would you like for me to stay here tonight?" Phil ventured. "Maybe you don't want to be alone."

Maybe *she* didn't want to be alone, I thought.

"I'd love that, Phil," I told her.

And why not? I wouldn't like to be alone on my first night home from a stay in a mental hospital. And she had everything she needed in Rose's room: clothes, toothbrush, pajamas—the memory of Rose, which still hung in the air like a lingering scent.

"Well," Gloria said, tossing back the last of her coffee and standing, "I'd better get back to the store. I have a baptism at six."

"The store?" I laughed.

"You know," Gloria said, headed for the front door, "the Jesus store. You sell books, I sell enlightenment."

"Not much money in either one, is there?" Phil asked, her attempt at a joke.

"You don't *sell* enlightenment," I objected.

Gloria stopped and turned. "What do you think the collection plate is? I talk about loving your neighbor and you put a fiver in a solid gold dish that costs more than a car."

"You should talk louder," Philomena said, staring into her coffee cup.

"What?" Gloria asked.

"Well, somebody didn't love their neighbor very much," Phil whispered, "if they broke somebody else's neck and buried the body in my front yard."

Gloria did not offer an immediate response.

3

I OPENED THE BOOKSHOP at ten o'clock the next morning utterly unprepared for the wild onslaught of sensation-seeking rubberneckers. There must have been twenty people on the front porch and another ten in the yard staring at the hole in the ground, the pile of dirt, and the perfunctory yellow crime scene tape strung between the bottom of the steps and the corner edge of the porch railing. When I unlocked the door, everything went silent for about five seconds before everybody started asking questions.

I was standing in the doorway in black jeans, a rust-colored T-shirt, and well-worn Crocs. I had a chipped mug of coffee in my hand and I held it up somehow thinking that the gesture would engender silence.

It did not.

I took in a breath to address the assembled, but before I could speak Dr. Waldrop appeared behind me dressed and ready for work.

"Children!" she bellowed.

She considered herself an old person, so everyone else was a child. Including me. But it worked. The throng fell silent.

"If you are here," she continued, near the top of her lungs, "to buy a book, please come in. If you are here for *any other reason*, please get your *petunias* off our lawn!"

The immediate population, mostly comprised of students from the college, gasped nearly as one. Phil's admonition was the closest she ever came to cursing, and the kids knew it. They weren't exactly certain what the word *petunias* represented, but they knew the tone of Phil's voice and they knew it probably substituted for some body part best omitted from polite company. So silence, at last, followed their gasp.

"The cops found a dead body buried in the yard," I said quickly. "We don't know who it was or how it happened. We don't know anything. So, as Dr. Waldrop suggested: if you're not here to buy a book, get lost."

No one moved.

I looked around the crowd. I recognized most of them. Repeat customers, Philomena's students, and Mae Etta, proprietor of the town's only diner. From the back of the porch crowd, Jennifer appeared.

"I tried to tell them," she said to me.

Jennifer Davis had been my elfin helper for nearly six months. She was a student at the college but she was about to leave for London and an internship at the Tate Modern. We had developed a unique work relationship: most of the time when she came to work, usually on her little sky-blue Vespa, she began our day with questions. They were almost always about my so-called acting career. She loved theatre and was planning on seeing a lot of it in London. Luckily, she *wasn't* planning on a life in the theatre, and even if she had been, my answers to her questions would have nipped that in the bud. But she seemed to delight in theatre stories, and I had a million of them. Not to mention that she was great with the shop's financials. In short, Jennifer was aces with me.

"Tried to tell them what?" I asked her as she made her way through the group.

"That there wouldn't be any news yet," she told me.

"Just because I haven't been around for the past few months," Phil announced, "doesn't mean that I don't know finals are right around the corner. So if you don't want to buy a book, go study! Go on, now!"

It took a second, but the crowd began to disperse. A few just wandered off, but most ended up coming into the shop. Jennifer went to the desk in what had been the parlor when the house had been a home, took her seat, and settled in. Phil and I repaired to the kitchen toward the back of the house.

Once at the kitchen table, French press between us, Phil heaved a sigh.

"I was so worried that my recent stay in the looney bin would undermine my authority with the children," she told me. "But they seemed to respond appropriately just now."

I nodded. "They love you, Phil. It's going to take a lot more than a few months in a *care facility* to erode years of reputation and respect."

She smiled. "You don't like to say the words *looney bin*. I do. It makes me laugh."

I put my hand on hers. "For one thing, you're not looney. For another, the word *bin* comes from Old Celtic and it means 'a cart with a woven wicker body.' Is that where you've been?"

"How on earth would you know that?" she asked.

"When you're in rehearsal for a play in which you have a very small part," I explained, "you do whatever you can to keep from losing your mind while you're waiting for your one big scene. Some actors drink or take drugs, some chat with other actors—if by *chat* we mean *gossip*—and some few of us would read."

"Rose was a gossip," she volunteered immediately.

"I know," I agreed, "but I was a reader, and years of backstage bibliophilia produced in me a nearly insufferable degree of useless etymological knowledge."

"Not to mention the ability to produce such dazzling sentences as that," she said.

"Exactly." I sat back. "But my point is that you say looney bin, I think, to preempt anyone else's judgment or derision. Like a kid who's funny first to keep other kids from making fun."

"Hmm," she fussed. "It would appear that you may have read a psychology book on one of your backstage literary expeditions. And anyway, Whispering Pines is more *spa* than *bin*, so maybe you're right."

We could have gone on like that for hours. Lively, odd conversation was the glue that bound us. But Jennifer appeared in the kitchen doorway.

"Sorry," she began, "but Miss Mae Etta has a question and I can't quite give her the answer she wants."

"Mae Etta?" Phil whispered. "From the diner?"

"I saw her on the porch," I said, standing. "I wondered what she was doing here."

I followed Jennifer out of the kitchen and into the shop. Rose had created the original organizational system, a haphazard blend of chaos and personal preferences. I'd tried to make things a little more coherent, but I hadn't had much success.

Essentially each downstairs room in the house was supposed to be its own kingdom. For example, the dining room was supposed to be the mystery section, but there were also two cases of poetry, and an entire wall was dedicated to Rose's extensive record collection. The parlor, where the cash box and desk sat, was mostly for contemporary books of fiction and nonfiction. In the study: history, biography, and older nonfiction.

But Mae Etta was standing in the tiny room—had it been a second pantry, or maybe a very large linen closet?—filled with rare books and first editions. Books that weren't for sale; you could only look at them in the shop. Rose always called it "the private library." I had often asked her why she wouldn't put all those expensive volumes somewhere upstairs where they wouldn't be disturbed, but no answer ever materialized.

Mae Etta saw me coming.

"I want one of these books," she said. "And this little girl won't sell it to me."

Her voice always sounded a little like ice cracking. Her hair was in its usual bun. Her plain brown dress reached halfway down her shins. It was a warm day, but she was wearing a heavy gray cardigan. And her glasses hung around her neck thanks to a beaded necklace she always wore.

"I told her those books weren't for sale," Jennifer whispered to me.

"What is it you're looking for?" I asked Mae Etta.

"I got a great-granddaughter in Omega who likes to read," she said impatiently. "I say God bless that."

"Amen," I agreed.

"And for some reason she likes these Wizard of Oz books," she went on. "You got a bunch of them in the back corner there. I want one."

"Okay," I said as I arrived at her side. "Those are all first editions. And it's a complete set. So—"

"She wants *Ozma of Oz*," she snapped. "You got it back there."

That was the third in the series. While Dorothy is traveling to Australia, she's washed overboard and lands in Ev, a country separated from Oz by a desert. In that desert they meet Tik-Tok, a mechanical man, and Princess Ozma. They all save the royal family and return triumphantly to Oz.

"Right," I said. "That one runs anywhere from eight hundred to twenty-five hundred."

Mae Etta clutched her cardigan. "Dollars?"

I nodded.

"For a *book*?"

"For a first edition," Jennifer intervened. "But as I was trying to tell you, ma'am, I can order you a very nice *replica* of that same book for about thirty-five. Hardcover."

Mae Etta looked back and forth between me and Jennifer a couple of times.

"Why do you have those books back there, then?" she asked me. "If you won't sell them, and if they're that valuable—I don't understand this."

"Rose," I said as a complete explanation.

Jennifer nodded and shrugged.

Mae Etta pulled her cardigan around herself and charged toward the desk in the other room.

"Come on, then," she called to Jennifer over her shoulder. "Order me that thirty-five-dollar thing. I'll give it to her at Christmas, I guess."

Jennifer bounded to Mae Etta's side and turned on her best sorority-girl demeanor. "Is she your only great-granddaughter?"

Mae Etta offered a curt single nod. "There's two boys but they're both idiots. Felicia's the only one worth a toot."

"Felicia?" Jennifer cooed. "I like that name."

And with that they were gone into the other room.

A moment later Phil wandered in, coffee in hand.

"What did Billy Sanders say?" she asked me.

"Say? You mean about the bones we found?"

She sipped. "I mean, did he have any ideas?"

"There was some talk," I told her, "about the legality of burying a family member in your own yard."

"But wouldn't that have been in the backyard?" she asked me. "I sometimes told Rose that I'd like to be buried out there in the back by the azaleas."

"I prefer cremation for myself," I said.

I heard arguing voices on the front porch. I couldn't hear exactly what they were saying, but it sounded like the argument was about to escalate.

"I want a large ceremony of some sort," Phil mused. "Not anything especially religious. I've spoken with Gloria about it."

"Could we change the subject," I said, headed for the front porch. "I think we've got enough naturally occurring death and dying around here without projecting into the future about, you know . . ."

"Yes." That's all she said.

The voices on the porch were louder, so I picked up my pace a little. They sounded official. They weren't student voices or even curiosity seekers. I had the impression that they were older men with a notion that they had authority. Like rich businessmen or upper-level law enforcement. And I heard just enough of what they were saying to be on my guard.

I opened my front door to discover two middle-aged men in dark JCPenney suits. One was on the porch peering down, the other was in the yard, standing in the hole where the bones had been buried.

So I turned on my irritated small-town homeowner voice.

"Can I help you, gentlemen?" I snarled. "And would you mind keeping your voices down in my place of business?"

Both men turned my way.

The one on the porch said, "Are you Madeline Brimley?"

"I am," I confirmed curtly.

The guy on the ground nodded and hauled out his wallet.

"Georgia Bureau of Investigation, ma'am," he said softly, holding up his badge. "Is there someplace we could have a word that won't disturb your customers?"

"That was quick," Phil muttered, standing at my left elbow.

"Perhaps you'd care to join me in the backyard," I said.

"The gazebo is very pleasant," Phil volunteered.

The men looked at each other; the one on the ground sighed.

"Gazebo?" he said.

"We can sit out there away from the curiosity seekers and the impressionable students," I said.

But I was thinking about how difficult it would be for these men to intimidate me, or Philomena, if we were all sitting outside in the middle of my garden.

"It's around this way," I suggested.

I came off the porch, nodded at the man with the badge in his hand, and headed around the house toward the backyard garden. The men followed, and Philomena brought up the rear.

It had turned into a very pleasant April morning, seventy degrees and a pleasant easterly wind. As we came closer to the gazebo, the scent of juniper, momentarily aloft on the breeze, filled the air.

One of the men behind me said, "Nice garden."

I turned. He was gazing at the azaleas.

"I was going to put some azaleas like those in the front yard," I said, veering into the gazebo and taking a seat. "But I decided on roses instead. That's why we were digging there yesterday."

The one who'd shown me his badge stepped into the gazebo and appeared to be about to speak, but Phil beat him to it.

"Could we see everyone's badge, please?" she asked.

She only sounded curious, not irritated—almost like it would be fun to see another badge.

The other man produced their credentials; the one with me in the gazebo sat down.

The original gazebo had been built in the nineteenth century by the first owners of the house, railway magnates. Rebuilt, it was still seven-sided, for luck, and had been painted red for prosperity. Waist-high railings acted as backing for the wraparound benches inside. The roof was delicately curved outward seven times, one for each side, and decked with slate roof tiles. The ceiling inside was painted with clouds and blue sky, exactly the way it had been before Philomena burned it down.

"Ma'am—" the first GBI investigator began.

"This has got to be some kind of record," I interrupted.

"Record?" he asked me.

"We found those bones less than twenty-four hours ago, and we already have the GBI on the case? Seems really fast, like Dr. Waldrop said."

He stared at Phil. "You're Dr. Waldrop?"

She smiled. "That's me."

"Okay. We were notified late last night by the coroner in Tifton," he said.

"Why?" I asked, my voice still edged in annoyance.

"Well," he began, "the local law enforcement officer who discovered the remains—"

"I discovered the remains," I told him. "Along with an Episcopal priest."

"That would be Gloria Coleman?"

"Uh-huh," I answered. "Why did the coroner call the GBI?"

"As I was saying," he told me calmly, "local law enforcement officially requested our help, through the office of the coroner in Tifton. Local agencies may seek GBI assistance in a case of limited resources or expertise, which Officer Sanders believes is the case, so he called our office in Sylvester."

We all settled into the gazebo.

"I don't understand why Billy would request your help with a case like this," I continued.

"A case like what, ma'am?" he asked me.

"We were thinking," Phil intervened, "that some family member was interred in the yard by the distant relatives of the current owner, to wit: Madeline."

I threw her a look. "'To wit'?"

"He was using such official-sounding language," she whispered. "I thought I should too."

"So you haven't been notified," the second man spoke up at last.

"Notified of what?" I asked him.

"The medical examiner does not believe this is a case of home burial," the second man answered.

"What is it, then?" Phil asked before I could.

"Well, ma'am," the first man said calmly, looking between Phil and me. "According to the medical examiner, this was most likely a murder."

4

"THAT'S NOT REALLY such a shock," I said right back to Mr. GBI. "Billy noticed that the person buried in my yard had a broken neck. We all saw it."

"Which could have happened from a fall down the steps," Phil interjected.

"But it didn't," Mr. GBI said plainly. "There was also a sizable dent in the back of the skull."

"Somebody hit somebody in the head hard enough to break their neck?" I asked. "On my front porch?"

"Do you mind my asking your names, gentlemen?" Phil chimed in suddenly.

"Baxter," said the man we'd been talking with.

"Baker," the other one said, nearly at the same time.

"Well, Baxter-Baker," I began, "what I'd like—"

"The tests have determined that the incident happened a little more than six months ago, before you moved in," said Baxter.

"While your aunt Rose was in the hospital or after she was dead, and the house was unoccupied," Baker added. "Officer Sanders informed us of that."

I realized that they were telling me I wasn't a suspect. It

hadn't even occurred to me that they might think I was. So I really didn't feel like telling them about Tandy Fletcher, who had been living in the house during the time Rose was in the hospital, and who had been murdered just inside the door. I did wonder—for about half a second—if Tandy had known anything about the broken-neck burial. But I dismissed it just as quickly. She would have told me.

"Do we know who the poor soul was?" Phil asked. "The victim, I mean."

"We do," said Baker. But that was all.

After a beat of silence that lasted a little too long, I asked, "Will you tell us who it was?"

They looked at each other for a second, then Baxter shook his head.

"We need to do a little more research before we get into that," he said.

"Into *what*, exactly?" I wanted to know.

"This is an open investigation," Baker said, sounding a little irritated. "We really don't give out details at this point."

"The person's name isn't really a detail," Phil protested. "What if it's someone we knew? What if it was one of Madeline's family? Or someone Rose knew?"

"You used dental records," I said. "That's what they always do on television."

"They do that in real life too," Baxter acknowledged.

But again that was all he said.

I sat back. "Still curious about the speed of your *investigation*."

"How do you mean, exactly?" Baker asked.

"We just found the remains yesterday. Is there something about this particular situation that merits such snappy service?"

Baker took in a deep breath. "For one thing, the Sylvester office of the GBI rarely gets involved with local crimes, even murder. So when we do, we do it pretty quick."

"Because you ordinarily don't have much to do?" Phil asked innocently.

"When that young woman was murdered here in your bookshop last year," Baxter said patiently, "we weren't even notified. So this situation here is already an unusual circumstance."

"But frankly, the main reason for this," Baker concluded, "is Officer Sanders."

I didn't understand the sentence. Most of the time I still pictured Billy Sanders as being eight years old, with his Kermit the Frog T-shirt and his bright-red flip-flops. My face must have betrayed that confusion because Baxter piped up.

"Millie Sanders is our office manager at the Sylvester office," he said.

"She's Billy's aunt," Baker added.

"She runs our office," Baxter went on softly, "no matter what the director thinks."

"Billy called Millie," Baker concluded, "and Millie called us."

"Billy and Millie." Phil smiled. "Now *there's* a television show. Crime-fighting nephew and aunt! I'd watch that."

"The point is," Baxter interjected, "that Billy alerted Millie to the situation after he got the coroner's report and he found out the victim's identity."

"Which you don't seem to want to tell us," I pressed.

Before either of the detectives could answer, Jennifer called out to me from the back door of the house.

"Madeline? There's a problem."

I nodded and stood.

"Okay," I answered, then lowered my voice. "Will you gentlemen excuse me? I have a shop to run."

Phil jumped up. "I'll go with you."

And before either of the men from the GBI could completely get to their feet, Phil and I were off.

"Why are you being so harsh with those men?" Phil asked me, her voice lowered to a barely audible level. "They seem nice enough."

I stopped, turned around, and called to the men in the gazebo.

"By the way," I asked, "what were you two arguing about on my front porch?"

Baxter answered. "I wanted to shut this place down. It's a crime scene."

"I thought you should stay open," Baker said, "because we don't usually shut down a cold case scene."

"And you won," I said to Baker.

He shook his head. "We weren't through arguing when you came out on the porch."

I looked at Phil. "That's why I was being harsh."

"I see," Phil whispered. "You think they might close us down."

"Over my dead body," I told her, heading for the back door once more.

"Oh, sweetheart," she admonished, following me. "Don't we have enough of those in this house as it is?"

THE problem in the shop was, as it turned out, unusual; it involved Cannonball. Cannonball was a cat the size of a badger whose agility defied his girth. He had managed to get himself on a top shelf in the "private library" room. Then, unable or unwilling to find a way down, he had begun to yowl like a prehistoric animal dropped in hot water. It was alarming the customers.

Once I hit the back door I could hear the racket.

I turned to Philomena. "Feline difficulties."

She nodded.

I went through the kitchen, into the shop, and over to the source of the hideous brouhaha, to wit: Cannonball.

"What are you doing?" I said to him.

He stopped his noise and glared down at me, clearly expecting me to fetch him.

"You got yourself up there," I told him. "Get yourself down. Come on."

He extended his paw, steadied himself for some sort of jump, but abandoned the thought almost immediately and sat back, waiting for me to do something.

He was sitting on the only empty shelf space in the entire little room. It was a shelf half filled with unique editions of books by the Grimm Brothers; there were really only seven, the original from 1812—which was not in evidence on the shelf—and six subsequent editions, and there was Cannonball, nine feet above the floor, sitting next to the six volumes, waiting patiently to be rescued.

Jennifer stood at my side, staring up.

"At least he's stopped making that noise," Jennifer whispered.

"We have a step stool in the kitchen," I said. "It's in the pantry. Would you mind?"

She was off in a flash.

"There are people here from the GBI," I told Cannonball. "I don't really have time for this."

In response he opened his mouth, stuck out his tongue, rolled his head, and started licking his chest, cleaning it, ignoring me.

Several students had gathered to watch the show. Jennifer returned with the step stool. I unfolded it, put one foot on the bottom step, and Cannonball leapt. Parkour-cat-style, he bounded back and forth from one bookshelf to another until he landed gracefully, like a large feather, on the top step of the stool.

The students laughed and applauded. Jennifer heaved a sigh. I scratched Cannonball's jaw.

"There," I said to him. "Was that so hard?"

He hesitated, obviously forming a response, and then jumped down from the stool and sauntered away, tail straight up in the air.

I turned to the students. "Show's over. Nothing to see here."

They wandered off.

"What was he doing?" Jennifer whispered to me.

I watched him walk away. "Saving me from further interaction with the GBI?"

Jennifer just shook her head and walked away.

But where was Philomena?

I headed back toward the kitchen, and there was Phil at the front door of the shop talking with Billy.

"Hey!" I called to him.

He only looked. He didn't smile. He didn't wave. He didn't move.

"What is it?" I said as I headed his way.

"He knows who it was," Phil said softly. "He knows who was buried in our front yard."

I stepped up right next to him.

"So?" I demanded. "Who?"

He looked around. "I'm not supposed to say."

"But since you know that I'll pester you mercilessly until you do, you're going to tell me anyway."

He closed his eyes. "Probably."

"But hang on," I said. "There are two guys from the GBI in my backyard."

"Baxter and Baker," he said, then lowered his voice. "Aunt Millie calls them Tweedledumb and Tweedlestupid."

Phil tilted her head. "Shouldn't it be Tweedledumb and Tweedledumber?"

"Oh, no," Billy assured us. "They're *equal* in their lack of intellectual ability."

There. That was the kind of thing he'd say every once in a while that would remind me that he was not, in fact, an eight-year-old boy. He was a smart young man with a sense of subtlety that was uncommon in our little town.

"Why does she think that about them?" Phil asked.

"She believes that they go for the quick and easy solution to most of their cases," he answered. "Whatever's obvious or superficial. They don't put much effort into their investigations beyond the shallowest explanations and most cursory of examinations."

Phil put her hand on his forearm. "I'm so proud of your vocabulary."

He smiled. "That's all thanks to you, Dr. Waldrop. To the classes I been taking."

"*I've* been taking," she corrected.

He patted her hand. "That's enough for one day. Here comes the GBI."

"What was the problem?" Baker asked.

"Nothing," I said instantly. "Cat related."

"I don't understand," Baxter said.

"We have a cat," I explained. "He was the problem. Is there anything else I can do for you gentlemen, or can I get back to work?"

"They were talking about closing the shop," Phil said to Billy.

"Just wanted you all to know," Billy said to Baxter, "that the dental records are confirmed."

They both nodded silently, like it was an episode of *Dragnet*.

"So you know what to do," Baker said to Billy.

"Yes, sir," Billy said.

"All right," Baxter said to me. "I guess this place can stay open. For the time being."

That was it. No word of farewell or parting glance. They were gone.

We walked out onto the front porch, all three of us, and watched them drive away in their cliché of an SUV.

"So now are you going to tell me who I dug up on Sunday?" I asked Billy, watching the SUV disappear down the street.

"Aren't you surprised by how quickly all this happened?" he asked in response. "It ain't been much more than twenty-four hours since you discovered the remains. And don't correct my grammar, Dr. Waldrop."

"I already asked those men about that," I answered him. "They said it was your fault. You and your aunt Millie."

"Millie and Billy," Philomena said softly to herself, delighted.

"My aunt didn't do this," he said. "I called her because she works at the GBI and I didn't know who else to call. I just needed help. That's what she told her boss, and her *boss* got this thing going. Because he likes her."

"That can't be all there is to it," I mumbled.

"I just assumed it was because there isn't much to do at the branch of the GBI in Sylvester, Georgia," Phil said.

"I'm sure that's part of it," he agreed. "But there's something else, I believe."

He didn't say anything else, but it was obvious his mind was working overtime.

"Who was the body in my front yard, Billy?" I asked again, almost at the end of my patience.

"Well." He sighed. "That's the problem. Turns out . . . the victim was Beatrice Glassie."

That *was* a problem. Beatrice Glassie was a problem. She was rich, entitled, more than a little crazy, and a pillar of the town. I'd never met her, but people talked and that was the kind of thing they always said.

Her younger sister, Idell, on the other hand, was one of my regulars at the shop. She was odd but sweet; she liked mysteries involving cats.

Curiously, Beatrice hadn't been seen in Enigma for quite a while, but it had generally been assumed that she was traveling, as she often did. No one in town knew her well or liked her very much, so no one had been the least bit curious about her absence.

Beatrice was also the most troubled and troublesome parishioner at Gloria's church. She was on the church's board of directors. She'd been vociferously opposed to the new female priest and had petitioned the bishop to remove Gloria Coleman and send a man to take her place. That had all happened before I'd come back to town, but I'd heard the stories, and they weren't pretty.

Philomena only raised her eyebrows. "So that's where she's been all this time. In our front yard."

"Gone for all that time," Billy mused, "and no one ever asked anything about her."

"She was *not* a likeable person," Phil added.

Billy sighed. "So, anyway, that's where I'm going next, to tell Idell that her sister's dead."

I turned to Billy. "That's not going to be any fun."

He shook his head and took to the steps down from the porch.

"Never is," he told me without looking back.

"You've had to do that before?" I asked him.

But he didn't respond. He just got into his police car and drove away.

5

EARLY THE NEXT day, the news was all over town. For most people it was little more than exciting gossip. "Did you hear? Y'all! They found Bea Glassie buried in the front yard of the Old Juniper Bookshop!"

But for Bea's sister, Idell, it was a life-changing event. Idell was ordinarily, at least in my experience, a lovely older woman. In her eighties, wrapped in shin-length black dresses two sizes too big, her white hair always in a neat braid down her back, she cut a distinct figure in the bookshop, sometimes standing for hours going through the rare books room, the books you couldn't buy. And always in red high-top tennis shoes.

After Billy told her what had happened, Idell spent the day crying and fuming. She got up at eight o'clock the next morning, walked (she didn't own a car) to St. Thomas Aquinas Church, Gloria Coleman pastor, and unleashed holy hell.

I knew because the church was almost across the street from the bookshop. I was sitting on my front porch gulping coffee and waiting for the further onslaught of ghoulish curiosity seekers.

For some reason I'd picked out an uncharacteristically adult outfit, gray Frank & Eileen linen slacks and a pale gold linen shirt, short sleeved. I wanted to look authoritative enough to chase away the oddball visitors—and in case the GBI came back.

Gloria happened to be out in front of the church changing the sign. She wanted to make it say, "Just Love Everyone, I'll Sort It Out Later. God." She'd finished "Just Love" when Idell roared up and started screaming. I could hear it from the porch. I couldn't hear everything Idell was yelling, but one sentence stuck out.

"You killed my sister!"

That was enough to get me off my rocking chair and hustle over to defend my friend.

Gloria was in a black short-sleeved priest shirt with the full clerical collar. She was calm and her voice was reassuring.

"Idell," she was saying when I got close enough to hear, "I know you're in shock from the news. It's terrible. Would you like to come inside and talk?"

"You killed my sister!" Idell screeched again. "I know it! Everybody knows it! You hated her!"

I arrived at Gloria's side just in time to hear her say, "I didn't hate your sister."

"Well, she hated you!" Idell said, still at the top of her lungs.

"I don't know if she hated me or not," Gloria said softly. "I do know that she didn't want me to be the priest here at St. Thomas Aquinas. But that didn't have anything to do with me. She just didn't want a woman pastor. That's all."

"She wrote the bishop!" Idell snapped. "I know that! She wrote the bishop to have you removed and you didn't like it."

"She did more than that," Gloria said to me, politely

acknowledging my presence. "She filibustered every church council meeting, she took all her money out of the church renovation fund, and she even had her own Sunday bulletins printed encouraging everyone to stop attending St. Thomas until I was gone. Stood beside me in the doorway and handed them out."

Gloria didn't want to show it, but there was a touch of a smile on her face. She'd apparently found Bea more amusing than intimidating. And all of Bea's efforts came to exactly nothing. The bishop ignored her, the church renovations were proceeding nicely, and attendance at St. Thomas had, in fact, increased since Gloria Coleman had come to our town.

"What you don't know," Idell snarled, her voice lowered, "is that I heard you that night. Heard you arguing. Right in there, in the narthex."

Gloria turned back to Bea. "I don't know what you're talking about."

"I had come with her that night, you see," Idell went on, barely above a hoarse whisper.

"You didn't know I was standing out here in the grass. It was a September night, still a little too warm, but you'd already turned the air conditioner off in the church, so it was cooler outside. And there I was. That door was open. I heard what my sister said. I heard what you said."

Gloria stared. "Are you talking about the night she came here drunk?"

"My sister was never drunk!" Idell took a deep breath. "We had been drinking gin and tonic, of course, with mint in it, because it was hot. She said we shouldn't be drinking such a thing since it was almost autumn, but I said I needed the quinine, so we kept drinking. She may have been *tipsy* . . ."

"She couldn't pronounce the word *harlot*," Gloria answered, even more amused. "She tried three times. The closest she got was *hurler*."

"She told me that you were making a play for her beau." Idell squinted hard. "That's why she tried to call you . . . that."

"Idell," Gloria said, finally laughing out loud. "I had no interest whatsoever in Kell Brady *and* I had no idea he was Bea's beau."

Idell looked down then, and some of the steam seemed to leave her.

"Don't say his name," she muttered.

I could read on Idell's face, and in her posture, that there was more to that particular story, but Gloria kept things moving.

"Why don't you come inside, have a seat, and let's talk," she said sweetly to Idell.

Idell looked up. "You won't be doing *any* talking in that church when I'm through with you."

With that she turned and marched away.

Gloria took a deep breath, let it out, and then called after Idell.

"Okay, bye, then," she chirped.

Idell did not respond.

"Well, *now* I'm awake," I said to Gloria.

Gloria grinned. "Yeah. I didn't know Idell could be that loud. She generally seems so . . . mousy. You want some more coffee? I just made it."

"No." I looked back at the bookshop. "I have a feeling this is going to be another weird day at the old homestead. I need to man the battlements."

"Right." She examined her half-finished sign. "I'm going to finish this sign, but if you need help, just holler."

I headed back to the shop. "Will do," I said, waiving my empty coffee cup in the air.

By ten o'clock the shop was busier than usual, and there were occasional non-customers loitering in the front yard. But the morning brightened up considerably when David showed up. The black jeans, brown T-shirt, and heavy work boots gave no hint of the poet inside the clothes; he looked the part of a small-town gardener.

His truck pulled up, the gray Jeep Gladiator, right when I was about to go fetch my shovel and swing it hard at two high school boys who would not stop saying annoying things about buried bodies to anyone coming in or going out of the shop. I'd had it with them, and was just set to launch a tirade, when David stepped out of his truck.

"Morning." He smiled, and most of my ire evaporated.

"Hi," I said, "give me a minute."

I strode very deliberately up to the troublemaking boys.

"Time to go to school now, guys," I said to them tersely. "I think you've had enough fun here for the morning."

"How many more dead people you got buried here?" one of the boys asked.

He was dressed in dirty blue jeans and a Metallica T-shirt.

I stepped up to him so suddenly that he flinched.

"One of the cute college girls in the shop, here," I said softly, "just asked me what was wrong with you. I told her you had syphilis and it caused your brain to go bad."

"Lady," the other began.

He was in camo pants and a fishnet shirt.

"You," I interrupted. "I told that same cute girl that you shot a dog and left him at the Berrien County dump. By lunchtime that's going to be all over town. You know how fast gossip travels in this town."

"True," David said, coming up behind me. "I already heard about it over at the college."

"Hello, David," I said sweetly.

"And you, Derek," David said to the Metallica fan, "you need to get up to the free clinic in Tifton and get some penicillin, like, today, don't you?"

And right on cue, two coeds bounded down the front steps, leaving the shop and giggling.

The boys were trying to come up with some kind of response to me or to David, but the phenomenon of two college girls laughing—maybe at them—was enough to make them skitter away without a word.

"That was fun," David said, watching the boys disappear down the street.

"This is my morning," I said. "Jennifer is inside selling books; I'm outside dealing with . . . I mean, that's the third time in an hour I've had to . . . plus, Idell Glassie was yelling at Gloria, and Billy doesn't think the GBI is going to do anything, so."

David smiled. "I see. Well. That's some morning."

I sipped a quick breath. "I'm not usually incoherent, am I?"

"No," he said as we headed up the steps. "But these are unusual circumstances. You know, what with the dead body and all."

"You want to sit out here with me for a bit?" I suggested.

"More than anything else in the world," he said, "but I'm actually here at the request of the other owner, Dr. Waldrop."

I turned to him at the top of the stairs. "Really?"

"She wanted to know if I still had any of your aunt Rose's hybrid—"

"Ophelia's Last Laugh," I interrupted.

"Yes," he went on, "and I do, as it happens. Rose gave me two dozen before she tore up all the ones she had growing in the back here. She wanted me to see how many you'd need if you wanted to plant all along the front of the porch. So, I came to assess the situation."

"I see," I told him. "And what's your assessment, doctor?"

He turned, looked down at the area of land surrounded by yellow police tape, concentrated, and then nodded.

"I'm going to suggest a dozen," he said. "Soon as the constabulary allows, I'll bring in some really good dirt and compost. We'll dig a nice trench, two feet deep—which is really twice as deep as you need to create a good bed for roses, then we'll plant, fit in a soaker hose, and mulch it with pine bark. Your front yard won't be the showplace that your backyard garden is, but at least this house won't look like it's been abandoned. By the Addams Family."

"Ha-ha," I told him, deadpan. "I'm the only one allowed to make the Addams Family reference."

"Sorry." He wasn't.

"This sounds like an expensive project you're proposing and I'm only a poor ex-actor trying to make a living selling books."

"That's not a problem," he said, nodding. "The rosebushes themselves won't cost anything because technically you own them, since Rose developed them and she left you everything in her will, right?"

"Absolutely," I confirmed.

"And I'll do the design and labor for free, even though I am a *very* important master gardener—at the college—because technically I'm your boyfriend, right?"

"Technically," I said.

"Of course you'll have to pay Frank."

Ah. Frank Fletcher. He was David's assistant at the college, but he was also the brother of Tandy Fletcher, my assistant before Jennifer. Tandy was killed just inside my front door. I finally outed the person responsible, and Frank had been at least deferential toward me since then. But I reckoned I would still have to pay him to do the kind of labor it would take to make the front yard of the Old Juniper Bookshop look even modestly presentable with respect to shrubbery.

So I said, "Yes, I'll pay Frank. Now let's get back to this notion that you're my technical boyfriend. And, PS, I don't really care for the term *boyfriend* in this particular case."

"Why?" he asked affably.

"Because I'm not in high school," I told him. "And you're not a boy."

"So how would you like to describe our relationship?" He smiled and raised his eyebrows.

"Personally? I'd like to describe it as 'further along,' but that's just me."

"We've been carrying on for nearly six months," he said, looking down at the ground. "I'm not seeing anyone else. We spend almost every day together. How much further along do we want to get today?"

"'Carrying on'?" I shook my head. "What is this, an episode of *The Andy Griffith Show*?"

His eyes wandered to the police tape. "Don't remember anybody being buried in Andy's front yard."

I didn't mean for my voice to get louder, but it did. "Faye! You still haven't told me everything about the mysterious relationship you had with Faye Dillard."

"This again?" He didn't sound mad, just tired.

The Dillard family owned the only completely organic farm anywhere near Enigma. David had met her at Wendell Berry's farm; she'd brought him back to Georgia, to her family's enterprise. She'd also been a fan of my aunt Rose, so she'd introduced David to the bookshop. He'd told me that they had kind of been expecting to get married, but he'd never told me anything more than that. And now Faye Dillard was gone, although I didn't know where she'd gone or when she'd left.

"Where is she," I wanted to know, "this alleged *Faye*? Why didn't you two get married? Do you still have feelings for her? That kind of thing."

I tried to sound matter-of-fact, but I could hear the insecurity in my voice. And I hated that.

He looked around. "Could we not talk about this on your front lawn?"

"You don't seem to talk about it at all," I objected.

He hesitated, then blew out his breath. "Yeah. Okay. It's just a little embarrassing, that's all. I haven't really talked about it, I guess, because I want you to like me. And I don't want to tell you anything about myself that you might *not* like. Can you understand that? Don't you have stuff like that too?"

"God, yes," I answered. "I'm a little embarrassed about *all* my previous relationships and I don't like to talk about *any* of them. But, of course, most of those relationships were with actors, so they were, by definition, embarrassing."

He laughed, which was my intention.

"But I still have to know about Faye," I went on.

He nodded. "Right. So, I'll go by Mona and Memaw's Barbecue tonight, we'll have dinner in your kitchen, and I will reveal the awful truth."

"Oh." I swallowed. "Okay. Should I prepare for the worst?"

"No." He finally looked at me. "It's not actually *awful*. I'm just sorry I haven't told you more before now. The thing is . . ."

But before he could explore the subject any more deeply, Billy Sanders's squad car roared up and Billy sprang out, slamming the door behind him.

"David, I'm glad you're here," Billy snapped. "You want to be sheriff? I quit."

"You can't quit," David told him. "You haven't even been elected yet."

"I think I'm going to go back into the drywall business," Billy muttered.

"What's the matter?" I asked.

"Idell Glassie is the matter." He took off his policeman's hat and fanned himself with it for a moment, even though it wasn't an especially hot day.

"She was just over at the Episcopal church giving Gloria what-for," I said. "And I mean at the top of her lungs."

"I know," Billy said, shaking his head. "She stood out in the street and flagged me down. I was going for coffee at Mae Etta's and she stopped me. She demanded that I arrest Gloria Coleman."

"Because she thinks Gloria killed Beatrice Glassie," I explained to David.

Which produced another hearty bit of laughter from David.

"Seriously?" he asked. "The only thing Gloria Coleman ever killed was an alligator when she lived in the swamp with her parents. And she was a kid then. And I think she might even have made that story up."

But I saw the concern on Billy's face. Idell and Beatrice

Glassie were by far the wealthiest people in Enigma. I wouldn't have used the term *old maids* as most of the people in Enigma did when they talked about the sisters, but neither had ever married and both rivaled Louisa May Alcott in the spinster department.

"Billy, you *know* Gloria didn't do anything to Bea Glassie."

"What I *know* does not, in this case, cut any mustard with that old woman," he said quietly.

David turned my way. "You don't hear a good 'cut the mustard' reference very often here in the twenty-first century."

"I got to go talk to Gloria now." But Billy didn't move.

"Why did you come here first," I asked him, "instead of just going right to the church?"

"Because I don't really want to go ask Gloria Coleman if she killed somebody," he said, irritated, "and I thought maybe you could talk me out of it."

"What good would that do?" David intervened. "It would only postpone the inevitable. Idell Glassie is not one to take no for an answer."

"And, really, what could I have said to you that would have helped?" I asked him. "I wasn't even in town when all this happened. Bea was—and excuse me for sounding callous or something—but Bea was buried in this yard before I left Atlanta. And after Rose was dead. So I wouldn't really have any . . ."

My voice trailed off and Billy nodded.

"Yeah," Billy said. "The thing is, Idell is all het up about this. I've only seen her like this once or twice before, but you're right. She won't let go. And sooner or later she'll get the governor or the president or the pope involved somehow, and my life—as I know it now—will be over."

I could see that what he'd really wanted was a buffer,

something between his obviously unsettling encounter with Idell and the entirely unwanted conversation with our Episcopal priest. And I was sorry I couldn't help.

Because it seemed clear to me that he might eventually have to arrest Gloria Coleman for murder.

6

BILLY LEFT HIS police car in my front yard, David got in his Jeep and trundled away, and I went back inside the bookshop. It was pleasantly crowded. A lesson that they probably don't teach in college economic courses is that a dead body can be good for business. I could have taught that course: Bad News equals Good Commerce 101.

I went to Jennifer, seated at the antique desk we used as a customer counter, the place where the books were purchased. She was wearing a familiar cotton T-shirt dress, white with horizontal blue stripes, that she told me she'd gotten from H&M. She was just finishing up with a customer.

"You are going to love this book," she told the young woman in torn jeans and an ABBA T-shirt. "Barbara Kingsolver is a genius."

Miss Torn Jeans appeared to be unconvinced. "It looks long."

"Not really," Jennifer chirped. "It flies. And besides, you're taking Jenkins's Twenty-first Century Fem Lit, right?"

Jeans nodded.

"Well." Jennifer shrugged. "It's required, so . . ."

The customer sighed, picked up her book, and shuffled toward the door.

"We're having a really good morning," Jennifer whispered to me.

I looked around. "I can see."

"I thought the news would keep people away," she went on, still sotto voce.

"Never underestimate the power of persnickety, macabre curiosity," I told her.

She looked up. "I don't know what *persnickety* is."

"Ah," I said. "It means finicky, fussy, picky, nit-picking."

"Oh." She sat back. "You mean like everyone in town."

"I do," I assured her.

"Okay," she said, squinting, "so maybe you don't want to add the GBI to your list of worries, but they called."

"The GBI called you?"

"They called this number." Jennifer glared down at the old-fashioned black dial phone. "They wanted to talk to you, but I told them you were in a meeting."

I gazed out the window and looked at the spot where David's Jeep had been.

"I *was* in a meeting," I said. "Thank you. What did they want?"

"They wanted to ask you about Idell Glassie."

I blinked. "What about her?"

Jennifer shifted in her seat and shook her head. "Okay, well, apparently, she's related to their boss, these GBI guys' boss."

"That can't be good," I said. "Which one did you talk with?"

"He announced himself, very grandly, as Special Agent Baxter," she said, nearly rolling her eyes. "I didn't talk with him for very long, and I got the impression that he didn't really want to take Idell seriously. Only his boss told him he had to. So I said you'd call back. Here's the number."

She handed me the note.

I stared at the number, then back at Jennifer. "All right, I'm going to take my new cell phone," I told her, mock anger filling my words, "go out to the gazebo, and call this Baxter guy back. I'm going to tell him that Idell Glassie is not a stable individual *nor* a reliable source of, really, anything."

"Did you just use the word *nor*, grandma?" she asked me.

I headed for the kitchen and the back door. "Somebody has to hold decent grammar together in this town, don't they?"

"And you're just the woman to do it," she said to my back.

Out in the yard, the day did its best to remind me that it was spring. Dahlias, zinnias, black-eyed Susans were everywhere, and Lady Banks roses covered the gazebo. But the fact that I was about to talk to Baxter of the GBI—the worst title for a television series ever—took a major portion of the beauty away from the garden.

I dialed the number on the note and waited. Baxter took forever to answer.

"Baxter," was all he said.

"This is Madeline Brimley," I said, "at the Old Juniper Bookshop in Enigma."

I could actually hear his shoulders slump as he shuffled paper on his desk.

"Yes, ma'am, we've heard from an . . . Idell Glassie—" he began.

"There's only one," I interrupted. "She's *the* Idell Glassie, and she ought to be institutionalized."

"Ma'am?"

"Stop calling me that. And Idell is nuts."

"Nevertheless," he said wearily, "she believes that Gloria Coleman murdered her sister."

"That's *Reverend* Gloria Coleman," I insisted.

"We have to follow up on her complaint," he said coldly.

"Ask anybody in town," I went on. "Idell Glassie is not a stable individual. And Gloria is a respected Episcopal priest, for God's sake."

"Gloria Coleman was heard arguing with Beatrice Glassie shortly before Glassie disappeared," he said.

"Find me somebody that didn't argue with Bea," I insisted, not really knowing what I was talking about. "Then you'll have something. And anyway Officer Sanders is interviewing Reverend Coleman as we speak."

"He is?"

"Idell got to him too," I said.

"Of course she did," he said, but it was mostly to himself. "But Idell Glassie is a regular customer at your store, isn't she?"

"She's a regular customer at my *shop*," I corrected.

"So we thought you might tell us a little something about her," he went on, "which you have now done. A little."

"She's a lonely older person who doesn't have many friends," I said, "despite her wealth and standing in our tiny little community. She's never mentioned her sister to me. Our conversations, brief as they were, never touched on anything except books, cats, and petunias."

"Petunias?"

"She likes purple petunias. Does that help solve the case?"

"Listen, *ma'am*," he snapped. "Is there some reason for you to be so belligerent with me?"

"There is, in fact," I insisted. "You seem to think that my good friend, a fine Episcopal priest, is a murder suspect!"

But in fact he was right. I took a deep breath and tried to get ahold of what was making me so uncharacteristically agitated. The guy was only trying to do his job.

"Officer Baxter—" I began.

"Special Agent," he interrupted. "Special Agent Baxter."

"You know that someone was killed in my shop very shortly after I inherited it," I went on. "You mentioned it to me yesterday. And now, finding a body buried in the front yard—I may be having a harder time coping with this than I want to admit. I *have* been a little antagonistic toward you and your partner and I apologize. But seriously, Gloria Coleman is the last person on earth who would harm anybody. She didn't do this."

"We just need to proceed with our investigation," he said, warming just a little. "And, by the way, I did know about what happened at your place because I knew Tandy Fletcher. My sister lives in Ty Ty and Tandy used to babysit my nieces. She was a real sweet girl."

That turned me around a good bit. I was still getting used to what a small community I lived in. Suddenly Baxter wasn't a foreign interloper. He was family, of a sort.

"Yeah," I agreed. "She was. And, by the way, I know that Idell has some kind of influence in high places or whatever, and you have to do what you have to do."

It wasn't quite the last line from *Casablanca*, but I still felt that Special Agent Baxter and I had made a bond, however superficial and tentative.

"Well," he concluded, "I'm going to call Officer Sanders now and see if his interview with Gloria Coleman told him anything we didn't already know."

"He's probably still talking with her," I said. "He just went over to the church."

"How do you know that?" he asked, a hint of suspicion in his voice.

"He stopped by here before he went over there," I said. "You know the church is across the street and only a little way down from my shop."

"Why did he stop by your place first?" Still wary.

"He wanted me to talk him out of going to see her," I told him. "I couldn't think of anything to say that might stop him, and I feel a little guilty about that."

"Oh." He seemed relieved, for some reason, and gave out with a little laugh. "Well, if you come up with anything that might stop *me*, call this number, hear?"

"Absolutely," I said.

And he hung up.

I looked around the garden. Right next to the gazebo there was a butterfly bush and flitting around it I saw a hummingbird moth. I'd never heard of hummingbird moths before I came to Enigma. The first time I saw one I thought it was one of Titania's fairies and I said so out loud, although that may have been the tequila talking. Gloria Coleman happened to be sitting with me at the time. She'd had as much to drink as I had, but she still managed to explain to me what I was seeing.

"*Hemaris diffinis*," she pronounced perfectly. "The snowberry clearwing, sometimes known as the 'hummingbird moth.' But if you prefer to call this one Peaseblossom or Cobweb, I will not object."

I was overwhelmingly impressed that she knew the Latin and common names of the insect *and* the Shakespeare names of the fairies. That was the exact moment she went from acquaintance to good friend in my estimation. And I'd only grown to love her more since then.

"All right, Cobweb," I said to the little moth as it went from one tiny purple blossom to another. "Message received. I'll go over and see what I can do to help Gloria."

The moth hovered in the air for a moment, staring at me, and then took off in the direction of the church. What could I do but follow?

7

I HADN'T EVEN CROSSED the street before I recognized that the conversation between Gloria and Billy was not going very well. The reason was obvious: Idell Glassie. She was pounding her fist into her other hand and mumbling. She saw me approaching and turned her ire my way.

"This has nothing to do with you!" she began. "This is between me and the woman who killed my sister!"

The three of them were gathered around the still-uncompleted church sign. Gloria had made it to "Just Love, I'll Sort It Ou—"

"You haven't finished that sign yet?" I asked Gloria as I arrived at the curb.

"People keep interrupting me," Gloria said, glancing sideways.

Idell snarled at Billy. "Tell her to leave!"

"Miss Glassie—" Billy began.

"You look here, Billy Sanders," Idell interrupted. "I have influence. I have money. I have standing. What are *you*?"

Billy had been raised in the traditional Southern method. He always said "Yes, ma'am" and "Yes, sir" to everyone, no matter who they were. He didn't drink, he didn't smoke, and

I'd never heard him curse. He would never even dream of arguing with an older woman no matter what she'd said. So it came as a surprise when he tensed, took a barely perceptible step back, straightened up to his full six-foot height, squared his shoulders, and took a deep breath.

"I represent the law," he said. "That's who I am." He was calm, but I could tell that it was taking an effort.

"And now that Finlay is retiring," I added, "he's about to be our new sheriff."

"Not if he don't arrest this woman right this minute," Idell said through her teeth. "I'll see to it that he don't get a job anywhere in this *state*!"

"Well, ma'am," he said to her, the soul of patience, however strained, "I'm not going to arrest anyone today."

"I'll get those GBI men here," Idell assured him. "They'll do your job if you won't. Then you'll see! And I'm telling *everyone* not to vote for you!"

With that she turned and motored away as fast as her eighty-something legs would carry her.

"He's running unopposed," I called after her.

She didn't turn around, she just mumbled something. I couldn't hear what it was. I waited until she was far enough away before I turned to Billy.

"Why is she in such a . . . why is she being like this?" I turned to Gloria. "She's always so quiet in the bookshop."

"I've been studying on that," Billy answered. "I believe it's guilt."

My eyes widened. "You don't think that *she* killed her sister!"

He shook his head. "Not that kind of guilt. Bea Glassie just kind of disappeared and no one, including Idell, took any notice at all. No missing person complaint, no questions from anyone, not even a whisper of gossip. Which, I can tell you, is a complete anomaly in this town."

"'Anomaly'?" Gloria poked at him, grinning. "Look who's using fancy words all of a sudden."

He smiled back, all trace of tension gone.

"I'm one year away from being the first college graduate in my entire family," he said. "I got all kinds of vocabulary."

"Well, I think you're right about Idell," Gloria went on. "I think that the discovery of her sister's body was shocking, and she turned shock into guilt for having ignored her sister's disappearance. And guilt sometimes has a way of turning into anger, don't you think?"

I thought for a moment.

"But, why *didn't* she ask any questions when her sister disappeared?" I asked Billy. "Why didn't she make a complaint then?"

He looked down the street. We could still see Idell in the distance, making her way back to her house, presumably to call the GBI.

"Yeah, that's just what I can't figure out," Billy answered. "They didn't get along, not one bit. Fought all the time. They sometimes went for months on end without speaking to each other. My mama used to say they were just two sour old maids, but I believe there was more to it than that."

Now, sometimes my brain gets the better of me and makes me do things that I don't particularly want to do. At that moment, my brain absolutely demanded that I look into the Glassie sisters, a dark well into which I did not really want to dive. But what if Idell *had* killed her sister? Wouldn't pointing an immediate and outraged finger at someone else be the perfect misdirection?

So I heard myself ask Billy, "What did they fight about?"

He shook his head. "Everything. I remember one time when I was a kid, they were at Mae Etta's having breakfast and Bea threw her ham biscuit at Idell and called her a gnashnab. I was in there getting me a Co-Cola and it was quite a scene. Of course Idell wasn't hurt, you know how fluffy them biscuits are at Mae Etta's. But Idell stood up, tossed her coffee in Bea's face, and stormed out. I asked Mae Etta what a gnashnab was, but she didn't know."

"It's a nitpicker," Gloria volunteered. "Someone who complains all the time."

Billy and I turned her way.

"Now who's got the vocabulary?" I asked Gloria.

She shrugged. "I do a lot of crossword puzzles."

"To tell the truth," Billy said, "I kind of forgot all about their cussedness."

But that just made me more determined to investigate the exact nature of said cussedness. Because even if it didn't tell me anything directly related to the murder, I thought it might at least enlighten me as to Idell's outsized ire toward my friend.

So I said, "Billy, you wouldn't mind if I asked around about that particular aspect of the relationship between the sisters, would you?"

"First place," he began, "yes, I would mind, because this is an official police investigation and I don't want you confusing things. But second place, the fact that I don't want you to do it won't have any effect on you, will it?"

"What if I just happen to run into Idell at the diner?" I asked innocently. "Or, you know, she comes into the shop all the time. What if I just happen to strike up a conversation with her?"

"About her sister." He shook his head.

"I guess the topic might come up," I said.

"Maddy," he said.

"Okay," I conceded. "I'll lay off. But if she comes at Gloria again, I'm talking to Idell with a two-by-four in my hand."

"As the presumptive sheriff of this town," he said with just a hint of a smile, "I would have to warn you against any such threat of bodily harm to a citizen of our fair city."

"And as an Episcopal priest," Gloria chimed in, "I would have to remind you that Jesus never threatened anybody with a two-by-four."

"Didn't he say, 'Walk softly but carry a big stick'?" I asked, grinning.

"That was Teddy Roosevelt," Gloria answered, laughing.

"Right," I said. "I always get those two confused."

"Heathen," Gloria chided.

"I'm serious as a heart attack, Maddy," Billy concluded. "Stay out of this. You could end up making more trouble for Reverend Coleman. And it's not just me. You got to stay *especially* out of the way of the GBI. You hear me?"

"I said *okay*," I told him.

I could see from the look in his eyes that he didn't believe me, but I really meant it.

At the time.

So I just said goodbye and walked back to the shop. The crowd of customers had dwindled. Jennifer was counting the money in the cash box. When Rose ran the place, it was a cash-only establishment. But I'd modernized. We had one of those little card-reading thingies that plugged into our Mac.

Jen looked up when I walked in.

"I think this might be our best day since I started working here," she told me. "I guess your 'bad news equals good business' rule applied heavily today."

"Yeah, but how's that going to help you at the Tate Modern this summer?" I said on my way into the kitchen.

"My London internship? Not at all. But the Tate Modern doesn't really need extra help with their business, whereas a dinky bookstore south of nowhere—"

"I'm fixing a late lunch," I interrupted. "You want something?"

She finished her counting and closed the cash box. "I could eat."

I loved the kitchen in that house. The creaking floorboards, the hiss of the gas stove, the clinking of dishes, the hum of the fridge, the rush of water from the faucet—they were all music to me. And if I closed my eyes, I could still smell Aunt Rose's cornbread and Philomena's collard greens. For me it was a time machine just as much as it was a place to cook. I rarely failed to be transported to my childhood, even if only for a moment, every time I stepped up into the pantry.

And in that pantry, there was pickled okra that Philomena had put up the previous summer. There were also pickled peaches, food of the gods. And lest we dine exclusively on pickles, I found some cold fried chicken and potato salad in the fridge.

Jennifer surveyed the table as I laid everything out.

"You didn't so much *fix* lunch as find it," she sniffed. "But, okay."

I ignored her, found silverware, and sat.

"You forgot the iced tea," she said, opening the fridge back up.

She found the tea, fetched two glasses, and joined me at the table.

"Now, then," she said, falling into her seat. "What's going to happen tonight?"

I looked up at her. We hadn't gotten any plates or bowls. We were going to eat straight from the serving plates or Ball jars. Fewer dishes to wash.

"Tonight?" I asked, skewering a pickled okra.

"Don't play coy with me," she said, a drumstick in her hand. "What's the hubbub with David tonight at dinner, here in this very kitchen? That's what I want to know."

"Hubbub?" I nabbed a spoonful of potato salad.

"I overheard what you said to him on the porch, for one thing," she said. "And for another thing, everybody in town knows that David doesn't like to talk about his past, and you seem intent on making him do just that."

"Everybody in town knows that?"

"I believe that you keep questioning my words because you're deflecting," she said, waving her drumstick at me.

"That's Dr. Waldrop talking," I told her. "Not you. You can't take one class in psychology and suddenly think you know what everyone is doing inside their little brains."

"I don't think I know what *everyone* is doing," she fired back. "I just know that you're pushing David to do something before he's willing to do it and that could result in pushing him away."

"So now you're a therapist *and* a relationship counselor?"

"Oh, I'm sure you're right," she said, "what does a cute twenty-year-old girl with three boyfriends and a rich social life know about romantic relationships? Pass me the pickled peaches. Please."

I nudged the jar her way.

"Well, if you must know," I said, surrendering just a little, "there's a *Faye* in the ointment."

She stopped moving. "There's a *what* now?"

"David was engaged to Faye Dillard a while back," I explained. "Everyone was certain they were going to marry. She was the reason he came to Enigma in the first place."

"So?" She jabbed a pickled peach with her fork.

"So what happened?" I wanted to know. "Why didn't they get hitched? Where's this alleged Faye now? That sort of thing."

She just shrugged. "Like that's any of your business."

"No, but I've asked him about it a lot," I began, sounding a lot more needy than I wanted to. "Why won't he talk about it?"

"Because it's none of your business!" Jennifer insisted.

"I know." I sat back. "I know that."

"I'll tell you what *is* your business," she said, reaching for another piece of cold chicken.

"What's that? *Man* these peaches are good."

"Who killed the person that was buried in your front yard?" She took a bite, then went on with her mouth full. "That's what I want to know. That's what you want to know too."

"Yeah, but I was just warned about looking into all that," I informed her, "by the local lawman."

"No." She brushed that objection aside immediately. "Billy says stuff like that. But he secretly wants you to help him."

"He does, huh?" I knew that wasn't true and I hoped that my tone of voice conveyed that conviction.

"He's in my Foundations of Education class," she went on, undaunted by my attitude. "He tries to act all tough and old-school, twentieth-century manly, or something, but I can tell he wants to reach out."

"How can you tell that?" I was beginning to be amused by her twenty-something assessment.

"I'm an empath," she told me primly. "I can feel what other people are feeling."

Before I could explain to her that being mildly observant was a long way away from being a certified empath, I heard the front door slam open.

"Maddy?" Billy called from the other room.

"In the kitchen," I told him.

A second later he appeared, and the look on his face made me stand up.

"What is it?" I asked him.

He looked at Jennifer, then back at me, and shook his head, eyes wide.

"Baxter." That was all he managed to say, but not for lack of trying.

I waited for a second before I asked, "Officer Baxter from the GBI?"

"Special Agent," he corrected absently. "He roared up in that big old black car. Jumped out holding his ID. Arrested Gloria Coleman, over my strenuous objection, and put her in the back of his car. She's gone."

"What?" I took an involuntary step forward. "Where did he take her?"

"Their office in Sylvester," Billy said.

"I don't understand." I felt an odd kind of panic rising from my stomach.

"He said he got a call from his superior," Billy told me. "They said bring her in. Direct order. I just came over to get the squad car to follow him. And to tell you what happened."

"Let's go." I turned to Jennifer. "Lock up!"

I headed out of the kitchen without waiting for any kind of response. I grabbed my purse out of the desk drawer and shot straight to the front door.

I was sitting in the front seat of the squad car before Billy made it out of the house.

8

THE FORTY-MINUTE DRIVE to Sylvester seemed like five hours, even though Billy had the siren on and we were going close to a hundred. When we finally got there, the GBI offices didn't look like what I'd pictured. Sure, it was a government building, brick, squat, unimaginative. But it was set back from Highway 82, surrounded by trees, pleasantly landscaped, and seemed calm.

"Do they have, like, a jail here?" I asked Billy.

"Not that I know of." His eyes were glued to the front door of the building.

"Is it unusual for the GBI to bring someone into their offices?" I got out of the squad car and headed for the glass double doors.

"I don't know," Billy answered, catching up to me.

We made what I considered to be a dramatic entrance, but there was only one guy at the front desk and he seemed unimpressed.

"Where's Millie?" Billy asked before he arrived at the desk.

The man behind the desk blinked. He was wearing the

same kind of cheap suit as Baxter and Baker; he was balding and his eyes were rimmed in red. He stared at Billy's badge and name plate.

"Break." That was all the man said. "Why?"

"She's my aunt," he said.

"Oh." He shrugged. "She's on break."

"Okay. We're actually here to see Baxter and Baker."

The man glared. "Concerning?"

"An ongoing murder investigation in Enigma," Billy snapped back, strong. "Of which I am the local liaison. I initiated the GBI's involvement in the case. So all I need from you is a room number."

The man behind the desk looked at me.

"The dead body was found in my front yard," I said, doing my best to sound timid. "I think I might be a suspect."

It was clear that the man behind the desk was utterly uncertain as to what to do or say. He looked down at his phone, then over his left shoulder.

"Down that hall, room G, interrogation," he said uncertainly. "I believe they might have a suspect in there right now."

"I know they do," Billy said, pulling away from the desk. "That's why I'm here."

I followed Billy down the hall to room G. We barged in. Speaking for myself, I was surprised by what I found.

Gloria and Baxter were laughing so hard they had tears in their eyes. Baker was shaking his head. All three turned our way.

"So I guess they haven't dragged out the rubber hoses yet," I said.

"We don't use those on people of the cloth anymore," Baker assured me. "We reserve those for small-town booksellers."

"You okay?" Billy asked Gloria.

"Oh, yeah," she said, continuing to laugh. "This guy just told me the best joke. Do you know what Moses said right before the Red Sea parted?"

"Do y'all have any actual reason to keep Reverend Coleman in custody?" Billy demanded.

Baker nodded. "It's not a good reason, but, yes, we have one."

"Our boss told us to," Baxter added.

"Let me guess," I said. "Your boss was somehow influenced by Idell Glassie."

Baker looked down. "I wouldn't care to speculate on the director's motivation. And I'm sure that Idell Glassie calling him a dozen times in the past twenty-four hours has nothing to do with anything."

"But we've been instructed to detain her during our ongoing investigation," Baxter added.

Billy looked around. "Where?"

"Where would we detain her?" Baker asked. "Not certain yet. I'm not inclined to put a priest in the Worth County Jail," Baker continued. "Maybe the Sylvester Inn?"

"How crazy would that make Idell," Gloria asked, "if you put me up in a motel?"

Baker nodded. "I don't think she can get much crazier than she already is, do you?"

There was a moment of silent nodding all around before I had to ask.

"Do you really have to put her anywhere?" I asked. "Can't she just go home? We'll give her a ride."

Baxter lowered his head. "This is a tricky situation."

Baker agreed. "We can't just let her go. This is, like, official GBI business."

"There's paperwork," Baxter added.

"With our names on it," Baker concluded.

I stared.

"You know," I told the men from the GBI, "when you're not standing in front of me—I mean when I'm not right there with you—I can't tell you guys apart. You wear the same basic suit. Your names are too similar. You kind of look alike. And neither one of you has much of a personality. No offense."

Baker smiled. "That's all on purpose."

"What?" I looked back and forth between them several times.

"The GBI has an unofficial directive that encourages us to be nondescript," Baxter began.

"Encourages us to dress alike, act alike," Baker continued.

"So that we can work without arousing suspicion," Baxter concluded. "Even undercover, incognito, or otherwise anonymously occupied."

"I see," I told them. "Then, good job."

"If I may interject here, for a moment," Gloria said softly. "I wonder if I might suggest something that may be a bit unorthodox, GBI-wise."

Everyone turned her way.

"Last fall," Gloria said, "when Madeline came back home to Enigma, someone tried to chase her out of town, and then someone killed a young woman in her shop."

"Tandy Fletcher," Baxter said.

"Yes." Gloria seemed surprised to hear the name. "And, anyway, Madeline pretty much figured out who killed Tandy, and then Madeline captured the killer. Bonked her in the head with a big old book. So I think we should turn Madeline Brimley loose on this particular caper. She'll figure it out."

Baker took a breath as if he might be about to object, but Baxter beat him to it.

"Out of the question," he said. "Miss Brimley, you stay out of this and I mean *completely*, you hear me?"

"Of course," I said instantly.

Billy licked his lips. Gloria smiled nearly imperceptibly. Baker nodded.

"All right, that's settled," Baker said. "Now, Reverend Coleman, I'm afraid we actually do have to remand you to a holding cell here in town while we complete our investigation."

"No!" I objected.

"Because," Baker went on as if I hadn't interrupted him, "an official directive to that effect has been issued."

"That's some backroom bull," Billy objected.

"Yes, it is," Baker said, "but it's official backroom bull, so . . ."

"How is this possible," I fumed. "You don't have any *kind* of evidence—"

"We have motive, opportunity, and means," Baxter said, holding up a finger for each of his ridiculous suggestions. "Bea Glassie intended to get rid of Reverend Coleman at their church and Coleman knew it. There was a confrontation for which we have an eyewitness. And the murder occurred right across the street from Coleman's church, in what was at the time an abandoned building."

I held up three fingers of my own. "Nobody in that church except Bea wanted to get rid of Gloria. The eyewitness in this scenario was the drunken sister of the *very* drunken deceased. And the bookshop was not abandoned. Tandy Fletcher was living there at the time this was supposed to have happened."

That only evoked a single second of silence.

"That's why there's an investigation," Baker said. "We're only holding Reverend Coleman for ninety-six hours, that's the maximum without the kind of evidence that would satisfy a DA."

"That's why we're eager to put Reverend Coleman in a nice comfortable cell," Baxter concluded. "We've got four days to find out who really killed Bea Glassie, because nobody except for Idell Glassie thinks that Coleman did it. So. If you would like to have a word with the Reverend, to say your goodbyes, we'll step out of the room. But then we're taking her over to the Worth County Jail."

"Absolutely not," I said, planting my feet.

Gloria smiled. "It's okay. I've been in jail before. Probably will be again. I think it makes me colorful. I'm a jailbird priest. That's a tradition. Didn't you ever hear of the Berrigan brothers?"

"Yeah," I said, "but they were Catholics."

Baxter stood. "We'll step out now."

He left, walked a few steps down the hall.

Baker stared hard into my eyes and said, loud enough so that Baxter could hear. "If we hear that you're impeding our investigation, I'll personally lock you up on a charge of obstruction."

"What if you *don't* hear about it?" I asked.

He paused, looked at Gloria, then back at me, lowered his voice, and said, "Then I guess you'd probably get away with it."

That was all. He was gone. But Gloria and Billy and I exchanged looks.

"Did you just get an unofficial, supersecret okay to investigate this thing?" Gloria whispered, grinning.

"No," Billy warned.

"And anyway, Gloria," I said, taking a seat beside her, "I didn't actually solve anything about Tandy. The killer came to the shop. I got lucky."

"Baloney," Gloria said, waving a hand. "You were like Miss Marple."

"Look, both of you," Billy told us sternly, "I don't like either of these GBI guys very much, so I hate to agree with them, but you really have to keep clear of all this, Maddy. Gloria's completely innocent. We all know it. Let this play itself out."

"Yeah, because nobody who was innocent has ever been convicted of murder," I snapped. "Don't get me started."

Gloria looked up at Billy. "*Please* don't get her started."

"Did you say you'd been in jail before?" Billy asked Gloria.

She stood. "Long story, but it's fairly amusing. It all started with a small disagreement; I was only fourteen at the time—"

But before she could go on, Baker came back into the room.

"Sorry," he said, and he sounded like he meant it. "Time to go, Reverend Coleman."

She smiled. "Okeydokey."

"We'll come back tomorrow and visit," I assured her.

"Oh, no, you won't," Baker snapped. "She won't be allowed visitors for the next ninety-six hours."

"Why not?" I objected.

"Because we don't have time for that," Baker told me, his irritation rising. "And because I said so!"

"I'd like to register one last objection to this—" Billy began.

Baker was about to respond when Gloria stepped up.

"Seriously, Billy," Gloria said. "It's all right. Madeline knows what to do."

With that, the Right Reverend Gloria Coleman, my favorite Episcopal priest, was carted off to jail, and there wasn't one thing that Billy or I could do about it.

9

THE RIDE HOME was interminable. At first all I could do was think of ways to break Gloria out of her unjust incarceration. That was before I remembered my dinner date with a certain master gardener. But I couldn't concentrate on that because Billy complained the whole way.

"Do you know how many times I've had to go over to Idell Glassie's house to investigate one of her 'urgent complaints'?" he grumbled.

"One million and seven," I suggested.

"Yes," he snapped. "That's the exact number. And it's always nothing. Kids walking too close to her house on their way to school. Dogs sniffing her hydrangeas. Once she called me because she couldn't reach a teacup on a high shelf. But did I ever complain?"

"Not to me," I said. I was trying to humor him.

"Not to anybody!" He slammed his hand into the steering wheel. "Not no more, buddy. My plan now is to go all over town and rile the general population against her."

"Pitchforks and torches," I agreed.

I wasn't about to tell him while he was in that kind of mood, but my own plan wasn't entirely different from his.

I was determined to find out about Idell and her sister, find out why Idell was being even more cussed than usual. And in the process, I thought I might see if I couldn't discover who actually killed Bea Glassie.

And when we finally got back to the bookshop, I bolted out of the squad car, partly to avoid any further conversation with the most irritated version of Billy Sanders I'd ever seen, but mostly because I wanted to change clothes and straighten up my kitchen before David arrived. Billy nodded in my direction when I got out, didn't say a word, and roared away just as soon as I slammed the car door.

I had no idea what time it was. The shop looked empty from the porch, and when I discovered that Jennifer had, indeed, locked up, I was relieved that I wouldn't have to deal with anyone. Just fly upstairs, change, and back down to arrange the kitchen in an illusion of organization.

I had the intuition that this was going to be a skirt or maybe even a dress occasion with David. He would probably still be in his work clothes, but I didn't care. I wasn't exactly going to dress up for a kitchen dinner of take-out barbecue, but I thought I could do a little better than slacks and a short-sleeved shirt. So dress it was, a Dolce & Gabbana Portofino print midi. I could never have afforded it; it was something I'd worn in a production of *Noises Off* that put more money into the costume budget than it had into the actor salaries, so I took the dress at the end of the run. It was nice. It had large roses on it.

But the second that I put it on and looked at myself in the mirror I saw that it was overkill. If I wore that, I realized, it would be obvious I was making too much of the encounter. All I really had in store was a bit of information about

David's fiancée—a phrase I was really hoping should include the word *former*.

So into the black jeans and a crisp olive-green short-sleeved pullover. I fixed my hair, but not too much. I put a dab of toothpaste on my tongue instead of actually brushing because I heard David at the door downstairs.

"Hey?" he called.

"Be right down." A last check in the mirror, and I launched myself in the direction of his voice.

I hadn't hit the last stairstep before I saw that David had, in fact, not worn his work clothes to pay me a visit. He was in noticeably clean khakis and a black short-sleeved shirt. He'd even gotten out of his work boots—he was wearing black Doc Martens. I was trying to think of the last time I'd seen him that dressed up when he held up two large take-out bags.

"Dinner." He smiled.

"Kitchen," I answered.

The kitchen was still kind of a mess from my haphazard lunch with Jennifer, but I don't think David noticed. He set the bags down on the table and looked around.

"Have a seat," I said. "I'll get silverware."

Did my voice sound nervous? I didn't want to be nervous. As an actor I'd always kind of depended on nerves, a little bump of adrenaline, right before going onstage. But my assumption was that I was going to be more audience than performer for this particular encounter, so I told my nerves to get lost. They didn't listen.

Silverware, plates, extra napkins, glasses of ice, an extra-large bowl for bones, and the table was set in what I might pretentiously refer to as a *rustic* style.

I sat. He sat. And for a very long moment, that's all that happened.

"So, where was I?" he finally said.

"Oh." I looked down. "Well. You were working on the Dillard farm, writing a little poetry, and it began to look like you and Faye would get married."

"Everybody thought we would." He nodded. "People said it was a good match. I guess it seemed like that, you know, on paper. The thing was . . ."

When he didn't finish his sentence after what seemed like an hour, I prompted.

"The thing was?" I said.

"She fell in love with the mayor of a small town around here," he said plainly. "Rather not say which one, and it doesn't really matter. I was relieved, to tell the truth."

"Why?" I tried to make it sound like a casual question.

He settled into his chair, took a breath, and thinned his lips, thinking.

"Sometimes you can be in love with the person you *want* somebody to be, not the person they actually are. You know?"

I nodded. "And it's hard to tell the difference."

"Exactly." He leaned forward. "And when I figured out that we were both in love with people who didn't really exist, the rest was easy."

I reached for the take-out bags and began to pull the food out, put it on the table. Because I didn't know what else to do.

Finally I was able to say, "I have to tell you that I'm greatly relieved myself, here."

"Oh?" He watched my busywork.

"Yeah," I went on. "Like, what if it was, 'I asked her to marry me and she turned me down and I'm still in love with her'? Like, what if that was your story?"

"Ah." He began helping me with the food. "Well, it's not."

"And that's why I'm relieved."

Food out, containers open, we began to dish up our dinner. Barbecued chicken, jalapeño corn bread, sweet slaw, baked beans—food of the gods.

We began to eat in silence because neither of us knew what to say next. Then, foolishly, I forged ahead.

"So maybe you're worried that having dinner with an actor is another episode of getting to know someone other than the *real* person." I took a forkful of coleslaw. "But, for good or ill, you've gotten to know the real me. The post-theatrical me. Not the actor."

He looked up from his plate. "I never thought I was having dinner with an actor. I'm having dinner with a woman who runs a bookshop. In a tiny little town in South Georgia. The fact that she's also been on Broadway, Off Broadway, and—as my extensive research has revealed—in lots of small television and film roles, that just makes her more fascinating to me."

I smiled. "Fascinating?"

"You heard me." He went back to his corn bread. "That's the word I used."

"*More* fascinating," I confirmed. Shamelessly.

He smiled and nodded.

"And you didn't want to tell me this little bit of information about Faye because . . . ?" I pressed.

He scowled, but only for a second. "How does it make me look? A person who was supposed to marry me ran off and married someone else?"

"It makes you look lucky," I said. "Pass the slaw, please."

"You don't think less of me?" he asked.

I was just about to tell him how much *more* I thought of

him when the front door opened and a familiar voice sang out.

"Yoo-hoo," Philomena called. "It's only me."

"We're in the kitchen," I answered. "David's here."

"Oh." I couldn't see her but I could tell that she wasn't moving, trying to decide whether or not to intrude.

"I got a mess of barbecue," David announced. "There's plenty for you to join us."

"Mona and Memaw's?" she asked, still not moving.

"Uh-huh," David answered. "Come on in."

"Well, I don't know." But I could hear her finally coming toward us.

She appeared in the wide doorway in all her glory: dress suit of the day—the brown one, along with black Tory Burch cap-toe pumps. Her hair pulled back in a severe bun, glasses around her neck on a pearl chain.

"I'm interrupting," she said, a slight smile on her lips.

"I think we're through with the embarrassing stuff," David said. "I told her about Faye."

"Oh, thank the Lord." With that she motored into the kitchen full force. "It's about time, too. You have no idea how much I've been dying to tell her about that."

"You knew?" I asked, getting up to fetch her a plate and some silverware.

"Everybody knows about that," she said, waving a dismissive hand. "But we all understood that David would tell you in his time, and it was his story to tell."

"Not much of a story," I told her. "Faye ran off with a small-town mayor. Sounds more like a country song in the making than an actual *story*."

"Is that barbecued chicken?" Phil asked, taking a seat.

I set a plate down in front of her. "Did you just come over for dinner or was there some other reason?"

"Yes!" She looked at both of us. "Gloria's been arrested!"

I nodded. "Yeah, I kind of watched it happen. Billy and I went to the GBI offices in Sylvester. They're 'holding' her. And they're not allowing visitors!"

"Why not?" Phil twisted in her seat. "That makes me so mad! This is nothing but Idell Glassie being a . . . a pistol!"

"The GBI is holding her for Bea's murder?" David shook his head. "That won't stick."

"The guys at the GBI don't think Gloria did it," I said, "but they still arrested, or, *detained* her."

Philomena snapped, "You have no idea the kind of influence the Glassie money has around here. Maddy, you were so young when you left you probably weren't aware of the way those sisters used to carry on. And David, you may have lived here for ten years, but you're still new in town to most people in Enigma, don't you think?"

David smiled, reaching for the chicken. "I don't think much about it one way or another. For the most part, I'm a stranger everywhere I go."

"Yes, very romantic," Phil said, eyelids low, "but there's a difference in our little town between families that have been here for generations and people who—"

"The point is," I interrupted a little too loudly, "that Gloria's in custody and I'm going to get her out because I'm going to find out who really killed Bea!"

That engendered an all-too-brief moment of silence followed by an avalanche of objections from the other two people at my kitchen table. But I was surprised to hear it end with Philomena's final pronouncement.

"I'll help," she said.

David swallowed his corn bread. "Me too."

I took a second to adjust to the moment, and then forged ahead.

"Okay, then let me tell you who's on my list of suspects," I said.

"Idell," Phil said instantly.

"Yes," I agreed.

"Also Mae Etta," Phil went on. "She hates both sisters."

"And I'd put Frank Fletcher on the list," David said quietly. "He did a lot of work for both sisters and they would often refuse to pay him or paid him less than they said they would. And Frank isn't what you'd call a forgiving sort of person."

"Oh, that's true," Phil confirmed. "I heard that Frank even cut off their water one time. You know, at the street? He was so mad."

"Good, he's on my list." I nodded. "And what about this guy who was supposed to have been Bea's boyfriend? Idell was going on about him when she confronted Gloria outside the church."

"Kell Brady?" Phil squinted. "I don't know if he's even still alive, but I don't think he's much of a suspect. Old, lots of money, not overly religious . . . lived in Hawkinsville. I only met him a few times. He walked with a cane. He never took much time getting to know anyone in Enigma that I'm aware of. I don't think there's anything there."

"Okay," I said, "but Idell, Mae Etta, and Frank are all good possibilities, right?"

The other two nodded.

"All right, then," I concluded, filling my fork full of slaw, "I'll have breakfast at the diner tomorrow morning and have a little chat with Mae Etta."

After that, no matter how much I wanted the conversation to return to the subject of my relationship with David, all we talked about was how to get Gloria out of custody. Food gone, dishes put up, sun set, Phil yawning, we said an early good night. I was hoping to get Phil to leave first and have a bit of personal time with David, but it was not to be. When I flipped on the front porch light switch, nothing happened. Dead bulb. David and I shared a meaningful look, but that was all. Phil took David's arm so that he could help her navigate the stairs in the dark, and moments later they were both gone.

The night was quiet. Tree frogs and crickets were the only noise; moon was the only light. I stayed out on the porch for a while. The air was soft and the light was dreamy. Too early in the year for fireflies, but the stars were blinking nicely. The peace of the night was hampered by the yellow police tape and the ravaged front yard, of course, but only a little.

It was hard to imagine, then, that anyone would kill anyone anywhere in the world, and I had the happy illusion, for just that half second, that Death had taken an infinitesimally short break, that murder had a tiny vacation—just in that second as I stood on the porch—and all life on the planet rejoiced.

Then there was a rattling of the screen door behind me, and Cannonball made his large presence known. Reality returned.

I looked his way. "You want me to come in?"

He batted at the screen door again.

"Okay, okay," I told him. "How about a little more dinner?"

He turned immediately and headed for the kitchen.

I went in and followed him. "You really do speak better English than some of our local residents."

Cannonball responded by sitting down next to his bowl and waiting patiently.

As I poured and he supervised, I had to ask.

"What's your take on all this?" I scratched his chin. "Who killed Bea Glassie? You were here when it happened, right?"

He looked at me like I was an idiot.

10

IT WAS RAINING the next morning when I woke up. Cannonball had decided that the pillow next to my head was the perfect place to be, staring out the window at the dreary drizzle. When I sat up, he turned his considerable head my way and glared, complaining about the damp.

"Still," I told him, "April showers bring Mae West, isn't that how the saying goes? Or is it May Flowers? Did I ever tell you that May Flowers was the name of a stripper who was in a show with me called *In Somnia*?"

Yes, that was the mood I was in. The surreal nature of events had finally gotten to me, and as I was getting dressed, staring out the window, I began to wonder if maybe everything was a dream. Whereas Cannonball, apparently unaffected by my mood, put his head on the pillow and went back to sleep.

Down the stairs in black slacks and a pale short-sleeved top, the mood continued. There had been a body buried in my front yard. That body had been murdered. And someone thought that an Episcopal priest had been the killer.

The shop was quiet, and the sound of the falling rain

seemed to lull the whole world into ... what? What was the rain trying to do?

After a moment I had the sense that I was in a play. Maybe something by Pinter, where the actors are supposed to make long silent pauses feel packed with emotional content. But of course, I thought to myself, an actor *would* think that life was a play. The play in God's mind. Just like Philomena would think that life was a class, something to be learned. Or how Gloria might have considered life just a prelude to heaven.

A sudden sound at the door startled me out of my contemplation, and I was very grateful to see Jennifer appear in the doorway. She sported a well-wrought French braid and she was wearing a springtime cotton dress. With black ankle-high army boots. Which momentarily broke my heart because it reminded me a little of Tandy Fletcher.

"Oh!" she said when she saw me. "You startled me! What are you doing?"

I looked around. "I'm pondering the nature of reality, and my own place in it."

She stared for a moment, and then: "Come to any conclusions?"

"Yes. Life is a play."

She nodded and closed the front door behind her. "I always heard that life was like a mountain railroad."

"What?"

"It's a song we sing in church sometimes." She ambled toward the desk in the living room. "You know, 'You will roll up grades of trial; you will cross the bridge of strife.'"

"Never heard the song," I confessed, "but I am familiar with the Bridge of Strife."

"There you go." She sat.

"Anyway, I'm going to the diner," I told her. "You want anything?"

She shook her head. "No, I already had breakfast. You know it's raining outside, right?"

"Yeah, I want to talk with Mae Etta."

"Oh, man," she complained. "Mae Etta. What a pain in the petunias she is."

Petunias, I thought. She got that from her college professor, Dr. Waldrop.

"You mean her insistence on getting that Oz book for—who was it for?"

"Great-granddaughter," Jennifer said. "She called here while you were out yesterday. She'll probably ask you about it."

"You've ordered it?"

"Of course."

I headed for the coat rack by the front door. It was a walnut antique. A bench flanked by rows of hooks on both sides and held together by a large, beveled mirror. The feet were huge bird claws holding a hard walnut sphere. Over the mirror there was a pattern of romantically posed deer. And just as I grabbed my raincoat, a Burberry gaberdine trench coat, I had an odd thought.

"Hey, Jen?" I sang out. "You know all those receipt books I showed you when you first started here? The ones that go back to the first day the shop was open?"

"Yes," she said, getting the desktop in order.

"How do you feel about going through them to see if Bea Glassie ever bought anything here. I hate to ask."

"Not at all!" she chirped. "It'll give me something to do in the slow moments. And the way it's raining, I have a feeling I'll have plenty of those today."

"You're going to be a *big* hit at the Tate Modern," I said.

"Oh, did I tell you they sent me my credentials?" she enthused. "A couple of documents that look really important, and they even sent me my official ID lanyard!"

"Exciting," I agreed. "So you don't mind going over the old books and stuff, see if you come across Bea's name?"

"Not a problem." She smiled. "But why do you want to know about that?"

"Not sure," I said, struggling into my raincoat. "Just suddenly wanted to know. I think the rain made me ask."

She didn't look my way. "The rain made you ask? Are you just trying to prepare me for the fabled English eccentrics you read about in Agatha Christie novels?"

"I'm just trying to figure out why Bea would have been buried in the front yard here." I opened the door and stared out at the rain. "Makes a *little* more sense if she was a customer, maybe."

"I'll get right on it."

I had the intuition that Jennifer was right, she *would* have plenty of time to wander through the old receipt books. We always had fewer customers when it rained, and it was really coming down.

I patted my back pocket for my wallet, my right front pocket for my keys, and hurried down the porch steps, into the deluge. I barely managed to get into Igor without drowning. Every time for the last six months that I'd sat behind the wheel, I wondered if I should pick a new name, since the car had been made into a gleaming showpiece by the highly estimable mechanic, Elbert, but every time I concluded that the name Igor was still right. After all, did movie stars change their names after a face-lift? The Globe Theatre was still the Globe no matter how many times it was rebuilt. And they're still called The Temptations even though there's only one original band member left alive.

I patted the steering wheel lovingly. "A rose by any other name, pal. You're stuck with *Igor*."

And with that, I was off.

THE diner was crowded. I had no idea what time it was, but Jennifer usually showed up for work at the bookshop around eight in the morning, so that was a clue. Most of the booths were taken, but there were a few stools at the counter, so I took the one right next to the cash register where Mae Etta sat in her tall chair, wrapped in a quilt she'd doubtless created herself.

She raised her head in my direction. "That little girl you got at your shop told me she ordered my book. That true?"

"If she said it," I confirmed, "it's true. She's pretty good."

She mumbled something that I couldn't hear.

"Maybe I could get a cup of coffee?" I suggested.

She got up, went to the pot, poured, and delivered a thick white mug with a single, oddly graceful motion. Decades of moving exactly that way over and over again had made her into a ballerina. Of sorts.

"I guess you heard about Gloria Coleman," I said, not looking at her.

She nodded once.

"You know she didn't do it," I said.

"I don't know anything," she told me.

"I think Idell did it," I said, mostly to see what response that would provoke.

Mae Etta remained nonplussed. "Wouldn't put it past her."

"Oh?" I leaned forward. "Why is that?"

"They argued all the time. The sisters."

I sipped my coffee. "I've heard about those arguments. Billy told me that Bea threw a biscuit at Idell in this very establishment."

"Ham biscuit." Mae Etta shook her head. "I'll never forget it. Bea threw a biscuit and then called her sister a dirty name."

"What were they arguing about?"

"Don't know. But I told them both right quick that my establishment would not tolerate that sort of behavior. And then Bea lit into me!"

"She did?"

"Said she'd convene a special meeting of the Downtown Development Committee and get my business license revoked."

I looked around the place. "But she didn't do it."

"Oh, she tried. But when they met, I brought ten people to the meeting, ten people that was in the diner that day. They all testified. Bea looked a fool." Mae Etta smiled, a rare phenomenon. "I even brought the biscuit she threw. You know, as evidence."

"Right," I said. "I'll bet she didn't take that too well."

"She did not."

Someone stepped up to the register then and our conversation took a momentary hiatus.

"Yeah," Mae Etta went on when she closed the register. "Bea didn't come back in the diner for over a year. Idell did, but she never said a single word to me. I don't believe we ever spoke again."

"So Bea was on the Downtown Development Committee," I prompted.

"She *was* the Downtown Development Committee," Mae Etta said. "Formed it, ran it, dissolved it when she got mad. Which was two or three times a year."

"Why did people put up with her?" I shook my head and tried to make it sound like a rhetorical question.

"Money," Mae Etta told me. "That woman had a hand in nearly everything on account of her family money. And not just in this town. All over the county. Building schools and tearing down old houses and trying her best to run everybody's life. Rich people. They think they can do anything and get away with it."

"Yeah, so you have no idea what they were arguing about. That day."

Mae Etta nodded slowly. "Not that day. But I *can* tell you what the problem was in general. Everybody knew it."

"Okay, what was the problem?"

"Well, what do you think it was?" she snapped. "What's always the problem? It was a man."

I sat waiting for her to go on, and when she didn't, I had to ask, "What man?"

She lowered her voice the way some people do when they tell you someone has cancer.

"That Kell Brady."

"In . . . what respect was he the problem?" I asked.

"Well, first place: he was sweet on Idell, and when she turned him down, he went after Bea. That's what caused Bea and Idell to split up and build separate houses. Bea's over there on that dirt road north of your place."

"They had separate houses? I thought they lived together. Like in a family manse or something."

"They did until they didn't," she pronounced. "Look, I know what you're doing."

"What am I doing?" I asked innocently.

"You want to get your friend, that lady preacher, out of trouble." Mae Etta sniffed. "That's why you're talking to me, because you think I might have done it. Truth be told, you'd have an easier time finding anybody around here that *didn't* want to hit Bea Glassie real hard in the head. I can tell you I would have done it with a glad heart and a clear conscience."

"Right, then," I said, laughing, "you're officially on my list of suspects."

Mae Etta gave me a look then that made the coffee in my cup tremble and the blood in my veins turn to ice.

"But you'd never be able to prove it," she whispered.

Before I could gather myself together to make any kind of response, another customer came to the register to pay her tab. By the time the transaction was done, Mae Etta was done talking with me about anything other than breakfast.

"We got blueberry pancakes this morning," she said, light as air. "You want you some?"

I pushed my coffee mug away from me. "No, thanks. I guess I'd better get on with my day."

"All right then," she said, not looking up at me. "Coffee's on the house. I had a good time messing with you. It was worth a cup of coffee."

And there was the faintest possible hint of a smile on her ancient lips.

I took that in, looked around the diner, and slid off my stool.

"You were just messing with me?" I asked, standing in front of her.

"I'm eighty-seven years old. What am I supposed to do for fun around here?" She finally looked me in the eye. "But on the other hand, you know what they say: many a truth is said in jest."

I didn't know what to believe—a continuation of the surreal mood in which I'd awakened. The rain showed no sign of letting up, and I stared out the glass door trying to decide what to do next.

Just as I was about to head for the door, I turned back to Mae Etta.

"Is Kell Brady still alive?" I asked.

"Far as I know," she answered.

"Where is he?"

"I believe he still lives in Hawkinsville."

"Okay." I leaned her way and whispered, "So who do you think killed Bea?"

"They say she was hit in the head," she answered, equally softly. "Don't seem like the kind of thing a woman would do. That's a man's occupation: hitting a woman. How much do you know about Frank Fletcher?"

I didn't want to tell her that I'd already considered Frank, mostly owing to what David and Philomena had told me about him. But I was resistant to the idea because I didn't like disturbing his sister Tandy's memory. Or her ghost. I had the romantic notion, without any evidence whatsoever, that Tandy's spirit still hung around the bookshop. And that her ghost would think ill of me if I hassled her brother.

So I just said, "Frank's okay."

I made it to the door and I was almost out of the diner before Mae Etta said, "I reckon you *have* to find out who really killed Bea, you hear me? Because don't nobody but Idell believe that the Coleman woman done it. And if Reverend Coleman gets put away, I believe it'll be a lot more people than Idell Glassie upset in this town."

So maybe, I thought, Mae Etta shouldn't be on my list of suspects. But wasn't that just the kind of thing that a clever murderer might say to throw off a decidedly amateur investigation? And despite the outward appearance of aged decrepitude, Mae Etta was sharp as a tack and twice as pointed.

So to *that* all I said was, "Yes, ma'am."

And I left the diner.

SINCE the diner was only a few blocks away from the sheriff's office, I thought I might pop in on Billy to see what he was up to, see if he had any new information or thoughts. I didn't really know why. I probably just wanted someone to talk with about the situation in general, think about how to proceed.

If it hadn't been raining, I probably would have walked, but as it was, I hopped into Igor and drove the two blocks to Billy. Then out of the car, into the pouring rain, through the sheriff's office door, I was suddenly aware of how significantly my coat was dripping. I really got the floor wet.

The office was only three rooms, really. There was the bigger main room, with a desk facing the door and a row of chairs against the wall where the door was, under a large plate glass window. To the right was a smaller office with the door closed. And the third space sported floor-to-ceiling bars, two bunks, no windows. The place had an uncomfortably sanitized smell, and it hadn't been painted since the Eisenhower administration.

It seemed empty, but as soon as I closed the outside door, I heard Billy's voice from the smaller office.

"Be right with you."

I took off my raincoat and hung it on the metal coatrack by the door.

"It's only me," I called out. "Got a minute?"

There was a moment of silence and then Billy appeared, uncharacteristically disheveled.

"Oh," I said, a little startled by his appearance. "Bad night?"

He squeezed his eyes shut for a second. "No sleep."

"Why?"

He shook his head. "Got a call from the GBI not that long after we came back from Sylvester. It was not good."

"Can you tell me about it?"

He motioned for me to come into his office and then disappeared.

"They think they found the murder weapon in Gloria's toolshed out back of the church," he told me as I was coming into the room.

"What?" I froze in the doorway. "What murder weapon?"

"Shovel," he answered, exhausted. "It's got old traces of blood on it. And there's more. Their background research on Gloria pulled up some . . . not good stuff."

I went in and sat down in the only chair, right in front of his desk. The office was small, there was nothing on the walls, no picture, no calendar, no decoration at all. It was painted gray and smelled like butterscotch, for some reason. The top of Billy's desk was immaculately clean and astonishingly well-organized.

"What *stuff*?" I asked him.

"Did you know that she has a criminal background?" He was staring, a little bleary-eyed, at his computer screen.

"What do you mean?" I leaned forward, trying to see what he was looking at on his computer.

"Multiple arrests for street fighting," he said. "And seven vagrancy charges. Pickpocketing, petty theft, disturbing the peace—it's kind of a long list."

"Is this from her home, like in the Okefenokee Swamp?"

"No." He turned the screen my way so that I could see the first of three pages of her arrest record. "Savannah."

I stared. There was her mug shot. And underneath it there were, just on the first page that Billy was showing me, a list of more than a dozen separate charges.

"Did you know anything about all this?" Billy went on.

"No." My voice sounded like it was made out of glass.

"They now consider her what they call a 'career criminal,'" he said, finally looking at me. "This sheet, combined with that shovel—Madeline, at six o'clock this morning, they officially charged Gloria with Bea Glassie's murder."

11

I COULD FEEL MY pulse double in three seconds flat.

"In the first place," I began, "the blood on the shovel would have to be more than six months old if it's Bea's. And dried blood samples aren't viable after a few weeks, so the GBI couldn't possibly test it to find out whose blood that is."

Billy glared. "How do you know a thing like that?"

"I was in a couple of episodes of *Coroner*," I told him. "It's a Canadian procedural. Not the point. There can't possibly be any forensic evidence on that shovel."

"Well, they knew it was blood for certain," Billy argued.

"Snake, rat, gopher, badger, possum—all of which I've seen around our neighborhood."

His head tilted sideways. "Badger?"

"I saw one once," I answered defensively.

"Okay but here's what you don't know," he went on. "The head of the Sylvester GBI office is some kind of second cousin to the Glassie clan, and he's apparently easily influenced by family ties."

I nodded. "Meaning that he wants to appease Idell."

"Yes, I think he just wants to get her off his back," Billy said. "And now I'm sorry I ever called the GBI in the first place."

But I could see Billy's dilemma. He was running for sheriff. He had to get this one right; the sooner he wrapped up the matter, the better. And being able to say that the whole thing was out of his hands, a GBI matter, had probably seemed like the smartest thing to do. At the time.

"What's his name?" I asked him. "The name of this head of the office."

"Oh, no," he told me. "You are *not* going to hassle that guy. He's the head of a GBI office and he's a relative of Idell Glassie's."

"How many different ways do you have of telling me not to go on investigating this thing?" I snapped.

"Not what I'm saying, Maddy," he said, clearly irritated. "I'm saying that if you bother that man, the next thing you know, *you'll* be in jail."

"Oh, come on."

"Would you put it past Idell at this point?" He shook his head. "And if you got locked up, how would you help Gloria then?"

I knew he was saying that to me just to keep me from flying down the road to Sylvester to jump down some bureaucrat's throat. But it was a good point. And it only made me more determined to find out who really killed Bea. Which was probably the second reason for Billy's question.

"Okay." I slumped down in my chair. "By the way, I'm having second thoughts about Mae Etta being the killer."

He leaned forward, elbows on his desk, hands together like he was about to pray.

"I didn't realize you had first thoughts about that." He shook his head.

"I went to talk with her this morning," I said. "Just now."

"And whatever she said made you doubt that she's your best suspect," he went on.

I nodded again.

"Which is exactly what she would want," he said, softer, "if she actually was the killer."

"I had a similar thought." I sat up. "But is that old woman really so . . . I don't know. Crafty?"

"That old woman has kept a business going in this tiny little town for almost fifty years," he answered. "What do you think it would take to make that happen?"

"Pact with the Devil?" I suggested.

"At least," he concurred.

"Well. Okay." I stood. "I'm going to consult the best source I know about gossip in this town."

"Dr. Waldrop."

"Exactly."

"Why?" he asked.

"Because I'm beginning to understand that we might have around a thousand suspects for Bea's murder."

"You mean most of the population of Enigma," he said. "You're only excluding the incapacitated elderly and the children too young to know about it. Everyone else has probably wanted, at one time or another, to hit Bea in the head with a shovel. Or whatever."

"Right." I headed for the door.

Billy stood to walk me to the exit, because, again, that's how he was raised.

"Hey, Maddy," he said, when we got to the door. "You know I can't officially help you with . . . I mean I have to tell you again, *officially*, that you're not to investigate this matter."

I nodded. "And I will swear in a court of law that you berated me about it."

"Okay, then."

The rain was beginning to abate a bit more, but I still put on my raincoat and dashed to Igor. I was eager to get to Philomena's office before her first class.

THE campus of Barnsley College always struck me as a shimmering anomaly in our part of South Georgia. It was a liberal arts institution, it attracted students from all over the East Coast, and, most of all, exhibited the most beautiful campus I'd ever seen, mostly due to the ministrations of its master gardener, one David Madison.

As you went through the stone entrance gate, all you could see at first were the gardens. David had planted pomegranate trees the previous fall, and they were coming along nicely, already blooming, so a kind of red and orange fire was the first thing you saw. They were underplanted with huge, variegated impatiens and a groundcover of sugar plum ajuga.

But their beauty was somewhat wasted on me. All I wanted to see was Philomena's face. I parked Igor in the open-air lot nearest the psychology building and headed in. The building was a nineteenth-century brick and stone structure with the occasional granite gargoyle and a cathedral entranceway. Phil's office was first on the left as you came into the darkwood hallway.

Her door was open and she was leaning forward in her chair, hunched over her laptop. She was in her navy blue suit, and her hair was in a more severe bun than usual. She didn't hear me come in.

So I said, as gently as I could so as not to startle her, "Hi."
She jumped. "Oh!"

She took a moment to adjust, and then saw me standing there dripping rain onto the ancient Persian rug that covered her hardwood floor.

"Maddy?" She said it like she wasn't sure I was really there, like I might be some sort of hallucination.

"Do you have a minute?" I asked softly.

"Of course!" She closed her laptop and took off her glasses. "You want to talk about the fact that as of this morning Gloria's been officially charged with Bea's murder."

"See?" I grinned and took a seat in one of the chairs in front of her desk. "I just told Billy I wanted to consult the foremost authority on Enigma gossip, and here you are, already ahead of me in that department."

"Yes, news travels fast." She sat back. "So."

"So. Who *did* kill Bea?"

Might as well start there, I thought. If Phil had an opinion, it would be an informed one, and she'd readily share it.

"I think the culprits we talked about last night are among the best possibilities," she hedged.

"I talked with Mae Etta this morning," I said. "Her suggestion is that the entire adult population of Enigma ought to be considered."

"True," she agreed. "Bea embarked on a career of offending just about everyone in town a long time ago. And she was good at it."

"Why?" I asked. "Was she just a cussed individual?"

"Well." Phil sat back and began to tap her fingers together. "I believe it all began with Enigma Elementary."

I waited, but when she didn't go on, I had to prompt. "Phil?"

She looked around. "Oh, did I stop talking?"

"You did."

"Sorry. The school burned down in 1973, when Bea was in her early twenties."

"I don't remember anything about a school," I began.

"You wouldn't," Phil went on. "It was originally a little bitty old one-room schoolhouse, but it was moved to a larger brick building on the north side of town just across from Highway 82 in, I believe, 1926. We could look that up if you like."

"It's not there now."

"No, it's Enigma City Park now. As I say, the building burned in October of 1973. The gym and cafeteria were still standing, and portable classrooms were brought in so the school could go on until it was rebuilt. Bea, for some reason, decided that she would single-handedly get it built back as 'Glassie Elementary.' She tried for ten years or more to get the construction going, but the mobile units—really just double-wide trailers—served as the school until it closed toward the end of the eighties. When Bea couldn't manage to get the thing rebuilt, she became increasingly bitter."

"Why couldn't she get it done?" I asked. "Money?"

"Oh, no," Phil answered. "Glassie family money could probably have gotten a grand building finished in six months. She wasn't trying to raise any outside money at all."

"Then what was the problem?"

"Bea!" Phil insisted. "Bea was the problem. She complained about everything. The site for the school wasn't right, the architect was all wrong—and, Lord, her admission policy... anyway, she tried to get elected to the original Downtown Development Committee, but no one would vote for her. She tried to get on the county Board of Education, same problem."

"So, she *was* just cussed," I said.

"All right," Phil acquiesced, "maybe she was."

"But what's this about her admission policy?"

Phil pinched her lips then lowered her head. She did that whenever she was trying not to say something that had to be said.

"It was the nineteen seventies," she began very softly, not lifting her head, "but Bea seemed to have a kind of Reconstruction mentality."

"How do you mean?"

Head still down, she went on. "Well, Bea wanted it to be a public, not a private school, but there were maybe twenty or so African American students in town at the time. And Bea wanted to make certain that they weren't allowed in her new school."

"Ah. That's why she couldn't get the thing built."

"At first," Phil agreed. "But as time went on and Bea offended everyone, even people who might have agreed with her, at least in theory, she just lost all . . . traction, or however you'd say it."

"But Mae Etta told me that Bea *was* on the Downtown Development Committee."

"Eventually she was." Phil finally looked up. "Money gets you nearly anywhere you want to go, doesn't it?"

"How would I know personally?" I shrugged. "But that's certainly my observation."

"I always used to think that a distant father and a nearly mute mother produced the Glassie sisters as we knew them," Phil mused. "But I quit thinking about them at all when your aunt Rose came back to town. After that, I mostly just thought about Rose."

She blushed a little.

"Did Idell come in the shop when Rose was alive?" I asked. "She certainly does now. At least once a week."

"Oh, yes," Phil said, "she was a good customer. Rarely spoke. Except to occasionally try to talk Rose into selling some of those books in the 'rare books' section. Which sometimes happened. And sometimes Rose even ordered first editions and obscure titles."

"Huh. Idell never approached me about that."

Phil shrugged. "Might be something to look into."

"I'll tell you what I want to look into," I told her. "I want to know more about Kell Brady."

"Oh!" Phil responded enthusiastically. "That *is* a juicy subject."

"So I'm given to understand. You said you met him a few times?"

"I did," she answered. "When old Father Glenn was the priest at our church, Kell would occasionally attend with both of the Glassie girls."

"Father Glenn was the guy right before Gloria."

"That's right."

"And do I remember this correctly: Father Glenn drank a lot, he was divorced a number of times, and his sermons were a little . . . windy."

She laughed. "I believe Gloria said that those were practically requirements for being an Episcopal priest. But in fact I think that Bea Glassie, owing to those very qualities, was the primary force in getting him out of the church and into his girlfriend's home on Saint Simons Island."

"Bea got him fired?"

"In essence."

"Man," I said. "Bea was a real . . . what's the word?"

"The *word*?" Phil looked down. "That word would be one not uttered in polite society, I believe."

"Isn't there an Episcopal church in Tifton?"

"St. Anne's," Phil confirmed.

"Why didn't Bea just go there?"

"Neither sister had a driver's license," she said. "Or a car. Their father didn't believe that women should drive."

I shook my head. "Welcome to the Old South."

"When they started seeing Kell Brady," Phil went on, "I thought they might get him to carry them to Tifton, but Bea seemed to thrive on ire."

"That's the picture I'm getting," I agreed. "Tell me more about their relationship with Kell."

"Did you know that both sisters were engaged to him at different times?"

"What?" I leaned forward. "No."

"Well, Kell was somehow involved in the project to rebuild the school," Phil said. "And at first, he preferred Idell. Because Idell's temperament was softer, in general. But Idell was always a little afraid of men, I think."

My inner amateur psychiatrist took over. "Because of the way her father treated her."

"Yes, probably. And when she refused Kell's advances, he turned to Bea."

"Right," I said. "This is basically what Mae Etta told me. After that the sisters fell out and built separate houses."

"And rarely spoke again."

"Really?" I said. "But I think Mae Etta told me that they split in . . . was it 1988?"

"That's right."

"So for forty years they stayed away from each other,"

I mused. "That's why Idell didn't complain to anyone when Bea disappeared last year."

"I think so." Phil hesitated. "Unless the reason she didn't complain is that she's the one who killed Bea."

"Yeah, but what would have provoked Idell that much after four decades? Enough to kill her sister. I mean, I get that they carried a grudge—they both sound like they're capable of that. But what could have happened to actualize that latent enmity enough to kill?"

"I don't know," Phil answered. "But it would appear that it was something that happened at the bookshop."

"Right." I sat back. "It would appear that way."

"Maybe it was something that happened with Kell."

"After all these years?"

"Well, Kell and Bea continued to see each other, you understand," Phil told me. "I think it may have been as much a business relationship as a romantic one. They were quite involved, for a while, in restoring the old opera house in Hawkinsville."

"Where Kell lives."

"He's still alive?"

"That's what Mae Etta said," I told her. "So, hey, why wouldn't we go pay him a visit?"

"Really?" Phil's eyes brightened to a rare degree. "Both of us?"

"Somebody's got to save Gloria Coleman," I said. "And who better than you and me? And Hawkinsville is only, what? An hour away?"

"Hour and a half," she answered worriedly. "And I have classes. And we don't know where he lives, exactly."

"I'll bet Billy could find out right quick." I hauled out my new iPhone, much to Philomena's astonishment.

"When did you get a cell phone?" She glared.

I don't think I blushed; I certainly didn't mean to. She knew it was my first such device, and it was certainly the first time I'd used it in her presence.

"David gave it to me for Christmas," I told Phil. "He said he wanted to drag me into the twenty-first century."

"Ooh," she cooed like she was a ten-year-old. "He's *so* sweet on you."

Okay, then I probably *did* blush. "Shut up."

I dialed Billy. He answered.

"Hey," I said without preamble. "Can you get me Kell Brady's address in Hawkinsville?"

"Who is this?" he mocked.

"I want to talk with him, as you may surmise, because of all the brouhaha between him and the Glassie sisters."

"You are *not* going to drive up there and bother that old man," he scolded.

"If you don't find his address for me," I responded, "I'll just go to Hawkinsville and drive up and down random streets shouting his name until I find him."

There was a brief moment of silence.

"If anybody else said that, I'd laugh. With you . . ."

"I'll take Philomena with me," I suggested.

"You'll do no such thing," he objected.

"I have classes," Phil repeated.

"Are you going to find his address for me or not?" I insisted.

A huge sigh was followed by rustling and clicking and various other desktop sounds until Billy eventually reported, very reluctantly, Kell Brady's home address.

"I won't tell anyone who gave me his address," I assured Billy.

"I won't either," Phil called out.

"I'd deny it if you did," he said wearily. "You know that Kell Brady is the reason the sisters hadn't spoken to each other all these years."

"I know," I said. "And I'm buying into your idea that guilt is the primary reason for Idell's zealous pursuit of her sister's killer—guilt about their sibling alienation. And that alienation was on account of Brady. Ergo: he's a factor in my hypothetical investigation into this entire sordid matter. Don't try to talk me out of this."

"I've already admitted that it wouldn't do me any good to try," he said, almost laughing. "And as a matter of fact, here's a new wrinkle that only supports my idea about Idell's motivation for all this. She just now petitioned the Downtown Development Committee to place a plaque in Enigma City Park to commemorate her sister's valiant but thwarted effort to save the elementary school that used to be there. I paraphrase the petition of which I have a copy on my desk, delivered in person by Idell herself not ten minutes ago."

I glanced at Phil. "Well. There you go. So, I'm going to Hawkinsville."

"Have a good trip," was all he said, and he hung up.

"What?" Phil asked. "What did Billy say?"

"Tell you in a second. I have to call Jennifer at the shop." And I dialed.

"Old Juniper Bookshop," Jennifer answered on the first ring.

"Hey, it's me," I said. "I've got to go on a little trip this morning and I probably won't be back until after lunch, are you okay?"

"Sure, practically nobody's here," she said in her usual spritely fashion. "But I found something interesting that you're going to want to see, I think."

"What is it?"

"It's . . . you know you asked me to go through all the old receipt books looking for anything that Bea Glassie might have ordered from your aunt Rose?"

"You got something?"

"Yeah, it's—"

"Save it 'til I get there, okay? I want to get going."

"Where?" she wanted to know. "Do you mind my asking?"

"Hawkinsville," I said.

"Oh. Okay. Safe trip. See you when you get back."

"Thanks, Jennifer," I said. "And nice work finding the thing about Bea."

"Sure!" I could tell she was smiling.

I stood. "Okay. Let's go."

Phil shook her head. "I told you. I have classes."

"When I was in college," I said, "and a professor canceled a class, I felt like I'd been let out of jail."

"I just got back to my job here, Madeline," she admonished. "I cannot cancel my classes. And, by the way, I don't believe my students think of my classroom as a jail cell."

She was right. Her students loved her, that much I knew.

"Okay," I surrendered. "Good point. But you're coming with me when I get back and go talk with Frank Fletcher."

"As long as it's after my classes," she said firmly.

"Okay, okay." I locked eyes with her. "I love you."

Her demeanor softened. "I love you too, sweetheart."

With that I abandoned her office, strode out of the building, and found that the rain had stopped. The sky was still gray, but on the horizon a single hard ray of sunlight was working overtime to dispel the gloom.

This has got to be a good omen, I thought as I cranked Igor into life and headed toward 129 North. Look out, Hawkinsville. Here I come.

12

THE DRIVE UP 129 was not entirely unpleasant. The road was wet but there was hardly any traffic, and I had a chance to think.

My first thought was that I'd been a little insensitive to Philomena. I shouldn't have goaded her about coming with me on my potentially ridiculous quest. She'd just spent months in a mental institution. And even though the place had been, for years, a kind of second home for her, there was always a little disorientation around the reentry back into her life as a college professor. I knew that, and still I'd pressured her, like a bad friend in high school, to skip classes and participate in what was probably going to be a fruitless endeavor.

That thought prompted me to meditate on a time in my life that I usually tried to forget: my childhood. I always envied people who thought of childhood as an idyll. Mine was spent almost entirely in an effort to grow up and get out. I had few friends, little in common with any other kids in Enigma, and a nonexistent relationship with my overworked and barely verbal parents. My only salvation was my aunt Rose and my non-aunt Philomena. I was in the bookshop every day, helping, talking, reading, and, best of all, listening to Rose's stories about her life as an actor in New York in the previous century.

My favorite stories were the ones in which the show went wrong. She was in a production of something called *Hamlet: The Musical!* She played Ophelia. Her first observation was that the exclamation point in the title was the most exciting thing about the production. But her best memory was of a night her character was onstage waiting for her brother, Laertes, to enter. But as the seconds turned into minutes, she began to do everything she could think of to occupy her solo time in front of a packed house. She sang, as she put it, "snatches of old tunes." She twirled in a brief interpretive dance. She was just at the point of going through her version of a Three Stooges routine when she, and all the audience, heard shouting from backstage.

"Laertes!"

"What?"

"You're *on*!"

"What?"

There followed a few of the vilest curse words I'd ever heard Rose say, the sound of furious running, and, at last, a disheveled Laertes entrance, sliding in like Tom Cruise in *Risky Business* and saying, with great passion, "O rose of May, dear maid, kind sister, sweet Ophelia!"

The moment brought the house down, and the director tried to convince the cast to keep the moment in the play, because it was hilarious. The actor who played Laertes was the sole dissenting voice, believing that it made him look like an idiot—which it did—and vowing never to miss an entrance again.

Hundreds of stories like that had instilled in me an overwhelming desire to be an actor. And it was only after half a dozen similarly horrendous occurrences of my own onstage that I came to believe they were better told as stories than lived as experiences. There was nothing quite so soul-freezing or nightmare-inducing as a moment like that in front of an audience.

Still, an actor's life for me, as they say in that song from *Pinocchio*.

But as I got older, I found that Philomena's stories about her times in her various mental institutions came to mean the most to me. Because to her, they were about a grander stage: life. And reality, for Philomena, was entirely subjective.

"Just because you don't see the pixies flitting about the doorway," she'd said to me on more than ten occasions, "doesn't mean they're not there. You can't see the wind either, but that doesn't mean it won't shake the barley free."

Her favorite movie was *Harvey*. When I saw it for the first time, I felt I understood her more—and loved her twice as much as I had before.

Such thoughts made my trip to Hawkinsville fly by. And thanks to some mysterious application on my relatively new iPhone, a kind woman's voice guided me quite accurately to a gigantic nineteenth-century mansion with a manicured front lawn that was four times the size of my backyard garden. The house was three stories high with a wraparound porch and imposing Doric columns. But what shocked me were the huge blooming rosebushes that seemed to surround the house. They were Aunt Rose's hybrids, "Ophelia's Last Laugh." Of course I was a little surprised by the coincidence that I'd just been thinking about Rose's stories. But mostly I was baffled as to how Kell Brady might have acquired these rarest of shrubberies.

I parked on the street, shut Igor down, and sat in the car

staring at the house for longer than I should have. Because after a while, a woman in a black uniform came out and stood on the porch staring at me.

I got out and waved.

"Hi," I said to the silent woman. "My name is Madeline Brimley, and these are my aunt's roses."

I had no idea why that had been my introductory thesis, but it seemed to have an effect

"Aren't they lovely?" the woman said, and her face entirely softened as she turned for a moment to look at the blossoms. "So you must be Rose's niece."

That was another oddity. How did she know Rose? How could she possibly have heard of me?

"Yes, I guess I must be," I told the woman.

"Please." She gestured. "Come in."

With that she turned and went back inside, leaving the door open.

I made my way down the flat stone walkway. After what seemed like a twenty-minute walk I arrived at the bottom of the porch steps. Up the steps and across the porch, I peeked into the house.

The foyer was intimidating. The gleamingly polished wooden floor was almost a mirror. The marble stairway in front of me was something from an antique government building. The paintings on the walls appeared to be genuine Turner landscapes. I was momentarily afraid that my presence might sully the otherworldly grace of the place. And it was only the entrance hall. The uniformed woman was standing just inside.

"Let me take your raincoat," she said.

I went in and surrendered my coat. She hung it on a very ornate coatrack by the door.

"Won't you have a seat in the library," she went on, indicating the room immediately to my left. "I'll tell Mr. Brady you're here."

And she vanished around one side of the stairs.

"Thank you," I managed to call out after she'd gone.

I actually tiptoed into the library, afraid of making too much noise.

The room was a parody of itself. There were floor-to-ceiling oak bookcases on every wall, some with glass doors. Two windows with beveled glass, one facing the front porch and one looking out on the lush side yard, flooded the room with light, even though the day was still overcast. There were two plush leather chairs, one with a cozy plaid blanket over an arm. A large cherrywood writing desk sat under the side-yard window. It wasn't for show. It was a working desk. There was also a slightly oversized leather sofa, a match for the chairs, strewn with pillows imitating tapestries. The floor was nearly covered by an ancient "oriental" rug, mauve and brown. I could almost hear a ghostly voice saying, "What's that you've got there, Holmes?"

I was not about to sit down anywhere, so I perused the bookcases. First editions abounded, but they were side by side with pulp paperbacks, old Fodor travel books, gardening manifestos, cookbooks, and, in one corner, what appeared to be nine different editions of *The Magus* by John Fowles, one of my favorite novels. I pulled one of the hardback versions, opened it up, and saw the inscription.

"Kell, thanks for the brandy, John."

I was startled by a bassoon baritone utterance behind me.

"I visited him in Lyme Regis," he said.

I whirled to face Kell Brady. He was clad in a burgundy waist-length housecoat, black silk pants, and opera shoes with white dragons on the toes. He looked to be over six feet tall and, except for the mane of thick white hair, looked a little like a benign manifestation of Thor.

"You met John Fowles?" My voice cracked as I spoke. "This might be my favorite novel of all times."

I held up the volume in my hand.

"Oh," he said instantly, "I envy that. At my age I no longer have a *favorite* anything. They all blend together: books, meals, places, music—even, alas, people."

"Well, you have a remarkable library here," I said, casting my eye about the place.

"Thank you," he said with just a touch of noblesse oblige. "I love these books. Probably more than anything else in my life, at this point. Certainly more than most people I know. But I was told that you were interested in roses."

"Yes, I was just telling your . . . the person who answered the door," I stuttered, "that you have my aunt's roses."

"Rose." He sighed. "I was so very sorry to hear of her passing. I didn't know her well, of course, but she was a remarkable woman as far as I could tell."

I smiled and returned the book in my hand to its place in the bookcase.

"She was," I said. "And it's because of her, sort of, that I've barged into your home uninvited."

"Please," he said, shaking his head, "you could not be more welcome. Won't you sit down?"

I turned to examine my seating options.

When he rightfully observed my momentary dilemma, he said, softly, "That chair with the blanket on it is very comfortable."

I took it. He moved, with astonishing grace despite his wooden cane, to the other leather chair.

Almost immediately, the woman in the black uniform entered with a silver tray. On it I saw a bone-white teapot, two cups, two short crystal glasses, and a clear bottle filled with amber liquid.

"Thank you, Donna," Kell said sweetly.

Donna set the tray down on the table in between us and left without a word.

He stared at the tray. "Donna apparently wasn't certain if you'd want tea or sherry. I recommend the sherry. This is a bottle of Barbadillo Versos 1891 Amontillado."

I tried not to gasp. In my research for a role in some staged version of Poe's "The Cask of Amontillado," I had come across information about that particular phenomenon. It was a ten-thousand-dollar bottle. And it was small.

I couldn't resist it, despite the fact that I had a long drive home ahead of me. I had to see what ten thousand dollars tasted like.

"I think this sherry would be insulted," I told him, "if I chose tea, don't you think?"

He laughed and reached immediately for the bottle. "I *do* think so."

He poured. I watched. Instantly the aroma of the nectar rose up, nutty and spicy and dried-fruity. He held up my glass and I took it.

I touched the sherry to my lips. If I had been a poet, I might have been able to describe the first taste. As it was, I could only close my eyes and make embarrassing, vaguely sexual sounds.

He laughed again, a delightful musical sound. "Yes, it is good, isn't it?"

"If you'd given this to John Fowles, his next novel would have been named after you," I said.

He sipped and then set down his glass.

"Now." He crossed his legs and folded his hands in front of him, his kind eyes locked on mine. "First, I'll tell you again that I lament the passing of your aunt Rose. She was, by all accounts, a true original."

"Agreed." I couldn't seem to relinquish my own glass. "There's never been another."

"Second," he went on, "Donna tells me that you were admiring the roses out front. I assume you know that they are your aunt's creation."

"Yes." I took another sip. "I was thinking of planting some in front of the bookshop but I wasn't exactly clear on what they looked like."

"Aren't they wonderful?" He sighed.

"Amazing," I agreed, finally able to set down my glass. "And I've just discovered that there are a few in the greenhouse at Barnsley College."

"Oh, that is lucky." His eyebrows rose. "I was momentarily afraid that you might want to take some of mine."

"Never," I assured him. "They're perfect for this house. I was just wondering, you know, since they're so rare, how you came by them. Rose gave them to you?"

"Not exactly. Do you know David Madison, the master gardener at Barnsley?"

I tried not to sound like a smitten coed. "I do know him."

"He's a remarkable young man," Kell said. "Did you know that he studied with no less than Wendell Berry?"

"I'd heard."

"Well, he helped Rose develop the hybrid, mostly by letting her use his greenhouse facilities at the college. And as I happened to endow the college with a particular emphasis on creating those facilities, he was kind enough to gift me the ones you see outside."

"A well-deserved gift," I said. "Those greenhouses are spectacular."

"In David's capable hands," he allowed, "they are."

I lifted my glass again, mostly stalling.

"I hope you've already heard about this," I began slowly, stopping to take a long sip. "Very recently, when I began, along with my friend Reverend Gloria Coleman, to dig up the yard in front of the bookshop to plant those very roses, we . . . I'm not quite sure how to say this. We dug up someone's bones."

"Good Lord," he gasped and actually sat forward. "Bones?"

"Yes." I fidgeted and then set down my glass again. "It gets worse. They turned out to belong to Beatrice Glassie."

His hand flew to cover his mouth and a good deal of color drained from his face. "No."

"I'm afraid so." I swallowed. "I was then given to understand that you knew her. And her sister Idell."

"I did," he told me, his voice greatly diminished. "I was, in fact, engaged to each of them for a time. Oh, my. Donna!"

Donna instantly appeared in the doorway to the library.

"Would you mind getting my Toprol?" he said.

She vanished without a word.

I suddenly felt terrible for the way I was handling the whole thing.

"I'm so sorry," I began.

"No, no, no," he said quickly. "I . . . I just can't believe it."

His breathing was labored and he was massaging his chest.

"I really shouldn't have . . . can I do anything?" I leaned forward.

But Donna appeared with a glass of water in one hand

and a pill in the other. He popped the pill into his mouth and then took the glass of water and drained it.

Donna turned to me.

"I think that's enough for today," she told me, but it wasn't an admonishment or a stern reproach. She said it gently, the way she might have spoken to a child.

"Of course." I stood.

"Please," Kell said. "Stay for a moment longer, Miss Brimley. I want to know more about this."

Donna shook her head, but she took the glass back from him, sighed, and left.

"Okay," I ventured, "but only for a minute. I personally agree with Donna."

"When did this happen?" He sat back. "And you say you were with Gloria Coleman? That had to have been unfortunate. They hated each other, Bea and Reverend Coleman."

"Well." I cleared my throat. "All we found were bones. We didn't know who they belonged to. But when we did, Idell went after Gloria. She believes that Gloria killed Bea."

Was that too much to tell a frail older man?

"Idell." The way he said her name was packed with regret. "I was in love with her, you know. But she refused me. Bea consoled me, and that brought me into a different kind of union."

"Oh?" I didn't want to press.

"Bea and I worked to restore the schoolhouse in Enigma," he said with a sigh. "And when that project did not come to fruition, she came here to Hawkinsville to help me restore the old opera house. She was a wonder when it came to dealing with obstinate city officials and recalcitrant day laborers. I was never any good at that sort of thing."

"And that project *was* successful?"

"Very." He nodded. "It's a lovely building, you should go see it before you leave. It was built in 1907 but nearly burned down in the early 1950s. I managed to get it placed on the National Historic Register in 1973. Lord, I was so young then. Anyway, it was, at various times, a city auditorium, a church, a movie house—until it succumbed to flame. It really wasn't until the year 2000 that we finally managed to open it as the state-of-the-art facility it is today."

As he spoke, the roses returned to his cheeks and his breathing seemed more normal.

"And Bea helped with all that," I said, hoping to sound kindly.

"She did." He managed to smile. "She even lived here in this house on and off for years. She didn't drive, you know. Neither sister did. I always had to go to Enigma. And sometimes when I did, I stayed with Beatrice, occasionally for weeks at a time. Of course there was nothing . . . untoward in the living arrangements."

"That's how you came to meet Rose," I assumed. "And why you went to St. Thomas Aquinas every once in a while."

He nodded. "I knew the church before I knew the bookshop, and mostly when old Father Glenn was there. Lord, *there* was a dusty specimen."

That made me laugh. "So I've been told."

"And then, of course, the bookshop is almost right across the street from the church. Your aunt told me once that *her* church was the theatre and was always open after the noon hour on Sunday. Much to the chagrin of the Baptists in the area."

He seemed to be delighted that the Baptists had been offended.

"So you didn't really know Gloria, I guess," I said.

"We met several times. I liked her. Bea, alas, did not care for even the *idea* of a female priest. They apparently quarreled quite a bit."

"Idell told me that Bea might have been jealous," I said, mostly in fun, "because Gloria flirted with you."

"A flirtatious priest?" he scoffed dramatically. "We weren't living in a pulpy romantic novel, dear."

I laughed. "That shows how much you remember about the atmosphere in Enigma. The entire town is just two steps away from Peyton Place."

He sighed heavily then.

"Poor Bea," he whispered and shook his head. "Poor, poor Bea. I should never have agreed to our engagement. It was her idea. Even though she knew how much I still cared for Idell. Here's my advice to you, Miss Brimley: stay well away from romantic entanglements."

"That's good advice," I agreed, "but how would you have taken it when you were younger?"

"When I was younger?" He smiled. "I would have ignored it altogether. I *did* ignore it altogether."

But before we could explore that particular philosophical territory further, Donna appeared again.

"I'm sorry," she said, and she sounded like she meant it. "I really do think that's enough for today. And Mr. Brady's luncheon is prepared."

"Oh!" he said excitedly. "You should stay for lunch. It's quiche today!"

"Absolutely not," I said before Donna had a chance to intervene. "I've imposed on your hospitality for far too long as it is."

I stood instantly. He took a little longer and extended his hand.

"I'm so glad you came," he told me as I took his hand.

"Even though the news I brought was so . . . grim," I told him apologetically.

"Yes." He put his other hand on top of mine. "You must come back some time and let me show you around my opera house."

"I would *love* that," I told him. "And thank you again for letting me invade your home."

He laughed.

Donna ushered me to the door and handed me my raincoat.

I lowered my voice and said to her, "Is he going to be all right?"

"His heart is not good," she answered.

"I'm sorry if I upset him."

She shook her head. "No, I think he enjoyed your visit. But the next time, you might call to give us a little warning. He'll be better prepared."

"Of course," I told her.

I left and Donna closed the door behind me.

I was down the steps, across the lawn, and almost in the car before I realized something.

Kell Brady hadn't really asked me anything about Bea's body or how it got into my front yard. And he especially hadn't asked me the question that almost anyone else might have: how she had died.

13

I SPENT MOST OF the drive back to Enigma kicking myself. Why hadn't I asked Kell Brady all the questions that were in my mind? I had so many questions about Kell's relationship with Bea. And with Idell. And hadn't it almost seemed, it suddenly occurred to me, that I'd been expected? How could that be? And why hadn't I confronted him when he didn't seem at all curious about Bea's bones? And then I spent a little time saying "Bea's bones" out loud over and over again for no reason I could think of other than that I was losing my mind.

Had it been because Kell was such a nice old guy? Would Dr. Freud have suggested that I still had unresolved issues concerning my father? Would Philomena have told me that I still harbored the "good Southern girl" manners with which I'd been raised? Or was I just an idiot?

By the time I pulled up in front of the bookshop, which was still decorated with yellow police tape, I was in a rare mood. The little buzz I'd gotten from the wildly expensive sherry had worn off, and I was hungrier than usual.

Up the porch stairs and into the shop, raincoat over my arm, I was a little surprised to see how busy we were. Jennifer was seated at the desk with a line in front of her. It was only three people, but still: a line.

I waved. "Hi."

She smiled in my direction but continued her customer service work. I went into the kitchen and glanced at the clock over the back door. It was nearly two o'clock. I tossed the coat over the back of a kitchen chair and opened the fridge to see what leftovers might save my life.

Half a dozen eggs and some fresh spinach would have made a nice omelet, but I opted for the cold pizza that Jennifer had ordered the day before and a large bottle of San Pellegrino.

I was chewing on the last of the crust when Jennifer came into the kitchen.

"How was your trip," she asked, "and why were you in Hawkinsville?"

"I went to see Kell Brady," I said with my mouth full.

"Who?"

"Some rich old guy who was engaged to Bea Glassie," I told her.

"Right! Bea!" She sat across from me. "Guess what I found?"

"Oh, yeah," I said, sliding the empty pizza box away from me. "You've got something about Bea?"

But before she could tell me, Philomena hurried into the room, fussy and impatient, her small black purse over her shoulder.

"Why didn't you come back to my office when you got home from Hawkinsville?" she demanded to know.

"Hi, Phil," I said calmly.

"Don't you 'Hi, Phil' me," she went on. "I sat around

waiting for you after both my classes. And here you are eating pizza!"

I glanced at the box. "It was Jennifer's leftover."

"It was," Jennifer confirmed.

"That's not the . . . What happened with Kell Brady?"

Her voice was high and I knew that I was going to have to report to her immediately, but I was also reticent to reveal my embarrassing shortcomings where the interview with Kell was concerned.

We heard the front door open and Jennifer hopped up to attend to what we assumed was a new customer, and Phil took her seat.

"So?" she demanded.

"So it turns out that Kell Brady is a lovely older gentleman who let me taste a ten-thousand-dollar sherry."

She glared. "What?"

I looked down. "He charmed me. He was kind, and then he was extremely shocked to hear about Bea. He even had to take a heart pill. And did you know that he has Rose's roses in his front yard?"

That gave her pause, but only for a moment.

"No he doesn't. Where would he have gotten them? Rose was still trying to convince the American Rose Society to allow—"

"David gave them to him," I interrupted, "because Kell Brady, apparently, endowed the college with enough money to build those state-of-the-art greenhouses with which David has been blessed."

"Oh." She nodded. "That's right. I forgot about that."

"And it's hard for me to imagine that he could muster the kind of aggressive action it would have taken to bash someone's head in and bury her in hard Georgia clay. For one thing, he just seems too *polite* to do anything like that."

She squinted. "Hmm. You should probably talk to a few folks around here. I think you might get a . . . a fuller picture of the man. Because as far as I've heard, he was a bit of a Jekyll-and-Hyde sort of person. You know, sweet as honey one minute, bitter as gall the next."

"Yes, I'm familiar with the type," I said. "I can't tell you how many actors I worked with who were members of that club. But he didn't seem that way to me. His gentility was deep down, the way it is with some of these old Southern gentlemen types. Genuine kindness backed up with just a touch of noblesse oblige."

"Well," she demurred. "Talk to Frank Fletcher before you completely make up your mind."

"I was planning to talk with Frank this afternoon, as a matter of fact."

"I want to go with you," she said.

"You do?"

"I'm feeling a little guilty," she told me. "I let you down this morning. I should have gone with you to visit Kell."

"No," I insisted immediately. "You should not have. That was on me. I should never have tried to talk you into it. I'll bet my guilt weighs more than yours does."

She smiled. "It's not a competition."

"Okay," I said, "but if it was, I'd win. So you want to go with me when I talk with Frank. Why?"

"I was around when he was working with Bea and Idell and Kell," she said, "and you weren't. You were in Atlanta being a great actor. I know what questions to ask. You don't."

"Well, I know what questions I *want* to ask," I argued.

"And I was only in Atlanta being a *working* actor. Very rarely a great one."

"How many actors are there in Atlanta who make their entire living on the stage?"

"Well," I admitted, "it's a relatively small group."

"Greatness isn't always about lots of money or superlative reviews."

I reached over and touched her hand. "I love you, Phil."

She put her hand on mine. "I've always loved you and I always will. Now let's go talk to Frank Fletcher. He's working with David today on the field behind the science building. You'll drive."

With that she was up and headed for the front door.

Only slightly fortified by the cold pizza, I felt a greater inclination toward a nap than I did to a sparring match with Frank, but Phil's enthusiasm was so palpable that I really couldn't refuse.

The sky was beginning to clear and the day had warmed up considerably, so I fished in my pocket for car keys, left the coat on the kitchen chair, and followed Phil into the shop.

There was only one customer, as it turned out: a young man who seemed more intent on flirting with Jennifer than on buying anything. I waved, but Jennifer barely noticed, equally intent on flirting back. Phil and I were out of the house and down the stairs seconds later.

"I need to check the gas," I realized. "It was a longer way to Hawkinsville than I thought."

"Well, I can't drive over there," she fretted. "I don't want my students to see my car. They'll pester me if they know I'm there, and I want to concentrate on talking with Frank. But if you park the car in the back lot behind the science building, I can slip in unaware."

She didn't wait for me to agree. She just opened Igor's passenger door. What could I do? I joined her. A quick check of the fuel gauge told me that I had a little more than an eighth of a tank left, plenty to get to the college without wasting time, so off we went.

BY the time we arrived at Barnsley, blue skies prevailed. There was a gentle spring breeze and it carried a subtle hint of the pomegranate blooms as we drove past them, windows open, on the way to the science building.

The science building itself was a lackluster blond brick edifice. Built in the 1950s, it was a big square box devoid of any architectural interest whatsoever. There were only a few cars parked in front, and none in back where we pulled in and got out of the car.

Across the wet fields I could see David and Frank. David had spent several years cultivating a wildflower meadow there, and this was, according to him, the first year it was actually working. It was a remarkable thing to see: baby's breath, bugleweed, cockscomb, yarrow, foxglove, amaranth, strawflower, zebra grass, and—my favorite—the dramatically named love-lies-bleeding.

The sun was heading for the western horizon and a sudden slant of after-the-rain light turned the meadow into an Impressionist landscape; I was momentarily mesmerized. From which state I was almost immediately plucked thanks to the fact that Phil decided to lay on Igor's horn to attract David and Frank's attention.

"Stop it!" I snapped, turning her way.

"But they didn't see us," she replied innocently.

I turned back to the real-life Monet to see David waving. I waved back. Philomena beckoned. They headed our way.

"Let me do the talking," Phil whispered.

"What? Why?"

"I already told you," she said impatiently. "I know more about this than you do. You asked for my help and so you're going to get it. All right?"

I smiled. "All right."

After a foolish and momentary impulse to run toward David in that most clichéd of romantic images, I held my ground—admirably, I thought. But I suspected that my face might have been described as "beaming."

Phil's impatience remained steady, and by the time the guys got to us she was ready to hurry inside and sit down for what I imagined would be an uncomfortable interrogation. David was in jeans and a T-shirt; Frank wore overalls and a pale shirt that appeared to be some kind of gardener's wonder fabric.

I said "Hi" to David.

And at the same time, Phil said, "Inside. Classroom A. Come on."

She turned and headed for one of the building's doors.

I started to explain, but David saved me.

"I already warned Frank that you might want to speak with him about the Glassie sisters," he said lightly.

"Hey, Miss Brimley," Frank said quietly.

"Hey, Frank. How're you doing?"

"Uh-huh." He nodded.

Phil stood at the door. "Come on!"

David laughed. "You know how she gets, Frank."

Frank sighed, hesitated, and then made for the door. Slowly.

"This was kind of Philomena's idea," I said to David apologetically.

"Like I said," he told me. "I prepared Frank for this eventuality. How was your conversation with Mae Etta?"

"You heard about that?"

"We had lunch at the diner," he said. "She was hilarious."

"What do you mean?"

We headed to the building, following Frank.

"The first thing she said to me when we walked in the door was 'Ooh, I know who's sweet on you!'"

"Well," I said matter-of-factly, "I'm not trying to keep it a secret."

He put his hand on my shoulder for a second. "Me neither."

"Lord!" Phil called out. "Y'all are slower than *Christmas*!"

We picked up our pace, all three of us, and found ourselves in a small classroom in no time.

The room was as bland as the exterior of the building. Beige walls, linoleum floors, and fluorescent lighting. There were no desks, only long tables with four chairs on one side and none on the other.

Phil grabbed a chair and dragged it around to the vacant side of the nearest table and began talking before she sat down.

"Frank," she announced, "I want you to tell Madeline about your work with the Glassie sisters."

He nodded, only a little sullenly, as he took his seat. Apparently, David's preparation had been magic.

"I . . ." Frank began, "I'm having a hard time with this."

"Why's that?" I asked, taking the chair next to him.

David remained standing, for some reason.

"Because I was raised to not say nothing about people if you couldn't say something nice," he answered pointedly, almost growling. "And I can't think of a single nice thing, at this moment, to say about them sisters."

"Tell them about the porch work you did for Bea last year," David prompted.

"It was spring a year ago," he said. "She had these two columns on her front porch that was not properly laid in, and, too, the wood was beginning to rot on account of whoever done it ain't put KILZ on before they painted, I believe."

"But the point is . . ." David encouraged.

"Miss Glassie said she'd pay me five hundred dollars to fix it," Frank continued. "I fixed it, and she ain't never pay me from that day to this."

"Why?" I asked.

"Well, first she was gone for two months after I finished," he said. "And when she come back, she acted like she ain't know what I was talking about. Like she ain't never ask me to do the work. I showed her the paint receipts, and the leftover wood, and she told me to get off her property or she'd call the sheriff."

"So you were actually *out* money," I said.

"Yes, ma'am, I was," he said. "And that was just the *final* time she done a thing like that. It was always some kind of hassle to get them to pay up, both of them. And they was none too kindly when I was working. Always complaining."

"Why did you keep taking jobs from them?" Phil asked.

He snorted like a horse. "You ever try to tell Bea Glassie no?"

"Good point," Phil admitted.

"One time a few years back," Frank went on, "I decided just not to show up when she wanted me to fix her attic fan and she went all over town talking about how I was no 'count. Even made a speech about it at a Downtown Development Committee meeting. It cost me work, I know that."

"I can vouch," David said. "I had to have a meeting with the administration here when I got an email memo that I was not to hire Frank anymore. A ridiculous, three-hour meeting."

"Still, that went in your favor," I said to Frank.

"Well," David hedged, "I can't hire Frank full time anymore. He has to be a short-term contract hire, and the contract has to be approved by the provost."

"So, long story short, I kept taking jobs from them women," Frank concluded. "Seem like I had to."

"And they kept not paying you," I assumed.

Frank nodded dourly.

"Well, I'm sorry that happened to you, Frank," Philomena told him sweetly. "That wasn't right."

"Yes, ma'am," Frank replied, staring down at the table in front of him. "Reckon I lost several thousand dollars all told."

Several thousand dollars was a lot for Frank to lose. I figured he only made twenty thousand or so a year. He still lived at home on his parents' farm and helped out there. If not for that, I wasn't sure how he'd have been able to live.

"So you weren't heartbroken," Phil said softly, "when you heard that Bea was dead."

"I did not shed a tear," he said.

"When was the last time you worked for her?" Phil asked.

"She called me over to her house first of the fall last year," he answered. "Early September. Wanted me to go with her to Hawkinsville, do some work for her there. Or, for that Mr. Brady, rather."

"Did you do that?" Phil glanced my way.

"We argued about it," he admitted. "She got real riled up. But I told her I couldn't do it because I had a contract with the college and they wouldn't let me go."

"Was that true?" I asked David.

"Yes," he said.

"She told me if I ain't go with her," Frank went on, "she'd get me fired permanent from the college."

"What did you do?" Phil wanted to know.

Frank didn't say anything for long enough to make us all uncomfortable.

"Frank," David urged after a minute.

"I just walked off her porch," he said hesitantly. "Turn my back on her."

"So what happened?" Phil asked.

"Ain't never hear from her after that." He looked up. "Reckon I know why now."

"All right, Frank." Philomena sighed. "Tell Madeline what you did next."

He looked at her coldly. "What I did?"

"You know what I'm talking about," Phil scolded. "Everybody in town knew it."

He scowled, then nodded, then looked me squarely in the eye, which he'd never done to me before that I could recall.

"Don't guess you'd know about this," he began, "but when you got a barn, you got rats."

"Of course I know that," I said, a little defensively.

"Hush, Maddy," Phil snapped. "Let him talk. Go on, Frank."

He looked around the room a little, trying to decide how to continue.

"Anyway," he said finally, "I caught a few in what they call a Havahart trap that's just a cage they get into and can't get back out of. And, so, I took the rats and I put them into Bea Glassie's house through a window, open kitchen window."

He stopped and he seemed to think that was the end of his story.

"And then?" Phil pressed.

"And then." He shifted in his seat. "Miss Glassie called me and said come over quick and help on account of she had rats in her house. And I said I would but she'd have to pay me up front, before I got rid of them rats. And she said she would. And I said I wouldn't do a thing until I saw the money. In cash."

Again, he felt he was done.

Phil turned my way. "Bea had locked herself in her upstairs bathroom, but she managed to get to her purse, take out some cash—she always had a lot of cash in her purse—went back to the bathroom, locked the door again, and waited for Frank to show up, right, Frank?"

He nodded.

"Then what, sugar," Phil prodded gently.

He sighed. "Well, then I stood under the window, that bathroom window where she told me to be, and she threw down a grocery sack with fifty dollars in it. Some of it was coins. So I said where was her shovel and she said she ain't got one and told me to run over to the church and get one out of the shed in back there. So that's what I done."

"Shovel?" I looked at David.

"Bop 'em on the head," he told me, "scoop 'em up, and bury the poor guys in the backyard."

"Do we have to talk about that part?" Phil actually shivered a little.

"Okay," David said, "but was that the idea, Frank?"

"Uh-huh," Frank acknowledged. "So, anyway, I run over to the church—"

"You mean St. Thomas Aquinas," I realized, since it was the church closest to Bea's house.

"That's right," Frank said. "So I run over to the church, got me a shovel, and, you know, done it."

"Took care of her rat problem," I confirmed.

"Right." He looked down. "I ain't proud of what I done, you understand. I was just so het up about the way they treated me. Truth be told, I was none too happy about the way they treated everybody in this town."

Phil smiled. "I was in Mae Etta's the next day and everybody in the place was laughing about it."

Frank grinned too, still looking down. "Mae Etta give me lunch on the house for a week."

I suddenly looked at Phil. "The shovel."

Phil nodded. "That's right."

"You used the shovel from the church," I said to Frank, "and then you put it back in the shed."

"Uh-huh," he said. "I ain't even know why they got a shed over there. Don't look to me like that lady preacher ever goes in it."

"I was right!" I said, a little too enthusiastically. "Rat blood!"

"Please!" Phil demanded. "Don't say that!"

Everyone else in the room just glared at me.

"When Billy told me that the GBI had found... *evidence* on that shovel," I explained, "I told Billy that it was probably rat evidence. Or badger."

That made David laugh. "Badger?"

"The point is," I breezed on, "it's not . . . human."

Frank finally looked up. "Why would it be human?"

"The GBI thinks that shovel is evidence that Gloria Coleman killed Bea," I said before I thought better of it. "That's just how wrong they are."

But Frank's eyes narrowed. "Well. It ain't no secret that Miss Coleman hated Bea, maybe worse than most."

"Why do you say that?" I asked him.

He shrugged. "Gossip, I guess."

"There was a lot of gossip about it last summer," Phil admitted to me. "Not long before you came back to town."

"You mind if I go get me a Co-Cola?" Frank asked David. "I'm a little dry."

"Sure," David answered. "You know where the machine is, right?"

He nodded, lifted himself up from the chair, and strode out of the room.

"So how about that?" Phil asked me once he was gone.

"I don't know," I said. "At first I thought it was a story about how Frank had the best motive for killing Bea, and then it turned into a reason to take him off my list, so I'm running out of suspects. Frank looks less guilty than I thought, Mae Etta doesn't seem quite up to a burial in hard dirt, and Kell Brady is a decidedly lovely old man from another town. Who's left?"

"But, see," Phil disagreed, "I don't believe you have the full story on Kell Brady. I'm telling you that he has a very troubled side which you just haven't seen yet or heard about. You need to talk to more people about him."

I turned to David. "You know him. What do you think?"

"I don't *know* him," he corrected, "but I'd have to say that he was very pleasant in all of my dealings with him. And his contributions to the college have been remarkably generous."

"Your greenhouses, for example," I said.

"He even kind of helped to design them," David added. "He's really very knowledgeable about . . . well, a lot of things. We had several discussions, standing out in that field in back of this building, about literature that I found superiorly engaging."

"'Superiorly engaging,'" I teased, turning to Phil. "I think Mr. Madison might be the one to watch in our current 'who's got the best vocabulary' contest?"

"What?" She was momentarily confused.

"You complimented Billy on his wordplay, remember?"

"Oh." She looked up, as if the ceiling would help her recall the moment. "That's right, I think."

"Yes," David went on, "I am, in fact, severely handicapped, especially in this town, by my effete education. But I'm telling you that Kell Brady has always been smart and kind to me."

"*And* he met John Fowles, by the way," I felt compelled to say. "Went to Lyme Regis, where Fowles lived, and delivered a brandy that Fowles memorialized in an inscription written directly to Mr. Brady."

"I love John Fowles," David said, almost under his breath. "*The Magus* is my favorite twentieth-century novel."

I started to say about a hundred things, but when they all wouldn't come out at once, and I began to stutter like an idiot, I stopped, took a breath, and smiled.

"I would like to discuss that with you over dinner, Mr. Madison," I told him. "Tonight?"

"Ooh," Phil cooed like a teenager. Again. "Lovebirds."

"Your place?" was all David said.

"Oh, I would think so. But no takeout, this time. I'll cook."

Phil leaned forward. "That means you're in for a treat, David. Maddy is a great cook. I would almost call her a *chef*."

"Call me anything," I replied, "just don't call me late for dinner."

"Who said that?" David asked, laughing. "I mean, who said it first?"

"It's from a short story called 'Mercantile Drumming,'" Phil reported without hesitation, "published in 1833. I can't quite recall the author's name but give me a minute."

David and I stared.

"Is it possible that you know *everything*?" David asked her.

"Yes," she joked. "Quite possible."

"In that case," I said in the same jocular vein, "do you know who killed Bea Glassie? Because I seem to be out of suspects."

Her face darkened and the entire room seemed to be filled with a sudden solemnity.

"I'm afraid to say it," she answered almost inaudibly. "But maybe we have to consider the worst possibility of all."

"What is it, Phil?" I asked her, concerned about her abrupt mood shift.

She avoided looking at either David or me, choosing instead to consult the ceiling once again.

After a second, she whispered, "What if Gloria actually did it?"

14

IT WAS IMPOSSIBLE for me to believe that my friend—a kind, gentle, loving, mama bear of a person—could kill anything beyond a fifth of Scotch. So for a minute I just stood there, stunned that Philomena would even suggest such a thing.

But David spoke up. "Why would you consider that, Dr. Waldrop?"

The fact that he'd called her by her last name instead of Philomena carried some import. Maybe it was an effort on his part to invite her to consider the situation from her more professional perspective; maybe it was just an effort to demonstrate how cold he was to her suggestion. Whatever it was, her demeanor shifted.

"Oh, my," she said. "You're right. Why did I say that?"

The sound of her voice, filled to the top with self-doubt and confused reproach, made me come to her aid.

"Well," I said, deliberately controlling the sound of my voice, "Billy found out some uncomfortable things about Gloria this morning. Did you know that she's got an arrest record in Savannah?"

Phil's eyes widened. "She does?"

"A long one." I looked at David. "The GBI thinks she's a career criminal: street fighting, vagrancy, petty theft."

He thought for a moment, then said, "That sounds more like a homeless kid than a career criminal. To me."

"Oh," Phil chimed in. "She did tell Rose and me that she went to Savannah after her parents died and lived on the streets until she got a job as a janitor at a church there."

"Right!" I remembered. "The pastor there kind of took her under his wing. That's what made her want to be a priest. He turned her life around, she said."

"But it's the job of law enforcement to see the life of crime, not the life turned around," David observed.

"We know a wonderful woman," Philomena said carefully. "But maybe we don't know the *whole* woman."

"My understanding of the Buddha," David said in what seemed like a non sequitur, "is that he was nothing but a spoiled rich kid at first. But he went outside of his palace a couple of times and saw things his parents didn't want him to see, like poverty, sickness, and death. He couldn't understand these things, so he spent years trying to figure them out. And his conclusion was that everything that lives knows suffering, but there's a way out of it."

Phil and I only stared.

"I'm saying that it doesn't matter to the over five hundred million Buddhists in the world that he started out a pampered layabout. What matters to them is that he became the Buddha."

"I'm pretty sure Gloria would laugh out loud at being compared to the Buddha," I insisted.

"Doubtless," David agreed. "But that's not my point. Would you rather be judged by the things you did when you were a teenager, or for the person that you are right now?"

Phil and I reacted at the same time. Several stammering sentences assured him that we'd rather be assessed for who we were that day.

"When I was a teenager, I wanted to kill myself," Phil concluded. "I don't want to anymore."

"When I was fifteen, I hated this town," I admitted. "All I could think about was how to get out. I obviously don't feel that way now."

"And when *I* was fifteen," David said softly, "I got into street fights, I was arrested for vagrancy, and I was a petty thief. Now I'm a gardener-poet. I'll take life *after* the turn-around. Every time."

"Agreed," I told him softly. "So, let's prove to the GBI that Gloria Coleman isn't a street tough or a career criminal. She's a wonderful person filled with an almost mystical, loving acceptance of everything and everyone on the planet."

"How do we do that?" Phil asked.

"We could start by talking to her mentor," I suggested. "The priest in Savannah."

"Good idea," David said.

Frank wandered back in then with a can of Coca-Cola in his hand.

"Here's what I been studying on," he announced. "I been thinking about that shovel I got from the church shed. You said the GBI took it on account of they think that's what killed Miss Glassie, right?"

"Right," David answered.

"But then the body was buried in front of the bookshop," Frank went on, obviously deep in thought. "So all that digging, in that cussed hard clay dirt there, there couldn't be a bit of what you call evidence left on that shovel, could there?"

"Oh, my, Frank," Phil said, deliberately demonstrating her admiration. "That's a very good point."

"So the GBI is just . . . stupid," Frank observed.

That made the three of us laugh a little too much. For my part, it was a tension release.

"And then," Frank went on, not quite understanding our laughter, "it come to me that y'all thought maybe I was the one that killed Miss Glassie."

"We did," David said immediately and straightforwardly. "But we don't now."

He nodded and downed the last of his Coke. "I can see why y'all might think that."

That was all. He made no explanation of his pronouncement. And when we made no comment, he went on.

"Now, when this happened," he said slowly, still thinking, staring at me, "this murder, it had to be when my sister was living at the bookshop, after Rose Brimley was in the hospital or after she was dead, and before you come to town, right?"

"Yes," I said.

"So that's around the time I was working on the roof at that church, Miss Coleman's church," he said. "I ain't know that my sister was there, at the bookshop, but ever so often it was some people coming and going over there. I paid it no mind. It was at the end of summer or so, and it was hot on that roof. I ain't think about much at all, tell the truth, but finish the work and drink about ten or twelve cold ones, you understand."

"Why are you telling us this, Frank?" David asked patiently.

"I just got it in my head to wonder if one of them people coming and going over there might have been Bea Glassie."

It slowly dawned on me. "Frank, are you saying you might have seen the murder?"

"Don't believe so," he answered slowly. "What I'm saying is: what was Bea Glassie doing at a closed-up bookshop? And she was *not* alone."

"Who was she with?" Phil asked, her voice hushed.

"Couldn't say." He seemed embarrassed then, for a second. "I don't see too good far away."

"So how did you know it was Bea that you saw?" David asked.

He smiled and shook his head. "Her voice could carry like it was on a loudspeaker."

"That's true," Phil confirmed.

"Was she with a man, do you think, Frank?" I asked.

He just shrugged.

"Okay, then," David said. "Let's get back to work."

Without a second's hesitation, Frank headed for the exit.

"We've got a couple more hours of work out there," David told me. "But after that?"

"Come on over," I said. "In the meantime I'll see if I can't get hold of Father whatever-his-name-is in Savannah."

"Can I help?" Phil asked me.

"I was hoping you'd say that," I told her.

"All *right*," David said, following Frank toward the door. "Let's reconvene at six or so and see if we can't figure all this out."

"Thanks for the lesson about the Buddha, by the way," I teased.

He didn't look back. "I do what I can to enlighten the troubled."

"He thinks he's funny," I said loudly to Philomena.

He waved as he headed out the door.

The second the door clanked closed, Phil whispered, "Frank did it!"

"What?" I couldn't help smiling. "Everything that just happened tells us that he absolutely did *not* do it."

She shook her head. "What you don't know about Frank is that he's smarter than he seems to be. His dumb farm boy act is a little too ridiculous, don't you think?"

"No, I don't think," I told her. "You know a hundred other guys around here who are just like that."

"He was deliberately trying to lead us away from the fact that he did it!" Phil's voice rose higher. "All that baloney about being on the roof and seeing Bea with someone . . . you can't possibly believe that."

"You think he made it up to keep us from thinking he . . . Phil, it didn't sound that way to me."

Before she could respond, students started coming into the classroom. They were curious about Phil and me, but not enough to keep them from continuing to talk to each other as they took their seats.

"Time to go," Phil said abruptly, heading for the back door.

I followed.

David and Frank were already back at work.

"What do you think they're doing?" I asked, staring out at them.

"Well," Phil answered, "a meadow garden takes a little more care than you might imagine. You have to encourage the things you want to be there and discourage the interlopers."

"So they're fertilizing and pulling weeds," I concluded.

"Mostly," she agreed. "But it's a little trickier than that. What if you come across something that you didn't plant, something unexpected, that you fall in love with? For example, do you see those tall, spikey white things there? That's *fairy candle*. I know for a fact that they didn't plant that, it just happened. But isn't it lovely?"

I looked. The creamy foot-long spires were waving in the April breeze nearly everywhere in the meadow.

"They are lovely," I agreed.

"So it's not just a question of pulling all the weeds. You have to know which ones to take out and which ones to nurture."

As I nodded, I slowly began to wonder if that was a metaphor, something that ought to be informing my thinking about who killed Bea. But I couldn't quite get it into any tangible manifestation, any coherent thought.

So I just walked to my car. Phil got in, and I drove her back to the bookshop where her car was parked. All the way there, she kept trying different approaches.

"I can't really see Gloria or Mae Etta or even Idell wielding anything heavy enough to whack Bea in the head and kill her," she suggested.

"That's what Mae Etta said," I told Phil. "She said that hitting a woman like that was something only a man would do."

"A man like Frank."

"Phil," I began wearily.

"Who else, then?"

"Aren't there plenty of other men in Enigma who ran afoul of Bea's rancor?" I asked. "That's certainly the impression I've gotten."

"Well." She folded her arms and slouched down in the seat a little, pouting.

Maybe that's what the meadow garden metaphor was

trying to tell me, something about the unexpected, unplanted possibility.

We pulled up in front of the bookshop just in time to see Jennifer locking the front door.

"I'm going home to think," Phil said sullenly as she bounded out of the car.

That was that. She steamed into her car and roared away.

"Are we closing early?" I asked Jennifer as I got out of Igor.

She smiled. "Who's running this place, you or me?"

"You are today," I said. "And I'm sorry I've been so absent."

"You're worried about Reverend Coleman," she said, unlocking the door for me. "I am too. No way did she kill Bea Glassie. Right?"

"Right." I climbed the steps a little slower than usual. "Seriously, Jennifer, thank you for taking such good care of the shop. I don't know what I'll do when you go to London."

"I know," she joked. "You'll probably just go out of business."

"Uh-huh," I said. "And by the way, who was that cute boy you were flirting with when I left?"

"Oh, that's just Hedge Anderson." But she blushed a little. "He's in my Foundations of Education class."

"I see."

"He's from Tennessee." She was avoiding eye contact.

"Came *all* the way from Tennessee," I said, goading her, "just to flirt with you."

"Shut up," she told me, laughing. "Why are you teasing me when you know I'm saving your crazy little bookshop. You don't see me teasing you about David Madison."

"That's because there's nothing to tease," I told her. "The way we're going, you'll be a grandmother before anything happens between me and David Madison."

"Oh, no, I won't," she insisted. "I'm not having children. I don't see the point."

I shook my head slowly. "What will Hedge Anderson think about that?"

"He'll think I'm economically sensible and sociologically responsible."

"*Man* are you smarter than I was at your age," I said.

"That's right, grandma," she said, heading down the stairs. "See you tomorrow."

No Vespa in sight, I watched her walk away, her book satchel over one arm. It occurred to me then that I didn't know where she lived. I had just assumed that she stayed in one of the dorm rooms at the college, but that would have been a very long walk, and she wasn't walking in the direction of the college. Then it occurred to me that she might be headed to meet someone. Maybe the arcanely named Hedge Anderson.

It also occurred to me, as she faded from sight, that she hadn't told me whatever it was she'd found out about Bea and the bookshop. She'd tried to tell me about it. Twice.

But when I made it into the kitchen I was distracted from those thoughts by Cannonball, who was standing in the middle of the kitchen table and demanding attention.

"Yes," I told him. "I guess you're hungry. Sorry. I've been busy. Although it's not like it would kill you to miss a meal. Or ten."

He sat to ponder my assessment of his weight, which was, at the vet's last encounter, almost twenty pounds. After a brief moment of silence, his conclusion was that he was hungry no matter what and didn't really care about his girth, and so he began to yowl.

"All right, all right," I acquiesced.

I went to the pantry and dug into the bag of ZIWI Peak. I had to special order it, and it was the most expensive cat food I'd ever heard of. They were based in New Zealand and claimed to be the world leader in the air-dried pet food market. The quality of their ingredients, their website claimed, was second to none. All I knew was that it was the only thing Rose ever fed her cats, and so I had little choice but to continue the madness. Because Cannonball knew the difference. I'd tried several times to substitute other very fine brands, and he did everything but call the cops on me. Which I'm convinced he would have done if only he'd had opposable thumbs.

"Here we go," I said, emerging from the pantry with his porcelain bowl filled with the feline ambrosia.

I set it down on the kitchen table and he deigned to dine.

I went to the electric teakettle, filled it with water, and got out the French press. I was just reaching for the coffee beans when the phone on the desk in the other room rang. I thought about letting it go to voice mail, which Jennifer had set up for me, but my second thought was that it might be David, so I went to answer it.

"Old Juniper Bookshop," I said in my best mock-business manner.

"Madeline Brimley, please," the stern voice requested.

I hesitated because he sounded a little too official.

"Speaking," I said at length.

"This is Hugh Glassie from over in Sylvester," he announced. "I head up the local office of the GBI."

15

I CONSIDERED HANGING UP. I considered saying "wrong number" in maybe a Swedish accent. I considered just making strange squeaking noises to rattle the guy.

But in the end, hoping to sound righteous, I said, "I'm glad you called. How do you have the gall to lock up an Episcopal priest when there's a crazed killer on the loose in my little town?"

He was momentarily silenced, but it didn't last.

"Miss Brimley," he began with a deliberate show of patience. "I understand that you have recently paid a visit to Kell Brady in Hawkinsville."

My first inclination was to ask how he would know what I'd been doing, but I quickly realized that didn't make any difference. So I told the truth. Some of it.

"He has roses in his front yard," I told Mr. GBI, "that my aunt designed. I wanted to see them. I'm thinking of planting some in my front yard too."

"Uh-huh," he muttered, unconvinced. "My special agents tell me that you *might* be trying to subvert the proper course of our investigation into the murder of Beatrice Glassie."

"Do you mean your close relative Bea Glassie?" I snapped.

"How does a clear conflict of interest like that remotely compare to my little visit to some rich old guy in Hawkinsville? He was delighted with my visit, by the way. He let me taste a ten-thousand-dollar sherry. Did he tell you that?"

"He didn't tell me anything, Miss Brimley," the man said, still straining to show me his patience.

Then how did he know about my visit?

"He didn't call you?" I demanded to know. "He didn't tell you to warn me to stay away from him?"

"No, he did not," the man insisted.

But that was all.

"Then how did you know—"

"Miss Brimley," he interrupted, all pretense of patience gone, "I called to tell you, flat out, that you are to cease and desist any so-called investigation you think you're conducting into the murder of Beatrice Glassie. It's a GBI matter, and if I discover that you're impeding our inquiries, I will personally put you in the same cell as your friend Gloria Coleman!"

There it was, aggressive male anger, the *first* resort of a certain kind of man when he's confronted with a certain kind of woman. I'd seen it a million times. Directors, actors, boyfriends. Two seconds of pretend patience followed by an extended period of moderate to severe rage. I just smiled because I knew, then, who I was dealing with.

"I'd *love* to put that to the test," I said calmly. "I'd love to see how you'd prove that a conversation about roses was a threat to your nonexistent case against a beloved Episcopal priest. In fact, send somebody over right now. I'll just have time to call my lawyer in Tifton. Oh, and my *good* friends at *The Atlanta Journal-Constitution*—seems like they'd really be interested in a story like this."

"I don't think you understand what you're doing," he said slowly.

"Well, you may be right," I said cheerfully. "I haven't really known what I was doing since I left New York about ten years ago. But listen to this, Mr. Glassie—"

"*Director* Glassie," he corrected.

"Okay." I laughed. "But what I *do* know is that Gloria Coleman didn't even say a harsh word to your cousin Beatrice, let alone bury her in my yard. And I really don't care what you or your special agents tell me to do, nor not to do. I'm going to figure out who actually *did* kill your cousin, since apparently no one else is working on that."

"She's not my cousin." That's all he said.

Then there was a long pause, long enough to make me think that maybe he'd hung up the phone.

"Um . . ." I began.

"I believe that you have misunderstood . . . a couple of things," he said at last. "I guess you're probably too young to know who Otis Redding is."

That non sequitur nearly gave me whiplash.

"Well, of course I know who Otis Redding is," I managed to tell him.

"I was born in Macon, Georgia, just like Otis, and his music has always meant a lot to me," he went on. "Did you know that Bob Dylan wrote 'Just Like a Woman' for Otis? Dylan wanted Otis to sing it. And do you know what Otis said?"

It was about then that I began to wonder if the director of the local chapter of the GBI might be having a stroke. But I gamely played along.

"No," I said. "What did Otis say?"

"Too many words."

So I was forced to say, again, "Um . . ."

"Otis thought that Dylan's song had too many words in it," he explained. "Otis applied Occam's razor; he thought that Dylan had unnecessarily multiplied the essentials."

"I know Occam's razor—" I began.

"I find myself in the same position as Otis Redding, Miss Brimley," he interrupted. "You are needlessly complicating the issue with all your wild speculation."

"It's not wild speculation—" I said, trying again to get through to him.

"Plus, I'm in a no-win situation where . . . are you familiar with Otis's song '(Sittin' on) the Dock of the Bay,'" he interrupted again.

"What?"

"Do you know the song or not?" he grumbled.

"I do, but . . ." It took me a minute. "Wait. You can't do what ten people tell you to do."

"That's right!" He seemed cheered by my ability to paraphrase a song lyric. "I can't. I have a boss, a bureaucracy, a bunch of really good special agents, and a crazy old relative all telling me what they think I'm supposed to do. So would you *please* just quit doing what you're doing and let my guys do their job."

I felt a sudden blush of sympathy for the man. "I really hadn't thought of all that. I see what you're saying."

I had no intention of stopping my so-called investigation, but why confront poor old Hugh Glassie from Macon, Georgia, any more than I already had?

"Okay." He sighed and his weariness was palpable even over the phone. "I can check you off my Idell to-do list."

"May I ask you a question," I said, "Director Glassie?"

"What is it?" He was ready to get off the phone.

"How did you know I went to see Kell Brady. Can you tell me that?"

There was the briefest of pauses. "I guess that wouldn't do any harm. Maybe you met Mr. Brady's maid, Donna Dukes."

"*She* called you?"

"Idell says that Donna looks after Mr. Brady like she's his mother," he told me. "Even though I believe they're about the same age. Roughly."

I tried to picture Donna in my head. She was one of those people who didn't really *look* any certain age. She was just... older.

"But the last thing Donna said to me," I recalled, "was that I should call before I visited again. Not that I shouldn't visit at all."

"I don't know what to tell you," he said, obviously anxious to end the conversation. "She's very protective."

"Okay." I didn't know what else to say.

"Okay." And he hung up.

But when I hung up the phone, my brain was suddenly in one of its bossiest moods. It shoved me toward a most unlikely proposition. It was vague, but it had to do with Donna. Was she feeling not just protective but also possessive? What if Donna drove to Enigma to confront Bea Glassie, to tell Bea to leave her *little Kellie* alone? And when Bea acted like Bea and said she wouldn't do it, Donna Dukes bashed Bea in the noggin and buried her in front of a bookshop.

So I was forced to tell my brain to shut up. Because that seemed completely far-fetched. But it did make me wonder if I had a complete picture of Kell Brady. He'd really done his best to charm me: sweet talk about the Glassie sisters, a housecoat out of the nineteenth century, and the world's most expensive sherry.

And *then*, unbidden, I heard my aunt Rose's admonition, "Sometimes a rose is just a rose." It was her deliberate mix of Sigmund Freud and Gertrude Stein, a bit of odd acting advice. Subtext is good, in fact essential, but some things ought to be taken at face value. Then she'd go on to tell me what John Gielgud had said to her about Shakespeare. "Shakespeare is easy. All you have to do is pronounce the words correctly. The author's done all the rest of the work for you."

I was almost certain that Rose had never met John Gielgud, but I was equally certain that he'd said something like that about Shakespeare. So who was I to argue with my dead aunt Rose and her imaginary Gielgud? Maybe Kell Brady was just what he appeared to be, a sweet old guy who was shocked to hear about the death of someone he knew so well.

So, with some effort, I pushed that entire line of thinking out of my mind, wandered back into the kitchen, and set about the task of trying to remember the name of the priest in Savannah who had been Gloria's mentor, or even the name of that church.

I sat down at the table and watched Cannonball eat for a moment before I asked him, "You don't remember the name of Gloria's Savannah mentor, do you?"

He stopped eating, looked up, closed his eyes for a moment—thinking, I presumed—and then returned to his dinner.

"I'll take that as a no," I said.

Maybe Phil would remember, I thought. Should I call her?

I knew that Phil's state of mind was still a little precarious. She'd been so determined that Frank was a murderer, and when someone she loved disagreed, it gave her pause. Nervous pause. So a quick phone call to check on her seemed in order anyway. And her memory was, despite everything, formidable.

I didn't want to use my iPhone so I went back into the other room to use the landline.

I dialed and waited. She had no voice mail and it was not unusual for Philomena to wait for the phone to ring ten or twelve times before she would answer.

"That way I know that whoever is calling really wants to talk with me," she'd told me. More than once.

So I just sat in the calm of the early evening, surrounded by all the books and memories and gentle ghosts. I couldn't help recalling a line that Rose always used to quote. "The bookshop has a thousand books, all colors, hues, and tinges, and every cover is a door, that turns on magic hinges."

As a kid I'd always loved that thought. It was from a poem by Nancy Byrd Turner, who, my aunt delighted in telling me, had won something called the Golden Rose Award in 1930 from the New England Poetry Society. And it was true for me at age ten, lingering, reading in the shop with Rose and Philomena after hours. Every first time I turned a cover I also opened a door to another world, my only escape from Enigma then, my only refuge from an otherwise dreary world.

Then: "Hello?"

"Ah, Phil," I said, "help me."

"Sweetheart, of course," she cooed with concern. "What is it?

"I can't remember the name of Gloria's priest mentor in Savannah, or the name of his church."

"Yes." She took only a slight moment. "That was Father Davis at St. John's. I believe it's on Bull Street."

I marveled. "How on earth would you remember what street it's on?"

"Oh, that's nothing. It's like saying something in Atlanta

is on Peachtree Street. You're bound to be right more than half the time."

"But it's Father Davis," I confirmed.

"Definitely," she said. "Gloria talks about him all the time. He really changed her life."

"Right," I said, "that's what I'm looking for, what David was talking about. Gloria isn't the street tough she apparently was when she first got to Savannah. She's Reverend Coleman now, a loving, gentle, non-murderous priest and cherished town character."

"Well, remember that David said he was coming over to your place later," she murmured playfully. "So you'd better do it quickly. You said you'd cook him dinner."

"Okay," I said sternly, obviating any further teasing. "Thanks, and unless you know Father Davis's phone number, I'm hanging up now."

"Bye now," she sang cheerily.

So that was that. I set the phone down. A quick online check would get me the number for St. John's church in Savannah, and what I hoped would be an informative conversation with Father Davis. I just had to calm my mind a little so that I could ask the right questions. Because I realized that my brief talk with Director Glassie of the GBI had unsettled me a little more than I'd thought it had.

For one thing, he was a more complex character than I'd imagined. When he was just a monolith behind a fabricated witch hunt, I could think of him as some rancid bureaucrat. But after actually talking with him, he was an Otis Redding–loving, henpecked victim of family pressure and on-the-job harassment. It was confusing for me to feel sympathy for him. For another thing, he'd made me start thinking of Kell Brady's maid as a murderous maven, something out of a 1940s noir film and a sister cliché of "the butler did it." Which made me doubt my ability to successfully walk across a room, let alone help Gloria get out of her troubles. And finally, his admonition to stop investigating Bea's murder carried, obviously, more weight than the previous warnings I'd gotten from Billy, or even Baxter-Baker. They probably wouldn't really do anything to me if I kept on with my inquiries. But Director Glassie might.

So I sat at the desk for a moment and took a couple of deep breaths, trying to get back into the mood I'd been in when I was waiting for Phil to answer the phone. When that didn't happen, I reached for the laptop on the desk and found, quite easily, the phone number for St. John's Episcopal Church in Savannah, Georgia.

16

I HAD NO IDEA what time it was, but it was still light outside, however fading, so I was hoping someone would answer. And someone did, but her voice was icy.

"St. John's." That was all.

"Yes, hello," I said. "My name is Madeline Brimley; I'm hoping to speak with Father Davis."

"Regarding?" the stern voice asked.

"It's about Gloria Coleman," I said.

"Gloria." Her voice softened a little. "What about her?"

"Well," I said, trying to decide how much to reveal to a chilly anonymous Episcopalian.

"Is she in some sort of trouble?" the woman asked after I was silent for a little too long.

"Why would you ask that?" I wanted to know.

"She's . . . unorthodox in just about every sense of the word," the woman said. "When she was with us, she was in nearly every kind of trouble you can be in."

"Okay, then, yes," I admitted. "She's in trouble. In fact, she's in jail."

"Again?"

And for some reason, that made me smile. Gloria had said

she'd been in jail before and would be again. The fact that this Savannah stranger said it too—that amused me.

"Yes, again," I said, "but I'm afraid it's pretty serious this time. She's been arrested on a murder charge."

"Murder? Gloria?" The woman actually laughed. "Don't be ridiculous."

"It's true," I assured her.

Then the woman took the phone away from her mouth and hollered, "Gary? You're not going to believe this. Pick up the phone."

I heard a distant voice call, "What?"

The woman doubled her volume. "Pick up the phone!"

It hurt my ear. A second later a gravelly, ancient voice said, "Hello?"

I could tell that the woman who had answered the phone was still on the line, but I didn't care.

"Father Davis," I said, "my name is Madeline Brimley, I'm calling from Enigma. Gloria Coleman is my friend and she's in trouble."

"Again?" he asked.

And I could hear the woman on the other line stifle a giggle.

"Hang up, Betty, please," Father Davis said sweetly.

She did.

"Now," he went on, "what's she done this time?"

"She hasn't done anything," I said. "But she's been arrested on a murder charge."

"Oh, for God's sake," he said, and he was laughing about it almost as much as Betty had.

"I know," I assured him. "She didn't do it, obviously, but the GBI is involved, and they think they've got proof. And

I was shown her hefty arrest record. That's what makes the GBI think she's a career criminal."

"Mmm," he agreed. "She was in quite a bit of trouble when she first came to Savannah."

When he didn't elaborate, I was forced to press.

"It looked to me, when I saw her record," I told him, "that it was mostly stuff a homeless teenager would have done, right?"

He paused. "Tell me who you are again."

"Madeline Brimley," I said. "I run a bookshop that's sort of across the street from Gloria's church."

"St. Thomas Aquinas," he interrupted. "You're the person at the Old Juniper Bookshop. She's written to me about that."

"About the shop?"

"Yes, and about you." He sighed. "She writes to me once a month. Old-fashioned letter writing—something out of a quite distant past, don't you think?"

"Well."

"And I can tell you that I look forward to those letters like a birthday present."

"Yes, but what I'm calling about—"

"It's absolutely ridiculous, of course," he insisted, "that she could . . . you know, when she was our janitor, she would catch the rats in our church basement and take them out to the park. You understand? She wouldn't even kill a rat. It's not in her constitution."

"Right, I wonder if we might start from the beginning," I coaxed, "and you could tell me how she came to your church. She told me that you were the reason she became a priest, and I was wondering how all that, you know, came about."

"*God* is the reason she became a priest," he admonished.

"I may have been an instrument in that regard, but I believe that Gloria was born to the priesthood. As was I."

"Of course," I began.

"She didn't always *look* it, obviously," he mused. "My first encounter with her was not exactly . . . pious."

"Oh?" I said, hoping that might encourage him to tell me the story I wanted to hear.

"She was sleeping in the little graveyard behind our church," he said, clearly amused, "cradling three stolen purses in her arms."

"No." Keep going, I thought.

"Yes! Sound asleep. She was dressed in filthy overalls and combat boots, if you can believe it."

"I can."

"And when I woke her up, do you know what she said?"

"What?"

"She looked up at me," he told me, "and said, 'Oh, no—am I dead?'"

He gave out with a wheezing laugh that lasted a little too long for my comfort.

"When I told her that she wasn't, she sat up and belched like a sailor."

I smiled. "Yes, that sounds like the person I know."

"Well," he said. "That was the beginning of our journey together."

And at last he told me the story.

GLORIA Coleman headed for Savannah after her parents died. She'd heard it was an interesting town. She left her home in the Okefenokee Swamp and walked or hitchhiked over a hundred and seventy miles, making her way up the Georgia coast until she eventually landed in a place called Thunderbolt, about five miles outside of downtown Savannah. She was a short, stocky fifteen-year-old with no money, crushing self-doubts, and a hair-trigger temper.

Her first arrest in Thunderbolt was for simple vagrancy, a charge which apparently amused her greatly.

"I have nowhere to sleep and nothing to eat," she was heard by other vagrants to say, "and that's a *crime*? And the *punishment* is that you're giving me a place to sleep and something to eat? You don't see the irony?"

It was clear to her in very short order that the arresting officer was a stranger to streetwise satire. He broke her arm when she objected, in a very physical manner, to handcuffs. It went untreated and never healed correctly.

She was warned, on her release, that she was to get a means of gainful employment immediately. Her response was to leave Thunderbolt at the speed of light.

She stopped running when she hit River Street in Savannah and managed to get a job busing tables at the Night Flight Café, a moderately popular bar that provided musical entertainment. She slept in a park near the Night Flight, ate from the plates she bused, and kept to herself.

After a week, the manager of the Night Flight offered her a place to stay in exchange for some relatively lewd and probably illegal behavior. When she politely declined, he began to insist. Her response was, at first, only verbal.

"Back home I used to wrestle alligators," she told the manager. "I would not mess with me, if I were you."

When he laughed, she demonstrated her swamp talent. He ended up in the hospital, and she ended up in jail. With no identification, the court did not seem to recognize or to care how old she was, and she was given a six-month sentence only partially ameliorated by her claim of self-defense.

When she hit the street again, she decided against gainful employment in favor of stealing food when she could, swiping any unattended purse she saw, and sleeping in parks and churchyards. A string of arrests ensued, but she had come to think that it was to her advantage to report her age. Then, as a juvenile delinquent, she was remanded to a facility she later described as "a shoddy workhouse that would have made Dickens weep."

By the time Father Davis found her in his cemetery she was seventeen years old, angry all the time, and unkempt in the extreme. He stood over her and she awoke, looked up, remembered the stolen purses in her arms, and cursed.

"I guess you called the cops on me," she said, after asking the priest if she was dead.

Father Davis shook his head. "I was going to invite you to breakfast."

She sat up and eyed the priest with obvious suspicion. "What for?"

He just smiled. "Scrambled eggs?"

Gloria finally let go of the stolen purses, let them fall to the ground as she stood up.

"We'll return those purses afterward," he went on as he turned and headed back into the church. "We'll do that together."

She looked down at her loot. "I haven't even looked inside these yet."

"I assume there will be some kind of identification in them," he told her, disappearing through the door.

"What day is today?" she called out, following after him.

Once inside she found herself in a large fellowship hall: lots of tables, lots more chairs, a drop ceiling with acoustic tiles, stark white walls, a hardwood floor that was scratched and scraped beyond all repair.

"It's Maundy Thursday," he finally answered from the kitchen at the far end of the hall.

"It's *what* Thursday?" she asked; the smell of the food made her pick up her pace.

"Maundy Thursday," he repeated. "The day of the Last Supper, a few days before Easter."

She arrived in the kitchen to see a tall thin woman in a floor-length white dress dishing eggs and bacon and toast onto three large, hard plastic plates.

"This is Betty," Father Davis said, waving his hand in the direction of the woman.

Betty stopped her work, turned, and stared blankly at Gloria.

"And who is *this*?" she asked.

"This is Gloria Coleman," Gloria answered. The chip on her shoulder was almost visible.

"I see," Betty said, returning to her work. "Well, take off that filthy jacket and wash your hands over there."

Betty tilted her head in the direction of the kitchen sink.

Gloria hesitated, on the verge of giving some less than charitable response, but Father Davis raised a single finger to his lips. Something about the way he did it encouraged Gloria to keep her mouth shut. Instead of venting her ire, she took off her coat and washed her hands.

Betty carried two plates out of the kitchen and into the large, characterless hall. Father Davis followed with the third.

Without a word, they all sat down.

Gloria had a piece of bacon in her hand and almost to

her mouth before Father Coleman closed his eyes and spoke softly.

"Creator of the universe, you give us this gift of food to nourish us and give us life. Bless this food that you have made, and human hands have prepared. May it satisfy our hunger, and in sharing it together may we come closer to one another."

"Uh-huh," Betty sniffed and then began eating.

Gloria put the bacon in her mouth.

Father Coleman said, "Amen."

"Yes, *amen*," Betty repeated, duly chastised.

Father Davis took his time gathering up his paper napkin, putting it in his lap, and arranging his cutlery before he began to eat. Gloria was nearly done by the time he took his first bite of toast. Father Davis glanced just once at her plate.

"More?" was all he said.

Gloria looked at Betty a little sheepishly.

"There's more bacon and toast," Betty said, not looking up from her breakfast.

Gloria got up, hustled to the kitchen, took all of the rest of the bacon and three more pieces of toast. She returned to the table, sat down, and paused.

"Do I need to say the magic words over this plate too," she asked, "or did the first prayer cover me?"

Father Davis laughed out loud; Betty just shook her head.

After that, Father Davis told Gloria she could sleep and eat in the church in exchange for a simple list of custodial duties: cleaning, kitchen work, sorting hymnals in the nave. Gloria readily agreed and added yard work and handyman duties to the list. She told Father Davis that she'd practically built the house that she and her parents lived in, wired it (albeit illegally), even put in a complicated plumbing system from the well on their property.

Father Davis was enthusiastic. Betty allowed that there would be a trial period beginning with finding the owners of the stolen purses and returning them before anything else was decided.

So Gloria set about the task, rummaging through each purse and finding identification. There were driver's licenses in all but one; those were easy to return. Gloria simply went to the address, said she'd found the purse in the street, and handed each one over to the surprised and grateful recipient. And when they offered a reward, which they all did, Gloria turned them down. Every one of them.

The last purse was a more difficult enterprise. The only thing in it with any kind of address was a worn business card from a chiropractor on a side street near City Market. Gloria went to the address and asked the receptionist if she recognized the purse, which she did not. So Gloria asked if she could leave the purse there in some prominent place where its owner might see it if she came back for an appointment. The receptionist agreed, however suspiciously, and Gloria left the purse on top of a filing cabinet.

It was later revealed that Gloria went back to the chiropractor's every day for two weeks until she saw that the purse was gone and the receptionist reported a very relieved reaction from a Mrs. Lewis.

That was good enough for Betty, and Gloria's residency at St. John's Episcopal Church began in earnest.

Father Davis couldn't quite put his finger on an exact date, but at some point, Gloria began asking questions about the priesthood. He answered absently at first, but when it became apparent that Gloria's interest was more than idle curiosity, he took a more scholarly approach. Gloria was confirmed in the church just after she turned eighteen.

After that she began to say that she wanted to be a priest, if such a thing would be possible for a woman. She was surprised to hear that a third of Episcopal priests were women. So she began her intensive study.

Father Davis, and even Betty, could see the fervor in the young woman. They began, secretly, collecting funds—some from wealthier parishioners, some from their own meager salaries—that would put Gloria through seminary at Sewanee, where Father Davis had acquired his degree.

They presented Gloria with a possibility on her twentieth birthday. They told her that if she was accepted at Sewanee, they would pay for it. Pay for everything, including a small living expense. It was the only time either Father Davis or Betty saw Gloria cry.

And Gloria's first reaction was to turn down the offer. She didn't deserve it. She wouldn't get in. Tennessee was too far away.

In the end Father Davis presented Gloria with the application and stood over her while she completed it.

She was, of course, accepted and, in fact, she excelled, completing the two-year course of study near the top of her class. When she returned to Savannah as the Reverend Gloria Coleman, she requested—seven times—to become Father Davis's curate, but that was not to be. She was assigned to assist at the Church of the Annunciation in Vidalia, Georgia. Where the onions come from.

"OF course she did so well there," Father Davis concluded his story, "that she was given full charge of that congregation when Father Miller died. And then, as you know, she was offered the post in Enigma when Father Glenn . . . retired."

It was clear from his hesitation that he knew what had actually happened with Father Glenn.

"Did you know," I asked, "that there was concern in Enigma about having a female priest?"

He sighed. "Yes, Gloria called me nearly every day for a while. Some woman at St. Thomas Aquinas seemed to be the primary culprit."

"That's right," I told him. "Her name was Beatrice Glassie. Did Gloria ever mention that name?"

"Not the name," he said, "but I could tell that Gloria was having a difficult time controlling her temper whenever she talked about that person."

"Oh?"

"Yes." He paused. "Gloria's path has been a difficult one. Do you know anything about Buddhism?"

I was momentarily silenced by the question, but I managed to say, after a moment, "A little. In fact, a friend of mine was just talking about it."

"You don't ever really say that you *are* a Buddhist, as I understand it," he went on. "You say you have a daily practice in Buddhism. The way, I suppose, a doctor calls it a *practice*. You are supposed to realize that you never completely get *there*. You have to practice every day to remind yourself who and what you are."

"Okay." I had no idea what he was getting at.

"Gloria has a temper," he said. "She always will. She has to meditate and pray on it every day, she's told me a hundred times, to keep it in its place. And this woman certainly seemed to test Gloria's ability to control her . . . what she referred to as her darkest demon."

"I see."

What had at first seemed to me a great story of Gloria's redemption had, at the last possible moment, turned into a shadow of doubt.

Father Davis had heard the tone in my voice.

"What is it?" he asked, his voice hushed.

I took a deep breath and then told him.

"The woman who was causing Gloria such distress," I said, "is the person who was murdered. That's the murder Gloria's accused of."

"Oh," he said, all the energy gone from his voice. "I see the problem."

"But you don't remotely think that Gloria would be capable—"

"Of course not!" he snapped. But then, after a single breath, he said, barely above a whisper, "I don't think so."

17

I HUNG UP THE phone, instantly regretting making the call in the first place. I tried to calm down by reminding myself that I'd known Gloria for six months, been with her nearly every day, and I'd never seen even the slightest hint of a bad temper. I thought that Phil might know more about that, but she hadn't really known Gloria for much longer than I had.

I sat at the desk in the fading light and wondered if I should try to call someone at the Church of the Annunciation in Vidalia where she'd been before she came to Enigma. Then I wondered if I should ask Phil to introduce me to some of the people in Gloria's congregation in Enigma. *Then* I wondered who was going to conduct the services at St. Thomas Aquinas while Gloria was incarcerated.

Before I could spiral into further digression, I heard a noise at the front door. Someone was knocking.

I hadn't remembered locking the door behind me when I'd come in, but as I came into the vestibule, I could see David through the front door window. He was still dressed in his work clothes.

I shot to the door and opened it. "You got finished with your work earlier than I thought you would."

He smiled. There was a little smudge of dirt on his jaw.

"I got to talking with Frank," he said, "and something came up that I thought you might want to know about."

"Okay."

I stood aside, he came in.

"Sorry for the . . ." He indicated the grubby condition of his work clothes.

I touched his shoulder. "I don't care what your clothes look like. I mean, you look like a gardener, and isn't that what you are?"

"It is," he agreed cheerfully.

"I think I've got some iced tea in the fridge," I said, heading for the kitchen.

"It's not *iced* tea," he corrected. "Here in Enigma, it's *sweet* tea. You lived in New York too long."

"True," I agreed. "But the tea is, in fact, unsweetened."

"I guess it'll have to do," he groused, jokingly.

"So what did Frank say that prompted your early arrival?" I asked. "Not that I'm complaining. I actually have something to tell you too."

"What is it?" he asked.

We went into the kitchen and when he sat down at the table, David gave out a little groan.

I went to the fridge, got out the pitcher of tea and set it on the table.

"What was that little noise you made?" I asked, going to the cupboard for glasses.

"Frank and I spent most of our day pulling out a couple of stumps from the meadow," he told me. "We should have gone for the tractor. I am just about *wore out*."

"'Wore out,'" I mocked. "And bereft of diction."

"Ha," he responded halfheartedly.

I poured the tea and sat beside him at the table.

"Now, what did Frank say?" I asked.

"He was telling me a little more about Kell Brady," David began, "and the work he did for Bea and him in Hawkinsville."

"What about it?"

"Frank lied to us earlier today," David said. "Apparently, after he put the rats in Bea's house, he felt guilty. He didn't say how it happened, but he *did* go to Hawkinsville. He worked for Kell Brady, helping with the opera house there. He worked for a couple of weeks last summer. Not long before you came back into town to take over this place."

He picked up the glass in front of him and downed it all at once without a pause or a breath.

"More?" I asked.

He nodded. I poured.

"Why did he lie to us," I wanted to know, "and why did he have a change of heart and tell you the truth?"

David drank half of his second glass of tea before he answered.

"I don't pretend to understand Frank. Maybe he's the still waters that run deep, or maybe the waters are just still—all the way down. But he does have some sort of admiration for you, for the fact that you found out who killed his sister."

"I keep telling people—"

"Doesn't matter." David waved away my objection. "The point is, he has a slow-moving but nevertheless nagging conscience, and it poked at him until he had to confess. He said he couldn't tell you in person, but that I could."

"Tell me that he worked for Kell Brady for a couple of weeks?" I shook my head. "What difference does that make?"

"I wasn't finished, sorry." He downed his second glass of

tea. "He seemed to want me to tell you three things. First, that he called Bea to tell her that he'd changed his mind and he would, after all, go to Hawkinsville and help with the opera house, but he never got in touch with her, so he just went to the opera house and waited for Kell to show up, which he did, and then worked for almost two weeks."

"What work did he do?"

"Small stuff," David said. "Wiring, a little painting, some Sheetrock. But the second thing he wanted you to know was that every time he asked if Bea was coming, Kell would change the subject. He thought at the time that maybe they'd had some kind of argument, but he was just as happy that Bea didn't show up."

"Huh." I didn't quite know what to make of this information.

"And the third thing," David continued, "which he was dead serious about, was that the opera house was haunted."

That handed me a smile. "Aren't they all?"

"Yeah, I know," he acknowledged, "but it was Frank's idea that the ghost was Bea."

And *that* really handed me a laugh. Out loud.

"Oh, for God's sake," I said. "What in the world made him think it was Bea's ghost?"

"He said that whenever he sat down to take a break," David answered, "the ghost would turn the lights off and make noise. He interpreted that as Bea being bossy."

I just shook my head. "Frank."

But David leaned my way. "Look, I'm not remotely suggesting that Bea's ghost took up residence in Hawkinsville. What I'm thinking is that Frank may have sensed something in Kell Brady's demeanor that for some reason made him think about Bea. I'm saying that the psychology of the situation is that Frank was haunted by the guilt he felt for the way he'd treated Bea. Say what you will about Frank, but he's a good Southern boy, and playing a dirty trick on an older woman, a woman whose economic and social status was far above his, weighed on his mind."

"Steady there, Dr. Freud," I told David. "I don't really think of Frank as being that complex. Is it possible that he was just spooked by some faulty wiring and random noise?"

"Of course it is," David admitted. "But there's more to Frank than you seem to think there is."

"Okay." I looked down. "What do you think it means, then? This new information from Frank."

"Don't know." He sat back in his chair. "But have I correctly observed that you may have some ambivalence when it comes to your opinion of Kell Brady?"

And there, I realized instantly, was one of the five thousand reasons I was beginning to really care for David. He could read me, read beyond the words. As a few good theatrical directors had put it to me, you have to see what the words imply, not just what they say. And David seemed to have that ability, that understanding. Which made me almost as nervous as it made me excited, but there my thinking digressed.

So I just said, "Yes. Philomena seems to think he's a Jekyll and Hyde. All I met was Dr. Jekyll, so I might not have a complete picture of the guy."

"Right," David agreed. "So. Maybe you and I should pay the Hawkinsville Opera House a visit and see if Mr. Brady wants to show us around."

"Oh. You know, he was *very* proud of it, of his work to preserve and to renovate it. I think he might go for that."

"And together maybe we can suss him out with a bit more accuracy," David said. "Plumb the depths."

"Plus," I said, "road trip date!"

He smiled. "See? And you keep saying that our relationship is moving too slow."

"Our relationship *is* moving too slowly," I assured him. "But I can be patient."

"When?" His voice got a tiny bit higher. "When have you ever been patient?"

I took a breath. "Last Thursday. For almost ten full minutes."

"Well." He put his hand on mine. "That *is* progress."

"But just to be clear," I said, "if there's really more to Frank than I think there is, couldn't it be possible that Frank is deliberately trying to direct attention away from himself? Couldn't he be trying to make us think that Kell Brady is a more likely suspect than *he* is?"

"Yes," he admitted solidly. "So in our bid to spring the Right Reverend Coleman from her unjust incarceration, we are going to, in no particular order, watch Frank, pester Brady, keep an eye on Mae Etta . . ."

When he paused, thinking, I added, "And press Idell. I think she may currently be my prime culprit."

"Really?" He was clearly skeptical.

"Here's my thinking," I said. "Kell Brady was and maybe still is smitten with Idell, for reasons beyond my understanding. She rebuffed his advances, whatever *those* looked like, and so he turned to Bea. His relationship with Bea was, it would appear, more a business understanding than a romantic association. Still, what if Idell was jealous? What if Idell is the if-I-can't-have-him-then-nobody-can sort of person?"

"That's an actual sort?" He smiled.

And, entirely unbidden, I had a satori. A small-town satori.

"I just realized something," I said slowly. "Relationships in a small town are *really* different from relationships in a large urban environment. In my experience. And my observation."

"Hmm." David's voice had changed and he stared at me in a distinctly hesitant manner. "Maybe you should elucidate that philosophy."

"In a small town," I said, "especially one as small as Enigma, the range of possibilities is limited, the expectations are lowered, and the demands are more basic."

"I see." His voice was cold and he shifted in his chair. "I see what you're saying."

His face had hardened and his jaw was set.

"David," I began, mystified by the shift in his demeanor.

"No." He nodded. "I think I can interpret what you're saying. You're saying that the pickin's are slim, you have to take what you can get, and maybe all you can really hope for is someone who's not an idiot."

"Um..."

"Which dramatically reduces what I thought *our* burgeoning association was."

"What?" My head snapped back. "No, I didn't mean—"

"And since I'm one of only, like, seven or eight men our age within a fifty-mile radius," he went on a little higher, "I guess I qualify as the best of a bad lot, is that it?"

"David—"

He stood slowly and deliberately. "I'm going home now, I think."

"Wait." I stood.

"I need to get out of these clothes. And take a shower."

He headed for the front door.

"I think you're radically misinterpreting what I was saying,"

I said, following after him. "I wasn't talking about *us*; I was talking about the Glassie sisters..."

He stopped dead at the door and I nearly ran into him.

"I can read between the lines," he said softly, without turning around.

"*Stop!*" My voice was raised to an uncomfortable level. "This went from zero to a hundred *way* too fast. You have to know I didn't mean—what's going on?"

He turned. The look on his face was unmistakable. He was pulling away.

"I know that you probably had your pick of your fellow actors in New York," he told me, staring me in the eye, "and that Atlanta is a city of over six million people. Maybe..."

But he didn't finish that sentence. He just turned and left.

"I was going to make dinner," I said weakly.

He didn't hear me.

I stood there in the doorway, watched him get in his truck, back out, and drive away. I watched until I couldn't see his pickup anymore. And then I watched for a while after that, until the streetlights in Enigma came on in the distance. All seven of them.

18

EVENTUALLY I CLOSED the door. Eventually I turned on the porch light. Eventually I went back into the kitchen. But it was a different room than the one I'd left only a few minutes before. It looked different. It felt different. It even smelled different.

I didn't clear the kitchen table. I was afraid to touch David's glass. I was afraid to wash it and put it up. I didn't push in his chair either. I just stood there for a while, unable to make my brain turn on again, because it had most severely shut down.

After a very long while I was distracted by fireflies, thank God. There were, without exaggeration, a million of them in my back garden. So, taking their light to be an invitation, I quit the kitchen and ambled out into the yard. I made it to the gazebo. I sat down. I smelled the juniper on the light spring breeze and something else more floral that I couldn't identify.

I heard a soft rustling behind me. I turned to see a rabbit eating my parsley. He didn't seem to mind that I was only three or four feet away, and I knew it was good parsley. I had plenty. I didn't mind. But I had a few thoughts I wanted to share with him.

"David Madison planted that parsley for me," I told him, "and I do use it in lots of my so-called cooking, so save me some, okay?"

He looked up, considered what I was saying, and then continued to eat.

"Okay," I went on, "then maybe you can explain to me what just happened. Because that escalated at the speed of light. What was it about? Any thoughts?"

Once again, he stopped eating, twitched his nose, and stared at me. But then the sudden laughter of a barn owl somewhere in the trees behind us made him jump, and before I knew it, the rabbit was gone.

"I see," I called after him. "You're all alike. You leave in the middle of a sentence."

I don't know how long I sat there turning over first one thought and then another. What did I say to David? Why had he taken such quick offense? Then, slowly, the question became: What did it say about me that I hadn't realized what I was saying? What I was really saying about small-town romance. Because, upon very little reflection, what I'd said could have been interpreted as being quite offensive. I'd meant it to apply to Kell Brady's relationship with the Glassie sisters, but I'd clearly made a more general statement—without meaning to.

Or *had* I meant to? And wasn't that right? How many so-called eligible bachelors were there in Enigma? Sure, I'd only been back in town for six months or so, but David seemed to be alone in that category, at least for me. Was I going to get involved with Frank? Or Elbert? Or even that dishy but rude Captain Jordon, fireman from Albany?

On the other hand, what if I'd met David in Atlanta? I only had to think about that for about ten seconds. He was really smart, at least as well-read as I was; he knew more about plants than anyone I'd ever met, he was great looking, and he wrote *poetry*, for God's sake. Good poetry. I'd read some of it. If I'd met him in Atlanta I wouldn't have believed my good fortune. That's what I needed to say to him, that he wasn't the best of a bad lot, he was the best of . . . he was in a lot all by himself.

I was just on the point of trying to figure out how to use the word *destiny* in my speech to him without sounding like an idiot when someone appeared in the back doorway, holding the screen door open, silhouetted by the kitchen light.

"Maddy?" she called out. "That's you, right?"

I stood and waved. "Phil. Care to come out here and watch the fireflies with me?"

She took a second to look around. "There are quite a lot of them tonight, aren't there? But why don't you come into the kitchen? I have . . . ideas."

"Uh-oh," I said, heading her way. "That can't be good."

She didn't respond. She just turned around and went into the kitchen, letting the screen door slam behind her.

"Good night, fireflies," I said. "Good night, rabbit. Watch out for the owls."

When I got to the kitchen, Phil was seated. She'd gotten a glass and poured some tea for herself from the pitcher I'd left on the table.

"I see you've had company," she said, staring at David's empty glass. "I thought you were supposed to be making him dinner."

"Yeah." I sat beside her. "It did *not* go well."

"Oh?" She turned my way. "What happened?"

"I think I insulted him," I told her. "I didn't mean to."

"What did you say?" she asked accusingly.

"I'm going to fix it," I answered.

"You'd better." She shook her head. "He's the only person I know of within a hundred miles in any direction who could possibly understand you."

"I don't know," I demurred. "What about Captain Jordon?"

"Who?"

"The fireman from Albany," I reminded her. "You know, black hair, granite jaw . . . tall."

"So why haven't I heard more about him?" she asked.

"Well," I said, "he lives in Albany."

"You can't tell David that the reason you're dating him," Phil scolded, "is that he's *convenient*."

She rolled her head. "He can't understand you like David can."

"You're probably right," I agreed. "I should tell David something like that."

"What did you say to him that got him so upset?" she repeated.

"I was trying to get at the limits of love in a town the size of Enigma," I answered, "concerning Kell Brady and the Glassie sisters—"

"And he thought you were talking about your relationship with him."

I stared. "Yes. You really are the most insightful person."

"I had the same discussion with Rose," she told me softly, "when she first came back to town after being in New York for so long. About a hundred times. I couldn't believe she wanted to be friends with me. And every time she'd tell one of her stories, you know, one of her adventures in the land of downtown Oz, I'd get my feelings hurt."

"Why?"

"I don't really know," Phil said. "I think it made me see

how small my life had been compared to hers. And, of course, you'd have to figure in my *massive* inferiority complex."

"Massive?"

"It's the size of New Jersey," she assured me.

"Yeah, okay, but that's not David," I said.

"Isn't it?"

"No," I insisted. "He's done all that stuff. He played fiddle in a band, he birthed a baby, he raised a bear cub, he planted seaweed; he studied organic gardening *and* poetry with Wendell Berry!"

"Sweetheart." She smiled sadly. "Our greatest accomplishments don't stand a chance against even our smallest insecurities."

That hit harder than I wanted it to. I didn't want to think about what that meant to me. How it spoke to my reasons for leaving New York—or, worse, my reasons for coming to Enigma.

"And then there's Faye," Phil went on after a moment of silence. "He left Wendell Berry, followed her to Enigma, worked on her family's farm, thought he was going to marry her. And then she left him for someone else. He doesn't seem like the kind of person that would take something like that lightly, does he?"

"I hadn't thought about that," I admitted. "All I could think about where Faye was concerned was how insecure it made *me* feel. He even told me how it affected him. I think I just didn't believe it."

"Well." She went back to her glass of tea.

"Damn it," I muttered. "I'm kind of a moron."

"Language," she chastised absently.

"Sorry," I told her. "I try not to use the word *moron*, but sometimes it just slips out."

She just shook her head slowly.

"But you didn't come visit me to hear about how I'm ruining the best relationship I ever had," I went on.

"No." She set her glass down. "I came to talk about Idell."

"Good," I said. "Let's talk about that. Anything to change the subject."

"I've really been thinking about how Idell never went to Billy or anyone when Bea went missing," she mused.

"Yeah, I wonder about that too. Didn't we talk about it? But according to everyone, Bea and Idell spent a lot of time not speaking to each other. Billy and Mae Etta told me about one of their duels in the diner. Mae Etta thought they were at odds primarily about Kell Brady."

"Well, he was sweet on Idell," Phil agreed, "and then threw her over for Bea. And he stayed with Bea for . . . I don't know, for the rest of her life, as it happened."

"I thought the gossip was that Idell turned Kell down," I said. "And he only turned to Bea as a kind of rebound or something."

"Yes, the reports of their breakup were conflicting," she told me. "But Kell and Bea stayed together after that for a very long time."

"She even lived with him in Hawkinsville," I said, hoping that I was telling her something new, "and he stayed at her house here in town for extended visits."

"Yes," she said, "but no one thought there was anything untoward in that. Everybody thought they were really more business associates than they were romantic partners."

"Exactly what I've been told," I said, "but what if that was wrong? Or at least, what if Idell didn't believe that? What if Idell thought that Bea had stolen her beau?"

"Even though Idell had rebuffed him," Phil said slowly, "she wouldn't have wanted her sister to get involved with him. Certainly not in any romantic sense."

"Yes, that's what I've been thinking. Thank you for confirming my suspicions. I'm telling you, that puts Idell right back at the top of my list. People probably think that she's a frail old woman, but I happen to know what kind of energy anger can produce."

"The adrenaline alone," Phil agreed.

"And if Kell was really the only man around with whom Idell thought she might have some sort of life," I thought out loud, "then maybe all she really wanted was a little time to figure out her feelings for Kell. And in that little interim, bam. Her sister swoops in and scoops him up. Little old lady or not, that kind of thing could have engendered a solid bit of shovel-swinging time."

"Sounds like a bad country song," Phil giggled. "'Shovel-Swinging Time Down South.'"

That was, to me, one of Philomena's most endearing qualities. She very often digressed from a serious conversation into what she considered a diverting joke. It seemed like a virtue, the power of lightheartedness. But I had realized, over the years, that it was a wall she put up whenever anything threatened to invade her psyche too deeply. She made a joke to keep the demons away. The vision of Idell swinging a shovel hard enough to kill her sister was certainly demonic enough for me. And I hadn't just come home from a stay in a mental institution.

So I forged ahead. "The thing is, David suggested—before he got his feelings hurt, or whatever, and flew away—that we go visit Kell under the presumption that we were interested in the Hawkinsville Opera House; get him to show us around, see if we couldn't slip in some cogent questions while he was distracted by giving us the tour, you know?"

"Oh." She nodded. "Good idea."

"But it would appear, at the moment, that he is less inclined to go with me than he was only a little earlier this evening," I lamented. "So maybe you want to go with me?"

"Yes!" she answered at once, and a little too enthusiastically, standing up. "Let's go!"

"Hang on there, Sancho," I said, still seated. "It's a little late in the day to run off half-cocked to a haunted opera house, don't you think?"

She looked around as if, for a second, she couldn't remember where she was. Then: "Right. A little late. Good. So, tomorrow morning?"

"Tomorrow morning it is," I agreed.

"And, um—*Sancho*?"

"Don Quixote's sidekick," I reminded her. "The one with a clearer picture of reality."

"And you think that's *me*?" She shook her head. "Lord, we are in trouble."

"I'm the one taking a flying leap at the windmills," I assured her. "So you've got to be the one with the solid grasp of things."

She stuck out her lower lip just a little. "That's a new role for me, but I think I like the idea. I'm the solid one for a change. Yes. That might do me some good. Okay."

I could tell the gears in her brain were whirring faster than usual, and it made me happy to see her consider that she might be, at least for a moment, the stable phenomenon in this particular scenario.

"How do we do it?" she asked, eyes still a little wild trying to tame her innermost thoughts.

"I'll call the old guy up," I said. "I'll probably get Donna, but I'll remind her that she told me to call, which she did, and say that Kell piqued my interest in his opera house. She might go for it, and he might, in turn, agree to a tour."

"That does sound a little half-cocked, as you were saying."

"Oh, it's half-cocked all right," I concurred. "But I really want to talk with him again. There are so many unanswered questions in my head about that guy. And, by the way, about Donna."

"Yes." She sat back down at last. "Donna?"

"Donna Dukes," I said, mostly to myself. "She's apparently been his housekeeper-nursemaid for quite some time. Looks after him like she was his mother, it's been said. But between you and me, I think there might be something more to their relationship, at least on her part."

"You think she might have feelings for Kell?" Phil asked me.

"Yes," I said, "although the nature of those feelings is unclear to me at the moment. Is she in love with him? Does she mother him? Is she just a sincerely diligent employee? I'd like to know."

"And if I go with you," Phil said, "it might seem more like a visit than an interrogation."

"Exactly," I agreed.

"It'll be fun," she said then, almost to herself. "Of course, not as much fun as it would have been with David. Are you sure you don't want to talk with him before you decide that I'm your best companion for this adventure? It was his idea, after all. And you don't want to let this little fissure in your mutual affection grow into anything larger. Do you?"

She looked deeply into my eyes then.

"Yeah, I need to talk with David," I agreed, "but at the moment that's a separate issue."

"Separate from what?"

"From getting Gloria out of jail!" I said.

"Oh." She seemed startled. "Right. That's the reason we're going to Hawkinsville. Right."

I sat silent for a moment wondering if maybe I was making Phil do something that she really shouldn't be doing. Despite my Sancho Panza metaphor, I knew that she was, in fact, not the most stable cheerleader in the pyramid.

So I said, "Unless you'd rather not go."

Her eyes widened. "Are you kidding? I'm desperate to go! I want so much to help Gloria. She's . . . done so much to help me."

The way she said it told me that there was something more on her mind that just helping a friend in need.

"Really?" I said.

Philomena looked down at the kitchen tabletop, examining it as if the things she wanted to say to me might be written there. After a moment, she began.

"When Rose got sick," she said softly, "Gloria was with us every day. She didn't make a big fuss or pray or anything. She was just there. She told jokes and strange stories, she listened to Rose's endless adventures in the demi-world of the New York theatre; she even sang with Rose. Terrible versions of obscure musicals. For some reason, Gloria especially liked songs from *The Roar of the Greasepaint—The Smell of the Crowd*."

"I know that show," I said, smiling. "Anthony Newley. Nobody's interested in him much anymore, but I love him."

"Well, they bonded over it," Phil went on, "and other bits of obscure theatrical phenomena. It warmed my heart. And when Rose got too sick to sing, and had to go to the hospital, Gloria was still there. She held my hand. She talked to Rose, even after Rose slipped into her coma. She talked to me, even though all I could do was cry. I owe Gloria a lot."

I touched Phil's arm for a second. "But you know that Gloria wouldn't see it that way. She wouldn't think that you owed her a thing."

"All the more reason for me to help get her out of this horrible situation," Phil said, a little stronger. "Because everyone knows she didn't do a thing to Bea Glassie. Although the Lord knows that Bea was absolutely deserving of a good whack in the head."

I laughed. "You know what Mae Etta said? She said that it would be hard to find anyone in Enigma that *didn't* want to whack Bea in the head."

"Truer words were never spoken," Phil told me, a little more seriously than seemed called for.

"So, to return to the point, if I may," I went on, "you'll go with me to Hawkinsville tomorrow."

"I will," she said, "if Kell agrees to the opera house tour."

"Yeah," I said, "but even if he doesn't. What if we just go there, nose around, see if we can't arouse his interest."

"Or his ire," she warned.

"Either way."

"All right, then," she said, patting the tabletop. "I'd better head home and get to bed early. I want to be at my best."

She stood.

"I'll call this Donna person in the morning," I repeated, "but no matter what, you'll come over at . . . what time?"

"Is six too early?" She turned and started toward the front door.

"Yes," I told her emphatically. "How about nine or so, after Jennifer's gotten here and we've opened the shop?"

"Right." She gestured her agreement with a single index finger. "Good idea."

I followed her out of the kitchen, through the shop, to the front door, and out onto the porch.

She looked down at the destroyed yard and the yellow police tape.

"It's going to be so pretty there once you get the roses in, don't you think?" she asked me.

"Yes," I said. "I do think."

"I might have planted juniper there," she mused, almost to herself. "Lots less fussy than the roses, and, after all, the name of the shop . . ."

"Uh-huh," I answered after she was silent for too long. "But I want people to be reminded of Aunt Rose. The name of the shop is on the sign over the front door, right?"

She was halfway down the stairs before she stopped and turned around.

"It's going to be all right with David, sweetheart," she said. "Just give him a little bit of time to realize that he overreacted, and to figure out *why* he did. And when he apologizes, you apologize right back to him, you hear?"

"Yes, I do, Dr. Waldrop." I told her. "And I love you."

"I love you too, dear." She turned away again and continued down the steps. "And, just a thought: you might consider saying those very words to David, if you haven't already."

"I should tell him that I love him?" I shook my head. "I don't know if I *do*."

She stopped with her hand on the driver's side door handle and looked up at me in the first soft moonlight.

"Oh, sugar." She shook her head slowly. "I'm sorry to tell you this. But you do."

I watched her get into her car and back out of the yard before I thought of what to say to her in response. And, obviously, by then it was too late.

19

DAVID DIDN'T CALL that night before I went to bed. He didn't call the next morning before Jennifer arrived, bright as a new penny in her sunny yellow dress and her Crocs from the Penny Mart. He didn't call even after Jennifer had set up the desk, ready to open the shop, or even when Philomena's car pulled into the front yard.

I stared at the phone, but that didn't seem to encourage it to ring. Phil came in, her usual workplace uniform—navy dress, black flats, bun hair—crisp and smart. I felt a little like the poorly festooned cousin standing in the same room as the other two. Pale blue cotton pants and a French sailor top, horizontal blue stripes and all, I was barely dangling an empty coffee cup from one finger.

"Ready?" was all Phil said.

"Good morning, Dr. Waldrop," Jennifer sang out cheerfully.

"Look how organized you are." Phil smiled. "Where would this shop be without you, Jennifer?"

"Yes, Madeline and I have been over that." Jennifer looked around for a moment, assessing. "I concluded that it would probably be an abandoned building by now, don't you think?"

"I do," Phil agreed instantly.

"All right, all right," I groused good-naturedly. "That's enough of that."

Phil looked away to ask, "Did anyone call last night?"

"No." I glanced at Jennifer. "Not this morning either."

"Expecting a call?" Jennifer asked innocently.

"If David Madison calls," Phil snapped before I could speak, "you give him Maddy's cell phone number, okay?"

Jennifer smiled. "Like he doesn't already have it."

I set my cup on the desk in front of Jennifer. "If David Madison calls, please tell him that Dr. Waldrop and I have gone to Hawkinsville. Without him."

"Okay, here's what I'm actually going to do," Jennifer said seriously. "I'm going to answer the phone, and if it's David Madison I'm going to say that you're not here, and I'm going to take a message if he cares to leave one."

She picked up my cup and stood.

"Let's go, then," Phil said impatiently.

"I'll drive," I said.

Phil shrugged and made for the door.

Wallet in my back pocket, keys in hand, I glared at Jennifer.

"You actually do run this place better than I do," I told her. "What exactly *am* I going to do when you leave?"

"You have, as I was saying, asked me that, more or less, before," she told me, heading to the kitchen with my empty coffee cup.

"And did you ever give me an answer that wasn't built entirely out of *sass*?"

She spun around like a dancer and sang, "I did not."

I just shook my head and started toward the door.

"Oh!" she shouted suddenly. "Wait."

"Come *on*," Phil complained, already standing at the front door.

"What is it?" I asked Jennifer.

"I've been trying to tell you," she answered, coming back into the parlor. "The thing about Bea Glassie's bookstore purchase. It's fancy."

When she was back behind the desk, she set down the coffee cup, rummaged through some papers in front of her, and produced an older bound ledger. She flipped through the pages and found what she was looking for, then held the page up for me to see.

I squinted. "What am I looking at?"

"Your aunt Rose sold Bea Glassie a book," Jennifer said, a little excited. "And it was a whopper."

I looked over the top of the ledger and into Jennifer's eyes. "In what sense?" I asked hesitantly.

"It was a first volume of *Grimm's Fairy Tales*," Jennifer answered in a hushed voice. "It was published as . . ." She turned the book toward her face and read. "It was *Kinder- und Hausmärchen* and put out in 1812! And are you ready for this? Bea paid eighty thousand dollars for it!"

I actually twitched. "What?"

Phil heard, and she came back into the parlor. "*How* much?"

"Eighty *thousand*," Jennifer repeated. "But that's nothing. I couldn't believe it either. I thought maybe Rose just wrote it down wrong or something. So I did a little research on that particular volume and you'll never guess what I found!"

"You're right." I took a step closer to her. "I'll probably never guess so just tell me, okay?"

"A copy of that same book sold at Christie's in 2022." She

eyed us both and lowered her voice. "For a hundred thirty-eight thousand and six hundred dollars!"

I think I went numb for a second or two.

"Are you sure?" I managed to ask.

"See," Jennifer went on, "that particular copy, the one that sold at Christie's, I mean, was special because it was signed by both brothers *and* it had a personal inscription from them." She examined a piece of paper that was stuck in the ledger. "It said, 'We present you with this on your impending departure from childhood as a reminder of happy times.'"

"How very remarkable," Phil whispered.

"Yeah," Jennifer said. "So I looked up the one that Rose got for Bea—it was autographed too—and today it would sell for over a hundred thousand *easy*."

"This is huge," I said, still trying to understand it.

"I *know*," Jennifer agreed.

"So is that book still at Bea's house, I wonder?" Phil asked.

"I never thought about looking through Bea's house," I said, mentally kicking myself.

"We should do that," Phil said.

"I wonder if Idell's been over there," I thought out loud.

"Or Billy," Phil added. "Or the GBI."

"Seems like we should at least go over there and see if we can find the book in question," I said.

"Did Rose do that kind of thing?" Jennifer wanted to know.

"Do *what* kind of thing?" I asked.

"Did she usually sell such high-end stuff?"

"Oh." I meditated for a moment. "Not that I know of. Phil?"

She mused. "Well. Once in a while."

The way she said it made me know that there was more to it than that.

"Maybe we'll talk about it in the car," I said to Jennifer.

Jennifer lifted her eyebrows a bit but was otherwise noncommittal. She just took up the coffee cup again and left for the kitchen.

"Ready?" I asked Phil.

"*Ready?*" She rolled her eyes. "I was standing by the door . . ."

"All right then," I said. "Let's go."

We were down the front steps, into my car, and down the road before I began to ask Philomena all the questions I had in my head.

"What's going on?" That was my first.

"Hmm?" Phil asked. "What do you mean?"

"You know what I mean," I said as we drove at a maddeningly slow pace through Enigma to Highway 82. "What are you not saying about Rose's 'high end'?"

She giggled like a seven-year-old. "Did you just say, 'Rose's high end'?"

"Phil!" I snapped. "What about Rose selling that really expensive book to Bea Glassie? And while we're at it, what exactly *is* the deal with the whole section in the Old Juniper that's filled with expensive first editions that we can't sell? And does it have anything to do with how Rose kept the bookshop afloat? Actually, not just *afloat*, but profitable!"

She turned my way, adjusting her seat belt so that she could sit almost sideways.

"Which one of those questions should I answer first?" she asked calmly.

"I will pull this car over right now!" I threatened, as if she actually might be seven years old.

"Okay." She folded her hands primly.

Out of the corner of my eye I could see her staring into space the way she always did when she was preparing to make a certain kind of speech. That made me nervous since she usually did it when she had something both important and uncomfortable to tell me.

"Rose," she began at last, "did not come back to Enigma to start a bookstore, or to retire from the theatre. She was already a bookseller in New York—years before she came back. It's what enabled her to live so well in New York. Early on in her career, she met someone."

And she stopped talking. Philomena sometimes took maddeningly long pauses in her stories and I was in no mood.

"Philomena Waldrop . . ."

"Someone who sold rare books." Phil swallowed. "And this someone happened to see Rose in some show or other, and this someone asked Rose to help him sell his rare books."

"Did this *someone* have a name?" It sometimes helped to make her stories more coherent if you asked for specific information.

"Ralph." She said his name the way most people would say a four-letter word.

"Something wasn't quite right about Ralph?" I asked.

"He asked Rose to . . . he hired Rose to pretend to be various characters who were selling these unusual books from an alleged but nonexistent private collection, do you see?"

"Rose was a shill."

"I was never comfortable with that word," she objected.

"Nevertheless."

"It became clear to Rose after only a short while that some of the books might be stolen," Phil went on. "But she kept on with Ralph because the money was good. And as time went on, Rose learned more and more about the rare book trade. Not all of Ralph's transactions were questionable. In fact, Rose thought that most of them were legal, and it was only that Rose's fragile widows or grieving children could fetch a higher price for the books than Ralph could, seeing that he was an uncomfortably large and, apparently, smelly gentleman with some kind of skin condition."

I had to smile. "This is actually kind of great. Whenever I think I know all there is about Rose, along comes a story like this. So when Rose decided to retire, she brought home some of this book trade with her."

"Not . . . exactly." Phil looked away. "Ralph was procuring some apparently expensive volumes in upstate New York and—there's no other way to say this. He was shot dead. Killed."

I glanced at her. "What?"

"Mm-hmm," Phil asserted. "He was killed and Rose was scared."

"This is incredible," I said, mostly to myself.

"I *know*," Phil told me. "So, anyway, Rose gathered up all of Ralph's unsold inventory and shipped it back to Enigma. She was in *Forbidden Broadway Cleans Up Its Act* at the end of 1998. She finished her run, told her friends that she was going to London for a show in the East End, bought a shady used car, and drove back to Enigma. In the dead of night."

"In the dead of several nights, probably," I corrected. "It's a long drive."

"She came back to the Juniper house," Phil went on, "and did a little quiet mail-order business in the rare book trade—she was always nervous about it. But then she and I cooked up the scheme that's going on in the shop now: supplying most of the textbooks for Barnsley College. And then,

I mean, you know Rose. She had such a magnetic personality. The Old Juniper became something of a local gathering spot."

"I know," I said. "I was there for that, as a kid."

"Yes, you were," she said sweetly.

"And that's all?" I asked.

"All?" She sat back in her seat. "Not entirely. She created the rare book section in the shop, mostly out of Ralph's old collection, and still trafficked in the occasional hard-to-find volume of forgotten lore."

"Now you're just quoting Poe," I said. "Trying to make the story spookier?"

"Well." She settled. "Now you know."

"So it wasn't exactly an anomaly," I said, "that Rose sold the Grimm Brothers book to Bea Glassie."

"Right."

"Well, it's a fascinating story," I said, "but I don't see that it has anything to do with Bea's murder."

"Neither do I," she agreed. "But you asked."

"I did," I agreed.

We were on the highway at last, and I stepped down hard on the accelerator. The last buildings of Enigma faded from view, and we drove ninety miles per hour past woods and farms and great open pastures. I could have taken I-75, but I always preferred US 129. It was a prettier drive.

"You know that we didn't call Kell Brady before we left the shop," Phil worried. "Shouldn't we have done that? Ask him if it's all right to visit. Do we even have his phone number?"

"I looked up his number right when Billy gave me his address," I said. "When we get closer to Hawkinsville, I'll call and tell him that we're on the road, headed his way."

"I see," she said. "That'll make it harder for him to tell us not to come."

"That's my thinking," I agreed. "He was very polite to me when I saw him before. You seem to think, on the other hand, that maybe he's not always so nice."

"To be fair," she told me, "I only met him a few times. And it was always at St. Thomas Aquinas. But there was always gossip."

"About him or about Bea and him?"

"Well, yes, about their relationship." She turned suddenly. "Pygmy goats! Look!"

"Phil."

"Sorry." She looked back at me. "There was a time at the hardware store—this was before the hardware store closed—that they argued for ten minutes about what color to paint Bea's front porch."

"That's not much of anything," I said. "I remember you and Rose going five rounds about what wallpaper to put up in the kitchen."

"She wanted that awful *plaid*," Phil complained.

"Yes, plaid would have been a terrible choice," I said. "I was on your side in that argument, but my point is that you guys argued but you weren't really mad at each other."

"We weren't," Phil agreed. "Not ever."

"So," I went on. "Same for Kell and Bea, right?"

"Maybe." Phil sat quietly for a moment. "But they said that Kell called Bea an idiot. And there was a particularly objectionable description of just what *kind* of an idiot she was. They said it was bad."

"They."

"I know," she said. "Gossip. As widespread as it is unreliable."

"I don't think much of it," I confirmed. "But when we get back to Enigma, I'd really like to break into Bea's house and have a look around, wouldn't you?"

"You mean to see if she still has the Grimm Brothers book?"

"That," I said, "and just to see what else there is to see. You know, see if maybe there's anything there that might give us some idea of who killed her."

She nodded firmly. "Clues. Like in a mystery novel."

"Yes," I said. "Almost exactly like in a mystery novel."

That ended our discussion for a bit. I turned on the radio, the Sirius bluegrass station, and we watched the farms go by.

There had always been something intriguing about farm life to me. Not intriguing enough to actually experience it, but I had always had romantic notions about how wonderful it would be to wake up with the chickens and spend the day planting and feeding livestock and watching the sun go down over my own wheat field.

But peanuts and sweet corn were the main crops around Enigma, also soybeans. And if there was an orchard, it was likely to be a pecan or a peach orchard.

Still, my fantasy persisted the entire time I lived in both New York and Atlanta. It was only after I returned home, eyes a little widened, that I saw small farm work for what it was: backbreaking, never-ending, ulcer-inducing work. And that was just to break even. If you really wanted to make any real money, you had to find a few acres for weed. Or, if you were the Dillard family, you could be certified organic, let the land and the livestock work in your favor, and charge five times the money for most of your crops. The Dillards weren't rich the way the Glassie family was, but they were certainly better off than most of the other farms their size in our part of the state. And by all reports—by *reports* I meant *gossip*—Faye Dillard was a whiz at marketing and packaging and all the other nonagricultural abilities that it took to make a wildly successful enterprise out of a small organic farm in Enigma, Georgia. She'd even used the town name to her advantage; she somehow made the produce seem mysterious, even mystical. Enigma Pickled Okra was the highest selling pickled okra in America. If that's not damning with faint praise.

I suddenly honked the horn.

Phil jumped and put her hand to her heart. "What did you do *that* for?"

And she said it in her original accent: shy, small-town girl from the Deep South. Not the mode of speaking she'd adapted as a college professor.

"I was trying to exorcize the ghost of Faye Dillard," I said.

"Oh." She let go of her breath. "Well, stop it, you nearly scared the life out of me. And besides, Faye's not a ghost, she's very much alive."

"Yeah." I sighed. "I know."

"David will call you," she insisted.

"When?"

"Look!" She pointed to a field to my left. "Ostriches!"

Sometime in the past, no one in Enigma could accurately tell me when, some adventurous farmers had been convinced that ostrich was the white meat of the future. As was the case with a lot of other outrageous farm fads, no one got rich riding the ostrich wave. Still, some farmers kept on. I always thought it was just to introduce an element of the surreal into the landscape. And for that, ostriches were perfect. There was nothing quite like coming over a small hill and—instead of seeing slow cows or prize pigs—seeing a gaggle of ostriches galumphing along or staring at you in a vaguely accusatory fashion.

The highway bent gently around the edge of a farm pond where two fuzzy gray donkeys had convened. There were ducks. The sky was doing its impersonation of a robin's egg, and the sun, maybe apologizing for the recent rain, made gold out of a lot of the landscape.

And when the bend in the road resolved itself, Hawkinsville came into view. The WELCOME TO HAWKINSVILLE sign proudly bragged that its population was a solid four thousand one hundred and thirty-four.

Philomena fidgeted.

"What are we going to say when we get there?" she asked nervously.

I pulled my phone out of my pocket. "I'll call him right now."

"No!" she said. "Do not use that phone while you're driving!"

"Fine," I said. "I'll pull in at the Stop N Go up there on the left."

The Stop N Go was only a few blocks shy of the opera house. I pulled in and dialed Kell Brady's number. It rang eleven times before Donna Dukes answered.

"Brady residence."

"Oh, hi, Donna," I chirped. "It's me, Madeline Brimley. How are you?"

"Hello, Madeline," she answered in absolute neutral. "I'm fine, thank you for asking. How may I help you?"

"Well, Mr. Brady was so excited about the opera house," I said, hoping to sound excited about it myself, "that I just had to come and see it. I was hoping that he might consider giving us a tour."

"Us?" Chilly.

"Dr. Waldrop and I are here in Hawkinsville right now!" I answered. "We could come by and pick Mr. Brady up in five minutes."

"Philomena Waldrop?" Donna asked. "Rose's . . . friend?"

"Yes," I said. "Rose's friend."

Phil called out, "Hello!"

Donna tried and failed to hide a sigh. "Where are you?"

"Stop N Go," I said. "And look what a pretty day it is!"

"Just a moment," Donna told me and I heard her set the phone down.

"She's checking with Brady now," I told Phil. "She doesn't seem all that enthusiastic about our visit."

"Maybe we shouldn't have come," Phil whispered.

"Too late to chicken out now," I told her. "We're here."

"I know, but . . ." she trailed off.

There was a rustling on the other end of the phone and then Donna said, "Mr. Brady insists that you come here to his house for coffee and scones. He'll discuss a tour of the opera house."

"Great!" I said, just a little too loud. "See you in a few seconds."

And I hung up before Donna could say anything more.

"Man," I told Phil. "That Donna. She was so sweet to me at first. Now, apparently, I'm nothing but trouble."

"What do you think accounts for that?" Phil asked.

"Oh, I'm pretty sure I know." I pulled out of the Stop N Go, headed for Kell Brady's mansion. "I think it means that Donna's our killer."

20

DONNA WAS STANDING on the front porch beside the open door when we pulled up. She wore a shin-length black cotton dress and an expression that threatened to poison the roses not five feet away from where she stood.

"She doesn't look happy," Phil whispered.

"I think she looks like that most of the time," I said, staring at Donna's overly stern visage.

"Maybe we shouldn't go in," Phil fretted. "I mean, if she actually is the killer."

I just shook my head. "I was kidding. The butler didn't do it, the butler never does it, get out of the car."

I opened my car door and waved cheerfully to Donna. She did not wave back.

Phil was slower to get out of the car, but she followed me up the walkway. As we drew nearer to the house, Phil's attention was drawn to the remarkable rosebushes at the front of the house.

"Oh," she said, a little breathlessly. "Look at that *color*."

Donna melted just a little. "They are beautiful this time of year."

"You know," Phil went on, "this is a hybrid developed by my friend Rose Brimley."

"I know," Donna said more gently than I might have expected.

"I'm sorry to just show up like this," I began. "That's why I called. You said to call ahead."

"Yes." Donna turned and went into the house.

I was up the porch steps a second later. Philomena lingered at the roses.

Donna stood just inside the door.

"The library," she said, indicating it with a single, slow gesture.

"Dr. Waldrop," I called.

"Coming!" she answered and appeared beside me a moment later.

Together we stepped across the threshold and I had a sudden House of Usher feeling. Phil sensed it too and shivered involuntarily.

Once we were in, Donna disappeared. Phil and I wandered into the library.

"Look at all these books," Phil marveled.

"I am going to look for rare first editions," I said vaguely.

But before I could look for anything, Kell announced himself.

"Well," he said brightly as he breezed into the room with only a little help from his ornate cane, "my cup certainly runneth over this morning. Two charming guests!"

Phil spun around to see him. He was decked out in black pleated pants, shiny patent leather shoes, and an immaculate white button-down shirt with a scarlet cravat. An honest-to-God cravat.

"Mr. Brady," she told him breathlessly, "I'm so sorry to

assault your lovely home this way. My friend Madeline has no manners. None whatsoever."

"Please," he insisted. "I invited her to come back and tour the opera house." Here he took the slightest of pauses. "I just didn't think she would be back so soon."

Donna appeared behind him with a tray.

"Ah," he said. "Scones. Donna makes them herself. They're lighter than air."

Donna did not respond to the flattery. She just swished past Kell and brought the tray into the room: a French press, three blindingly white cups in saucers, a large plate of golden scones, linen napkins, and assorted silver cutlery. She set it down on the coffee table in front of the sofa, across from the two leather club chairs.

"Don't those look heavenly," Phil said, smiling in the general direction of the scones.

"Blueberry," Donna responded.

"From our blueberry bushes in the back," Kell added. "Of course not this year's blueberries, the bushes haven't produced yet. These are Donna's preserves from last year."

"Still," Philomena said.

"We'll serve ourselves, Donna," Kell said softly. "Thank you."

Donna nodded and was gone.

"Now then," Kell went on. "You're here to see the opera house. I couldn't be more delighted."

Philomena approached him as if he were the pope.

"I'm Philomena Waldrop," she said, holding out her hand and lowering her head a little. "We met—"

"Dr. Waldrop," he said warmly, taking her hand in both of his. "Of course I remember you. And David Madison speaks so highly of you."

"Oh." Phil actually blushed. "Well."

I realized then what a good idea it had been for her to come along with me. She was a shy and distracting buffer between me and Mr. Brady. I didn't know exactly how that would be useful, but I was sure it would be somehow.

"Shall we sit?" Kell said, moving to one of the club chairs.

Phil took the sofa, I sat in the other club chair, and before anyone else could move, Phil was pouring coffee for us.

"I should warn you," Kell said, "that these scones will crumble and you'll have bits of them all over for the rest of the day. I wrap mine in one of these napkins, dab it with butter, and throw caution to the wind."

I watched him talk. He seemed to be deliberately old-maidish. But he did, indeed, swaddle a scone in one of the linen napkins, dip the tip of the scone in the softened butter on the plate, and attack it with abandon.

"I watched someone eat these this way," he explained after he'd swallowed, "in the Lake District in England a long time ago and it stuck with me."

"Well, then," Phil said and she followed his example. "When in Rome."

I, instead, went for the nearest coffee cup.

"So could we convince you to take us on a private tour of the opera house?" I asked.

"I've always heard that it was haunted," Phil piped up, thrilled.

"It is," Kell assured us both. "Just when you're trying to do the most important things, the lights dim or go out. And twice I've seen a figure onstage, a flapper in a fringe dress, bowing to an invisible audience that only she can see."

It was a good spooky image, but it sounded like an invention, not an experience.

"And I would be delighted to show you around the place," Kell went on; and then he took another crumbling bite of his scone.

"If you're sure," Phil demurred. "I have a horrible feeling that we're imposing."

"Not at all," he assured her. "I love showing off the place; I worked so hard to get it restored."

"And by the way," Phil went on, "you've taken such good care of those roses out front. I love seeing them so full."

"Well," he said, "I mostly have David Madison to thank. He installed them so perfectly. And of course I have a service."

"A gardening service," Phil confirmed.

"Yes," he said, "the Lopez brothers. They're excellent."

"Did David suggest them?" I asked. "Not the service, I mean the roses."

"No," Kell answered. "I saw them in the greenhouse. I asked about them. He told me they were Rose Brimley's invention. I asked David for an introduction and I subsequently met your aunt at the college greenhouses. She certainly was a character."

"She was," I agreed.

"She asked me what my intentions were," he told me with a little laugh. "As if I might be inclined to court the roses. Which, I suppose, in some ways I might have been. So when I told her I wanted to plant them in front of my house, she approved."

"That was the only time you met her?" Phil asked, absently enjoying her scone.

"No." But that was all he said.

Donna was suddenly in the doorway to the library.

"The car is ready, Mr. Brady," she intoned.

"Ah." He set down his wrapped scone. "Why don't you go

in your car, Miss Brimley, and follow me. Perhaps Dr. Waldrop would like to ride with me. We can talk a little more about Rose and her roses!"

I didn't quite know what to make of that.

"I would like that," Phil said instantly, taking another huge bite of her scone. "What kind of car is it?"

"It's only an Escalade," Kell said, laughing.

"Oh," she said, trying not to sound disappointed. "I was hoping it might be that lovely Mercedes limousine you used to have when you came to visit us at St. Thomas Aquinas."

He nodded. "I love that car, but the Escalade doesn't need as much attention. The Mercedes goes to the mechanic on the order of once a month."

"I see," Phil said.

And I could hear in her voice the gentle rebuke, the delicate but righteous condemnation of a rich man's problems. Kell Brady did not appear to hear it. He simply levitated from his chair and offered Phil his arm. They both ignored me as they followed Donna out of the room.

"Okay," I said to no one.

I gulped back the last of my coffee and made for the front door alone. I got to Igor just in time to see the black Escalade moving in its stately fashion down the long driveway. What surprised me was the driver. There was no uniformed chauffeur nor scruffy but good-looking mechanic. Donna was driving.

WE pulled up right in front of the imposing two-story brick edifice. Donna got out of the driver's side and opened the back door. Kell stepped out and offered his help to Philomena, who was delighted to be treated in a less-than-contemporary manner. I parked behind the Escalade and joined them.

Kell had already begun his tour.

"When it was built in 1907," he was saying to Phil, "the place had the largest seating capacity of any public building in Pulaski County. And all during the years before WWII it hosted many, many well-known theatrical and entertainment acts. It was really the place to go for a fine evening out."

"When I was a little girl," Phil said, "we would always hear about the famous people who were performing here."

"You never came?" he asked her.

"Oh, no," she said. "We could never afford anything like that."

"You grew up in Enigma?" he asked.

"No." She looked down; she was often uncomfortable talking about her upbringing. "I was born and raised at Koinonia."

Kell only paused for a second. "I see."

Founded in 1942, Koinonia was a religious collective farm. They caused quite a stir in rural Georgia—Americus, to be specific—because they "welcomed and shared with anyone and everyone regardless of race, religion, no religion, background or anything else that divides people." Which made them quite popular targets in the Jim Crow South. And it was Phil's home until she went away to college. Because of their beliefs, Phil's parents were refused help when Phil contracted rheumatic fever. Only the intervention of no less than Rosalynn Carter saved Phil's life. Mrs. Carter brought in her personal physician to care for Phil, but not before some damage had been done. That damage accounted for Phil's occasional bouts of confusion.

"I always refer to the place as the *opera house*," Kell went on, "even though it was mostly used for anything *but* opera. It was a church, and then a movie house."

Phil and Kell were up the steps; Donna had keys in her hand, and she unlocked the front doors.

"But in 1973, I managed to have it placed on the National Historic Register." He held the door open for Phil. "Beatrice and I."

"It's absolutely lovely," Phil gushed, but I could tell that she was overacting just a little, for some reason.

"Well, the old girl had a one-point-seven-million-dollar face-lift in 2000," Kell told her, "which produced the lovely facility that we have today."

"You must be so proud," Phil said, beaming.

I thought I understood: Phil was using an older feminine paradigm to gain Kell Brady's trust, or something. Her version of flirting, trying to get Kell to let down his guard and maybe tell her something he didn't really want to tell her.

"Today, of course," he concluded, "the Old Hawkinsville Opera House is owned by the citizens of Hawkinsville; it's managed by the Hawkinsville–Pulaski County Arts Council. A nonprofit."

He managed to make the appellation *nonprofit* sound like an illness.

"Now," Phil said, touching his forearm. "Tell me about the ghost."

"I personally think," he answered confidentially, "that it's Oliver Hardy."

"Of Laurel and Hardy?" Phil asked, fascinated.

"Yes," Kell said. "He performed here as a solo act many, many years ago and was reported to have been very upset that there wasn't a golf course nearby. When he left, he told people he wouldn't be caught dead in the place ever again. But I think that's just what happened: he's been caught here *dead*."

He was speaking the way older men sometimes speak to younger children.

"Of course I didn't ever meet him," Phil said, "but it's hard to imagine the comedian I've seen on the screen being a very threatening ghost."

"Oh, no," Kell assured her. "He's just a prankster. Turns off the lights when you least expect it, laughs in the dressing rooms when there's no one there, and, best of all, leaves a beat-up golf club in the middle of the stage. Beside the ghost light!"

"The ghost light?" Phil asked.

Kell turned to me as I followed behind him.

"I'm certain Miss Brimley knows about the ghost light," he said.

I happened to know that Phil was quite aware of the ghost light phenomenon, but I was happy to play along.

"It's a light that's left on at center stage after all the other lights are turned off," I said. "Usually just a bare lightbulb on some kind of standing lamp."

"To keep the ghosts away?" Phil asked innocently.

"To keep people from breaking their necks in the dark," I answered instantly.

Rose always loved to indulge in theatre superstitions, but I hated them. I was of the opinion that they infantilized our entire profession, but Rose just thought they made things more fun.

"At any rate," Kell breezed on, "let's go into the theatre and see what Ollie's left us today."

Our parade, Kell and Philomena arm in arm in the lead,

Donna close behind, and I bringing up the rear, entered the theatre. It was lovely. The stage curtain was open and the houselights were on. There were plush red seats, a curving balcony, and a fair-sized proscenium stage. No ghost light and no bottle of Bordeaux.

"We loved working on this project," he said softly. "Beatrice and I."

"Is there a show tonight?" I asked.

Kell turned to look at me again. He stared and paused, and then, "Not tonight."

It was difficult for me to figure out what was going on with him. He was gallant and dull and nostalgic and romantic and icy all at the same time.

"Donna," Kell said abruptly, "would you mind going up into the booth and turning on the stage lights. I'd like to show our guests this fantastic lighting grid."

Donna nodded once, turned, brushed past me, and headed back up the aisle.

"Oh," Phil gushed, "you and Beatrice must have had such fun doing this together."

Kell chuckled. It sounded very deliberate.

"Well, you know how Beatrice could be," he said.

"She could be a little headstrong," Phil said, smiling, "but isn't that what made her such a juggernaut for her causes?"

He nodded a little too enthusiastically. "And I can assure you that I was twice as bad. I believe I do not exaggerate when I tell you that we argued over every brick and nail and two-by-four in this entire building."

"But look at it now," Phil said sweetly.

"Yes." He looked around. "Look at it now."

It was an effort for me to keep quiet. I'd been in a hundred small theatres that were much nicer, at least to my sensibilities. For one thing, the Hawkinsville Opera House was more auditorium than theatre, and that was a sincere dividing line for me.

It wasn't just that the place had been a church and a movie house and a school. It wasn't just that the proscenium was sterile, or that the seating had little character. It was the aura of the place. I'd worked in theatres in New York and London where John Gielgud and Maggie Smith and Mark Rylance and Idina Menzel had worked, and believe me when I say that the bricks and nails and two-by-fours know the difference. A building absorbs that energy, those performances; the air remains hung with a thousand versions of "To be or not to be" and "Stella!" and "Popular" and "Some Enchanted Evening."

I was glad for Hawkinsville that it had a good auditorium and that it was a historical building with a checkered past. It was just hard for me to ooh and aah the way Philomena was doing.

Dr. Philomena Waldrop had really dialed up the flirting. She was still attempting to get Kell Brady lulled into some sense of comfort wherein he might reveal something or other that would be important to our cause, that cause being the liberation of Gloria Coleman. I didn't quite know where it was all going, but I had a sudden and spontaneous appreciation of Phil's effort.

"Now," Phil went on, "are you certain we're not going to run into the ghost?"

Kell laughed again. "I think Ollie's probably resting somewhere backstage."

And just at that moment the stage lights came on. Donna had made it to the booth, turned on the light board, and brought up a basic stage look all in record time. Which told me how familiar she was with the booth. It probably didn't mean anything, but it was interesting to me for some reason.

Kell escorted Phil up some stairs to the right side of the stage and they disappeared through black curtains there.

I had a moment then, all alone in the theatre, that was like a thousand other moments I'd experienced, staring at an empty stage. I had the same feeling that some people report having in a quiet cathedral. I could almost hear a hundred years of audiences laughing, clapping, sighing. A hundred years or more.

"I know what you're trying to do," I said out loud to the building. "But I run a bookshop now; I don't want to be on the stage anymore. *Get thee behind me!*"

"Maddy?" Phil called out, invisible. "Are you all right?"

"Fine," I assured her. "Just putting demon theatre in its place."

Kell and Phil emerged from the backstage shadows and came to center stage.

"Madeline was an actor, just like Rose," Phil explained to Kell.

"Not *just* like Rose," I corrected.

Kell agreed. "My impression of Rose Brimley was that she was utterly inimitable."

Before I could respond to that, Kell went on.

"As you can see," he told Phil, pointing up at the lighting grid overhead, "we have a very serious array of lighting instruments."

"Now, when you and Bea were going through this remarkable renovation," Phil asked, "how did you know what lights to buy, what lighting board, all the . . . well, the more technical requirements of the theatre."

"Ah," Kell answered. "We had an array of experts; they knew everything. Not that it kept Bea from arguing with them, you understand. For example, Bea wanted a big old-fashioned spotlight. It must have taken the lighting designer a month to convince her that there were dozens of better alternatives."

I mulled over the virtues of a good old-fashioned spotlight. The old ones, the antiques, got really hot and they were loud and clanky, but there really wasn't a substitute for the history and nostalgia of those ancient behemoths.

"I know what you mean," Phil said. "Bea could argue the chrome off a trailer hitch."

I looked away and stifled a laugh at Phil's attempt to sound casual and folksy.

"Once," she went on, "she fought with Father Glenn about the Beatitudes for a whole week. Lord, I thought they would come to blows!"

"Yes," he concurred only a little under his breath, "I know that feeling."

"And when Bea tried to take away Mae Etta's business license at the diner," Phil continued, "I heard that Mae Etta threatened Bea with a baseball bat!"

Not true—or at least I had never heard that. But I was interested to see Kell's reaction.

"That woman's head was so hard," he told Phil jovially, "it would have splintered the bat."

Phil laughed and touched Kell's forearm.

"Would you like to see the dressing rooms?" he asked Phil.

"I would," she said.

He took her elbow and they both disappeared into the darkness upstage. When they did, the stage lights went off and the work lights came on. Donna's easy knowledge of the booth and the lighting system continued to nag at my interest.

I was about to sit down when all the lights went out, followed by Kell Brady's bellowing.

"Donna!"

Donna did not respond. Then a single light came on upstage right. It was the ghost light, previously obscured by shadows. Its buttery glow pulsated slowly but perceptibly, and for a long moment the entire theatre was silent.

21

I WORKED IN A theatre in Atlanta once—corner of Peachtree and Tenth—where the lights would come on at will, with no one anywhere near the lighting board or a light switch. The toilets would flush when there was no one using them. You could hear someone knocking on the women's dressing room door when there was no one there. And twice I personally heard someone singing "Stewball was a racehorse" from the locked basement underneath the place.

That was a haunted theatre.

"Sorry!" Donna called out. "Don't know what happened. Sorry. Just give me a second."

And sure enough, a second later the lights came back on. And the ghost light went off.

I started toward the stage. "Phil? Are you okay?"

"Yes," she answered.

"Miss Brimley," Kell announced, "would you please have a word with Oliver Hardy, actor to actor, and ask him not to do that again?"

She and Kell came back onto the stage.

"But wasn't that exciting," Kell said, grinning.

And it seemed to me that his delight was a little rehearsed.

I realized then that it was just possible that Kell and Donna played that little trick on all their private tours: cut the lights for a second, boost the ghost mythology.

"Could we go have a seat in the house for a moment?" Phil asked Kell. "I believe I might have to catch my breath."

Phil was really playing her Southern belle character to the hilt.

"Of course," Kell said instantly.

Moments later, all four of us were sitting in the plush red seats and Kell Brady got real.

"Now, I feel almost certain that you two ladies did not come to Hawkinsville for a tour of my opera house," he said, his voice low and rumbling. "Not really."

"Why else would we have come?" Phil asked blankly.

"You came, both of you together, to *vet* me," he answered. "You want to find out what sort of person I am. I mean, rather, to see if I am the sort of person who could murder Bea Glassie."

Phil said, "Oh, my!" at the exact moment I said, "Yes."

I could hear Donna rushing down the aisle but I didn't care. My eyes were glued on Kell. He was staring back at me.

And then he told us a little story.

KELL Brady first met the Glassie sisters of Enigma, Georgia, when Beatrice Glassie was trying to build a schoolhouse in the early 1970s. All three were in their early twenties and members of a rarified small-town social circle comprised of only twelve or thirteen good Southern Christian young people.

Kell was drawn to the project more for the company of two proper young women than any commitment to social phenomena. And his ardor first fell on Idell, the younger of the two sisters. Idell was, in her day, often compared to Bobbie Gentry, the singer-songwriter whose song "Ode to Billy Joe" had made an international splash. And Idell played the guitar in Sunday school classes.

The thoroughly entitled trio were seen all over the various counties of South Georgia for most of the 1970s, roaring through towns in one of the Brady family limousines (like the sleek black Mercedes that Philomena had hoped to ride in).

They went to the movies in Tifton. They rode horses in Hawkinsville. They even drove to Atlanta for the occasional big night out: the Metropolitan Opera when it came to the Fox Theatre, dinner at Sidney's Just South on the north side of town; to Rich's department store at Christmas to watch children ride the Pink Pig.

And then one night, after several jolly years of that sort of adventure, Kell found himself alone with Idell at a small county fair in Irwinville. It was coming on sunset, there was a scent of hay and cotton candy in the air. They were standing near the entrance to the corn maze. At the far end of the fairground there was a string band playing "Darlin' Cory." Bea had been asked to judge the fruit preserves competition, so Kell and Idell were momentarily at a loss since they were so used to being a trio.

Idell observed, looking out over the corn maze, that the sunset was going to be lovely. It was already touched with scarlet.

"Red sky at night," Kell said idly. "Sailor's delight."

Idell did not look at him. "We're so far from the sea, I don't know how that affects us."

Kell then made bold as to touch Idell's jaw with his right hand and turn her face toward his.

"Everything in this old world affects us, Idell," he told her. "Just the way everything you do in the world affects me."

She looked up at him. "I don't think I can talk."

"Why not?" he asked her.

"I think I might... my heart is pounding so fast." She closed her eyes.

"Mine is too," Kell said.

The difference was that Idell was frightened but Kell was... enthusiastic.

"I wonder if you might consider marrying me," Kell went on.

Idell's eyes flew open. "What?"

"I said—"

"Oh, no, no, no, no, no," Idell ranted, taking a step back.

Kell stood his ground. "Why not?"

"I—so *many* reasons," Idell gasped. "I wouldn't know how to be married. I wouldn't know how to tell Bea. I wouldn't know... where would we live?"

His head twitched sideways, surprised by the question.

"At my home, of course," he said as if it were obvious.

"All three of us?"

He laughed. "Of course not, sweetheart. Just you and I."

"But... what would Bea do?"

"We could still do the things we do, I suppose," Kell said slowly. "Except you and I would be married. That's all."

"But... why do you want to marry *me*?" Idell whispered.

"What man wouldn't want to marry you?" Kell began. "You're beautiful, you're charming, you're well-brought-up, you're quiet, and you come from an impeccable social standing. And, if I may say it, as we approach our thirties, the pool of eligible candidates for wedded bliss gets shallower and shallower, doesn't it?"

Idell looked down at the straw-covered red clay. "Do you love me?"

"For three years I've spent almost every free moment with you," he answered. "I've held your hand when no one was looking. I've given you presents. I've introduced you to my friends. I've even gone to your church in Enigma with that wheezing old Father Glenn at the helm. How can you ask me that question?"

Idell looked up at Kell then. For what may have been the first time in her life, she spoke for herself.

"That's not really the answer," she said softly, "for which I might have hoped."

Kell rolled his head. "Oh, for God's sake, Idell, what a ridiculous thing to say; of course I love you!"

But he didn't sound in love. He sounded angry.

"I'm so flustered," Idell said, taking another step backward. "I need to think."

And with that, Idell Glassie turned and ran into the corn maze.

The next Sunday, when the three of them were in church in Enigma, Idell waited until Bea got up to go to the altar and take communion before she touched Kell's arm.

"No." That was all she said.

"Hmm?" Kell asked, distracted by the fact that it was time for him to follow Bea to the communion rail.

"I must say no to your offer of marriage, Kell," Idell whispered.

Kell froze. Then he turned around to face Idell. Then he glared. Then he stood. Then he walked out of the church, got in his chauffeur-driven limousine, and went back to Hawkinsville, where he remained incommunicado for two months.

After that he emerged a slightly different man. He

trimmed his hair. He sold some timberland at an enormous profit. He took up working on the Old Hawkinsville Opera House. And when he turned thirty, he began to court Bea Glassie.

Bea was stockier and less waiflike than Idell, but she was also much livelier, more engaging in a social situation, and, best of all, ruthless in her business dealings. She and Kell cemented their relationship over financial matters. At some point in the late 1980s—because despite the heat in South Georgia, affairs of the heart often move at a glacial pace—they became engaged. Informally. There was no announcement in the paper or any church bulletin, and Bea's parents had passed on, so there was no family fuss about it. They were just known by all and sundry to be a solid item. They were seen everywhere. They worked together. They frequently lived together. They made a lot of money together.

All without Idell.

Idell and Bea were heard quarreling every night in their family manse, shouting, throwing things, breaking windows, until Bea exploded, took a fireplace poker to Idell's bedroom set, and then moved to Hawkinsville to live in Kell's home.

Idell built a home of her own almost immediately after that. She closed up the Glassie family mansion without telling Bea; neither sister ever went back inside that house that anyone knew of.

From then on, the sisters rarely saw each other except for services at St. Thomas Aquinas and the occasional unintended sighting at Mae Etta's diner.

When the century turned, Bea and Kell, with no effort whatsoever, came into their fifties. Kell retired from business. Bea built a house in Enigma far away from the abandoned Glassie mansion and her sister Idell's home. The geography was a little difficult to manage, but a suitable lot on the eastern outskirts of Enigma was found.

And while time did not exactly heal old wounds and soothe ancient injuries, things became less fraught with the more energetic presentments of youth. Or at least a veneer of peace was pasted over the storied trio, and they appeared to be led beside the still waters at last.

"BEA and I just . . . drifted apart," he concluded, his voice rife with sadness. "I didn't want to argue with her anymore. And now here I am: seventy-seven years old, alone, and reminiscing about a love that was gone a long, long time ago."

Phil touched his arm. "Bea was difficult to deal with," she said gently. "Everyone knew that."

He turned to her. "I meant Idell, of course."

"Of course," Phil said instantly.

Kell turned my way. "Is that the story you came to hear?"

"I just came to see the opera house," I lied.

"Well." He shrugged, and he suddenly sounded exhausted. "You've seen it. Shall we go?"

Donna moved quickly toward Kell. She helped him out of his seat, but it seemed like more a performance than an actual activity, as if they both were trying to give the impression that Kell was just a tired, frail old man.

Once on his feet, leaning on his cane, Kell looked around the opera house.

"Yes, this is all I have to show for my life, isn't it?" he mused with just the right tinge of self-pity in his voice. "An opera house that presents no opera, a venue for Christmas pageants and third-tier country music acts. And there I am, all alone in a very large house."

"But you have Donna," Phil pointed out gently, standing up.

Both Kell and Donna appeared to be shocked by her statement of the obvious.

"I certainly hope you're not implying . . ." Donna began indignantly.

"Oh! Of course not!" Phil was genuinely surprised by their show of pique.

"Donna is an *employee*," Kell said harshly.

"I only meant that Donna is there in your house," Phil said quickly. "So you're not *alone* alone." She shot me a glance. "If that's the right way to say it."

"Come on, Dr. Waldrop," I told her, coming to my feet. "Let's get you home."

Kell was racing up the aisle ahead of the rest of us, clearly trying to show that he was still energetic despite being seventy-seven.

Donna drew up next to me.

"I'm afraid I can't encourage any further visits," she told me, barely above a whisper. "But if you decide that you must, I *insist* that you call from Enigma, *before* you set out, to see if it's convenient for Mr. Brady. Will you do that, please?"

And she left my side without waiting for an answer. She caught up with Kell and they were both gone before Phil had moved much.

"How did we do?" she whispered after a second.

"Not sure," I answered. "But I think we might have just experienced a little bit of good old-fashioned performance art."

"I agree," she said as we both headed up the aisle toward the front door. "I know frail old men, and Kell Brady is most definitely *not* one. What I can't understand is why he wants us to think that about him, which he clearly does."

"Of course my first reaction," I said, "is that he's trying to convince us that he's too worn out to bash Bea in the head."

"And Donna was helping him with his little performance," Phil agreed.

"And all that phony-baloney ghost business," I went on. "What was that all about?"

"Why choose Oliver Hardy?" She was laughing. "Of all the least threatening personalities in the world to invoke."

"Well," I explained, "Ollie actually did perform here a very long time ago. I learned that from the website for this place."

"Oh." She looked around, then called out, "Sorry, Oliver!"

We emerged from the building into the relatively blinding light of the late morning. The Escalade was gone. Phil looked around for a moment.

"All right," she said as we headed toward Igor. "What now? I mean, we agree that Kell Brady is not what he seems to be. But what does that really mean?"

"Right," I said. "There's something he's not telling us. I'm just not sure what it is."

"And oddly it's *not*, I think, that he killed Bea." She shook her head. "I mean, I still don't think that he did it. Donna on the other hand . . ."

"Yeah." I opened my car door. "She's pretty frosty."

"What if Kell told her to get rid of Bea?" Phil asked, sliding into Igor's passenger side. "Would she have done it? Is she that sort of person?"

At that exact moment, three crows took off from the roof of the opera house. They cried out, swooped close to our car, and then vanished into the horizon.

I nodded, looking up into the sky. "Just . . . any kind of sign."

Phil laughed; we headed for home. And we didn't speak the whole way back. As it turned out, each of us was temporarily lost in some pretty strange thoughts.

22

I WAS FEELING RIDICULOUSLY hungry by the time we approached the outskirts of Enigma, for some reason, so I steered for Mae Etta's place.

"Bite to eat?" I suggested to Phil.

She looked at her watch. "I've already taken way too much time away from my classes—I guess another hour won't hurt. And I could eat."

The diner was crowded as it usually was by eleven thirty, and we had to wait for a booth. Neither of us felt like sitting on a stool at the counter. Mae Etta acknowledged us with a lift of her chin, but otherwise ignored us.

A back booth freed up in under five minutes, and we took it before the new bus person could clear it. Stained white coffee mugs and smeared hard plastic plates did not deter my appetite.

"Why am I so hungry?" I asked Phil.

"If I were an award-winning psychologist—which I am—I might suggest that you're concerned about David Madison."

"Isn't 'eating your feelings' kind of a cliché, Doctor?" I mocked.

"How many times do I have to tell you," she said breezily, "there's a reason that it's a cliché. Because it's so very true."

"Uh-huh—" I began.

That's when the new bus person appeared and started clearing the table.

"Sorry, Dr. Waldrop," she said. "Let me get this mess out of your way, and Marsha will be right over to take your order."

Phil looked up at the young woman.

"Hello, Judy," Phil said sweetly. "I didn't know you were working here."

"Just got the job," Judy reported proudly. "It fits in perfectly with all my classes, and Marsha splits her tips with me!"

"Isn't that wonderful," Phil said. "And by the way, you got an A on your quiz in the Intro class."

Judy stopped working for a second. "I did?"

Phil nodded. "You only missed one question."

"It was the one about the collective unconscious," Judy said knowingly. "I'm still confused about that."

Phil laughed. "Join the club, my dear. *Everyone* is confused about that."

Marsha swooped in then, bussed the last remaining plate, and patted Judy on the arm. Judy nodded once and breezed away.

"Isn't she just the cutest thing ever?" Marsha asked us both.

"A good student, too," Phil affirmed.

I wondered about Marsha then. All I knew about her was that she'd been working in the diner as long as I'd been back in Enigma, but that hadn't been very long, really.

"It's nice of you to split your tips with her," I said to Marsha.

"What am I going to spend money on?" she said, laughing. "My boyfriend pays for the movies, Mae Etta lets me stay in the apartment upstairs for free, and when our bunch goes up to Tifton to hear a band or dance in a club, I *always* get free drinks."

"Because you're the cutest one in the place," Phil suggested.

"Because I got legs as long as a day in July," she announced happily and without a hint of false pride, "and a skirt as short as a bad girl's memory."

Everyone in the place laughed out loud. And that, I realized, was why Marsha had plenty of tip money to spare, even if the skirt of her wait uniform came down below her knee. She was a beloved character. Just like Mae Etta herself.

"So what'd-y'all-want?" Marsha asked—it was all one word. "Special today is . . ." She consulted her pad. "Fried chicken livers!"

"That's for me," Phil said happily. "With collard greens and mashed potatoes."

"I need a vegetable plate," I told Marsha. "Collards, yellow squash and onions, field peas, and . . . I guess mashed potatoes too."

"Corn bread muffins?" she presumed.

"Right."

And Marsha was gone.

"Short as a bad girl's memory?" Phil whispered. "I don't know what that means."

"Some people don't remember how bad a hangover is," I said, also at a whisper, "or what a one-night stand feels like the next day. They forget. That's what makes them bad. They repeat the same mistakes over and over again."

Phil sat back. "Well, that's a rather sophisticated metaphor, don't you think?"

"There's more to Marsha than meets the eye," I said. "I was just thinking about that."

"Speaking of which," she said, "I think there's more to that *Donna* than meets the eye. She is *not* just an employee to Kell Brady."

"There is something weird about their relationship," I agreed.

"Do you still think that Donna might be our . . . you know, our suspect?"

"I never *really* thought that," I reminded her. "But if Kell did it, she's an accessory after the fact, at the very least."

"Because she'd know that Kell did it."

I nodded.

"And what was all that bizarre ghost show business about at the opera house?" Phil went on. "I thought about that the whole drive home just now."

"I was thinking about your impersonation of a Southern belle," I kidded her. "Flirting with Kell Brady like a high school girl."

"I think it worked," she said without a trace of embarrassment. "He told us things I've never heard before. And I am, as you have sometimes pointed out, a hub of local if not regional gossip. I've heard *everything*, and I'd never heard the relatively heartbreaking story of Kell and the Glassie sisters' ménage à *weird*."

"That was sad," I agreed. "Especially his bedraggled punch line: all alone in a big old house with nothing to show for his life but a bland special event venue in a tiny little town."

"Which brings us back to Donna," Phil insisted. "I say to

him that he has Donna, and he, a little indignantly, assures me that Donna is nothing but the *help*."

"When she's clearly more than that," I said.

"Caretaker, nursemaid, chief cook, and bottle washer," Phil rambled.

"Also, I have to say I was surprised that she was your chauffeur today."

"I was too!" Phil leaned forward. "Very unexpected. Who exactly is she *really*?"

"Sounds like a bit of after-lunch research is in order," I said.

At that, my phone buzzed from my back pocket. I retrieved it and looked at it just as Marsha brought us our sweet tea.

"Hello, Jennifer," I said. "Everything okay?"

"Tell her I said hello," Phil sang out.

"Slow day," Jennifer said quickly. "So, among other things, I was doing a little more digging about that Grimm Brothers book that Rose sold to Bea Glassie."

I looked at Phil. "Really?"

"Madeline," Jennifer said breathlessly, "someone is offering that very book for sale online for two hundred thousand dollars!"

"What do you mean 'that very book'?"

"The 1812 first edition of *Kinder- und Hausmärchen*!"

"Who's selling it?" I asked, still staring at Phil.

"Secret seller," Jennifer said, more delighted than ever. "Secret, *mystery* seller!"

"What if it's Bea," I concluded. "Bea got it from Rose, then tried to flip it, maybe?"

"Maybe," Jennifer said. "But then since Bea's dead, no one

could have responded to any of the offers to buy it, so it's still out there, the offer. How about that?"

"You really are a gem, you know it?" I said to Jennifer.

"This is so *cool*," she told me.

"We're at the diner," I said. "We'll be there in a flash."

I hung up the phone and put it back in my pocket.

"You didn't tell her I said hello," Phil objected.

"Wait until you hear what she found," I began.

But Marsha appeared abruptly with our food, and Phil and I both dug in like we hadn't eaten in a month. Apparently odd encounters with rich old men can make a person very hungry. We both only came up for air twenty minutes later.

"So what I was trying to say, before we were so rudely interrupted by food," Phil told me, dabbing the corners of her mouth with her paper napkin, "is that the entire ghost-in-the-opera-house scenario seemed made-up to me. Amateur theatrics."

"I thought the same thing," I agreed. "But why? What reason would he have for doing that?"

"Maybe he and Donna put on their little show for anyone who comes in the place," Phil suggested. "All a part of the building's mythology."

"Maybe." I hesitated. "Or maybe it was a preamble to his sad tale of unrequited Idell love, just to fill his whole narrative with romantic pathos. Sad little Laurel and Hardy ghost, sadder little tale of woe, lost love, and building permit anxieties."

She nodded. "It did seem all of a piece, didn't it."

Marsha breezed back then. "Pie."

It wasn't a question; it was an imperative.

"Cherry," Phil said without hesitation.

"What are my choices?" I asked.

"Same as always, hon," Marsha said tolerantly. "Cherry, lemon ice box, and chocolate meringue."

"Maybe just some coffee," I said.

"All right then," Marsha said, but it sounded like a condemnation. "By the way, did I hear y'all talking about the ghost at the Hawkinsville Opera House?"

We both looked up at her.

"Yes," Phil said finally.

"*Y'all!*" She leaned toward us. "Me and my old boyfriend Avis, we were up there at the last Christmas pageant, on account of Avis had this little sister who was in it? And anyway, right when she began to sing that song 'In the Bleak Midwinter'—she really did have such a pretty little voice—all the lights in the whole place went out! And then it was someone onstage, some man, not one of the children, some man was laughing. Real loud! And then, just like that, the lights came back on. I'm serious as a crutch. And there was nothing but little children on that stage. No man whatsoever. You don't believe me, you can go right over there to the Stop and Shop on Eighty-two and ask Avis. He works there now. Him and that Jaime Pritchet, she works there too. He's sweet on her now, don't ask me why. He's a big cheat and she's a big flirter—I guess they deserve each other. Did you know that she—"

"I think I'll have some coffee too," Phil intervened. "To go with my pie."

"Oh." Marsha straightened up. "Cherry, right?"

"That's right," Phil said gently.

And Marsha was gone.

"Tonight starring Oliver Hardy as the Ghost of Christmas Past," I intoned.

Phil laughed. "So maybe there really is a ghost. I can't see

Kell Brady bothering to interrupt a little girl's song for some cheap spectral antics."

"But can we agree that the whole enterprise this morning was so rife with melancholy that it made us both eat too much?" I asked.

"Yes." She looked down demurely. "*That's* what made us eat too much. I'm sure that in your case it had nothing to do with the fact that David hasn't called you yet."

I glared. "Why would you remind me of that?"

"You can torture me about flirting with Kell Brady but I can't tease you about your boyfriend?" She was still looking down, but she was smiling.

"He's not my boyfriend!"

"Why not?" She was more amused than ever.

"Because, as I said to him: I'm not in high school and he's not a boy."

"Oh." She laughed a little. "That explains it."

"So." I watched Marsha pour our coffee in back of the counter. "Do you want to hear what Jennifer discovered?"

"Oh, that's right!" Phil leaned toward me, elbows on the Formica tabletop. "What did she say?"

"Someone is offering the Grimm Brothers book for sale online for two hundred thousand dollars," I whispered.

"The book that Rose acquired for Bea," Phil marveled.

"I guess it was probably Bea," I said, watching Marsha's approach. "So even if there have been takers, Bea wouldn't have responded."

"Because she's been dead," Phil said absently.

Which made me laugh. "Yes, because she's been dead."

Coffee arrived. Without pie.

Phil looked down at the coffee, then up at Marsha.

"Cherry pie?" she suggested to Marsha.

Marsha looked down at the table. "Well, yes, looks like someone forgot to fetch your pie, Dr. Waldrop."

Phil was sympathetic. "Thinking about Avis?"

Marsha nodded. "You read me like a book."

"Well," Phil said, lowering her voice. "I think you're better off without him."

"Do you know that he made fun of me for being afraid about that ghost at the opera house?" She shifted her weight to one side. "But listen, y'all, I have seen things you wouldn't believe. Like the other day? I was out with Elbert—you know Elbert, Miss Brimley. He's the one who fixed up your car so nice?"

"He made my car a work of art," I confirmed.

"Anyway," she went on, "we were out driving around in one of his antique cars—it was an old MG convertible, pretty little red thing—and we parked up in front of Bea Glassie's house there, just past your house, because, you know, we figured it would be a quiet spot. Since she's passed on. But, y'all, we saw her inside! Saw her through the parlor window, I am *not* making this up!"

"When was this?" I asked her.

"It was the day . . ." Marsha looked around the diner, then lowered her voice. "It was the day after you dug her up. Dug up Bea Glassie. We saw Bea's ghost! I mean it."

"My," Phil said after a momentary pause. "That *is* something."

Marsha looked around again, then nodded once. "Bea Glassie's ghost."

With that she was away, presumably in search of cherry pie.

Phil only waited a second before she announced, barely

audibly, "Oh, we're going to Bea Glassie's house as soon as I'm done with my pie."

"Exactly," I concurred. "That way we can just *ask* Bea who bumped her off."

"If you think that's best," she answered me primly. "But I thought we might see if we could find the Grimm Brothers book. Couldn't you use two hundred thousand dollars?"

For a second I was distracted by all the things I could do with that kind of money. I could update the shop's plumbing and electrical systems. I could give the whole place a makeover. And then I could go to New York, or Paris, or the Isle of Skye.

But then I came back to earth.

"I should never have suggested that we go to a dead woman's house," I lamented. "What are we supposed to do? Break in and just rummage around for an old book?"

"No," she responded. "We should go and see if we can find out who broke into a dead woman's house the day after that dead woman's body was discovered—and why."

"Oh." I looked down at my coffee. "When you put it that way . . ."

Marsha returned moments later with cherry pie and the check.

"Listen," she told us confidentially. "I know y'all probably think I'm crazy."

I looked up at her. "What I think, Marsha, is that there are more things in heaven and earth than are dreamed of . . . et cetera. And that includes a ghost or two."

"Hmm." She thought about it. "Well, then."

And she was gone.

23

PIE GONE, BILL paid, Phil and I were on the road past the bookshop, into the more wooded area just outside the southern city limits of Enigma, and just about to Bea Glassie's mansion.

Old pines shaded the road, which would not have ordinarily been paved, but Bea's money, Phil told me, had ensured a nice two-lane blacktop that ended just beyond Bea's house. After that it was a dirt road that went on and on past farms into the next county.

I'd driven that way before, just exploring. Bea's house was a sight to see, and I only just then realized, as we were pulling up into the gravel driveway, how much it looked like Kell Brady's house in Hawkinsville. Three stories, wraparound front porch, a little too Hawthorne-looking and decidedly Victorian, even though it had been built in the twenty-first century. Painted light gray with strong burgundy accents, it proudly displayed copper gutters and a slate tile roof. There was a fairy-tale round turret at one corner and grand floor-to-ceiling windows on either side of the double front door.

"Well, if there was going to be a ghost," I said as I turned off the engine and Igor sputtered to a conclusion, "this would be the place for it."

"Spooky," Phil agreed.

We got out. The sun was collaborating with the Hammer Film atmosphere, hiding behind a series of high rain clouds. We walked, side by side, up the front steps, but when we got to the door we just stood there.

"Should we knock?" Phil suggested.

"Would you be comfortable if someone answered?" I asked her.

And then I tested the door handle. The door was locked.

"Maybe go around back?" I said.

I headed around the outside of the house on the porch, but it ended before the backyard. There was a window there that looked into a small office-like room. There was no screen, so I tested the window. It complained, but I was able to raise it.

Phil had followed me, but she suddenly seemed concerned about actually going into the house, at least through a window.

"I don't know about this," she told me, backing away.

"Well, I'm going in," I said. "Go back to the front door, I'll come and let you in."

"Oh." She didn't move.

But I was already climbing through the window.

The office was neat, but it also looked very much like a working office. There were stacks of paper on an old dark secretary's desk, there were books stacked on the floor next to a comfy-looking Queen Anne chair, and the fireplace screen had been moved to one side as if maybe someone were about to make a fire.

I found my way to the front door and let Phil in.

"Avon calling," she said nervously, stepping over the threshold as if it might explode.

"Haven't seen anyone so far," I told her.

"Uh-huh." She cast her eye about the place. "Does this house look a little like Kell Brady's house?"

"I was just thinking that," I told her.

"Then that would be the library," she said, pointing to a room to our right.

I agreed with a nod; we ventured in. It was, indeed, a library room. Same floor-to-ceiling built-in bookshelves as in Kell's place. The furniture was different though. There was a wicker and velvet sofa that would have been at least a hundred years old. It was flanked by equally arcane and nearly matching chairs. The velvet was wine-colored and there were intricately embroidered pillows, almost like tapestries, everywhere. Just like the ones in Kell's house.

Phil gasped suddenly and pointed. "Look!"

She appeared to be pointing at one of the pillows. I took a closer look. The image on it was a bundle of bones wrapped in a scarf, and the needlepoint quote said, "My sister Marlene gathered all my bones and laid them beneath the juniper tree."

"That's a quote from the most grotesque story the Grimm Brothers ever wrote," Phil whispered. "And it's called 'The Juniper Tree.'"

I started to say something about the bundle of coincidences involved in that discovery, but what I actually said was, "How do you know that?"

She looked at me as if I'd lost my mind.

"I read," she said, a little indignantly. "Unlike some people. Apparently."

"No," I protested, "I read too, but I don't remember tiny little quotes—"

"No," she interrupted. "You just remember whole Shakespeare plays and television scripts from ten years ago."

"Good point," I conceded, "but it's still strange to me that you know that this quote is from the book we're looking for."

"As strange as the fact that Bea embroidered it onto a pillow?" she asked me.

I nodded. "Another good point. *Man*, this is all suddenly very weird."

"Suddenly?" she railed. "You dug up a dead person's bones in your front yard! With an Episcopal priest who used to kill alligators! You drove past *weird* a while ago, dear."

I looked at her. "If you keep making such cogent arguments, I'm going to have to reassess my entire opinion of you."

"Like our friend Marsha at the diner," she told me, "there's more to *me* than meets the eye."

"Oh, I've known that all my life," I assured her. "I'm just trying to come to grips with the fact that, at the moment, you seem to be more coherent than I am. That's going to take some getting used to."

"Ha-ha," she said affectedly. "Very funny. Look for the book, why don't you?"

"All right, I will," I said in my best Stan Laurel impression.

Phil did not acknowledge my skillful impersonation. She just went to the nearest bookcase and started poring over the titles.

I went to one of the cases that had glass doors. I could tell right away that the books on those shelves were extraordinary. There was a tattered volume of Jung's *The Red Book*, two volumes of H. G. Wells's *The Outline of History*, a privately bound book that just said *R. Burns* on the spine—and dozens more in no immediately discernible order.

"Oh!" Phil cried out. "Maddy, come look at this!"

I turned to see her holding out a book opened to the front page.

"What is it?" I took a few steps toward her.

"It's *To the Lighthouse*," she whispered. "Virginia Woolf, first edition, 1927 . . . and it's *signed*."

I stared. "Do you have any idea how much that's worth?"

"My first guess," she said, "would be a whole *lot* too much money."

"That's the exact amount I was thinking," I agreed. "Who knew Bea was such a collector?"

Phil nodded. "But look."

Phil ran her finger over the tops of the pages and then showed me a prodigious amount of dust.

"Ah," I said. "A *collector*, not a reader."

"Right," Phil affirmed. "Rich people. They buy van Gogh as an investment; they collect books like this but they never read them. I mean, if Bea Glassie knew what was in this Virginia Woolf book, she would never have had it anywhere near her house. Not the Bea Glassie we all knew, anyway."

"Why do you say that?" I asked.

Phil closed the book. "This book is about unquenched desire. About always chasing an ever-receding horizon. That wasn't Bea. She got everything she ever wanted to get."

I only paused for a second. "Except a marriage to Kell Brady."

Before Phil could respond, there was a loud clatter at the front door. Phil dropped the book and hooted a little like a barn owl. I twisted around toward the library doorway, ready for a fight.

"Maddy!" Billy called out, and I could hear that he was angry.

"Billy Sanders, you nearly scared the life out of me!" Phil complained at the top of her lungs.

"Dr. Waldrop?" He appeared in the library doorway in full uniform including the hat. "What in *the* hell are you doing here?"

"Language," she chided. "And we're looking for a book."

"Why are *you* here?" I wanted to know.

He stood there for a second, hovering somewhere between anger and curiosity with just a hint of official police business in the mix.

"This house has a security system." He sighed and his shoulders relaxed a little. "It's a company in Tifton. There aren't but three houses in Enigma that use their service, so when something sets off their little bell or whatever it is, they call me."

"You got a call from Tifton that someone was breaking into this house here in Enigma?" I considered the absurdity of the moment.

"And when I pulled up and saw your car—" he began.

"I had no idea she had a security system," I interrupted.

"She had it installed," Billy went on wearily, "after somebody—and by *somebody* I mean Frank Fletcher—put rats in her kitchen. This is my third trip here since she put it in."

"Someone else broke into this house?" Phil asked, looking around.

"Well," Billy told her, "the last time I was out here it was Marsha from the diner who was parked in the yard and making out."

"There are outside sensors?" I asked.

"That's right," he assured me. "But also Marsha said she

saw someone in the house. So I checked inside, but there was no one here."

"Not even Bea's ghost?" Phil suggested softly.

"The call just now was that some car pulled into the yard," Billy said, ignoring Phil. "So I thought it might be Marsha up here again. But then another call said that the house had been 'compromised' in some way."

"Maddy came in through a window," Phil reported immediately.

"No kidding, Maddy," he said. "What are y'all doing here?"

I told him about the Grimm Brothers book, how much it was worth, how odd it was that it was for sale online. Unfortunately, Phil also told him all about our trip to the Hawkinsville Opera House, complete with the ghost story, the revelation of Kell Brady's confusing relationship with the Glassie sisters, and Marsha's experience at a Christmas pageant.

"Maddy," he seethed, "didn't I tell you not to bother Kell Brady?"

"Yes, but you also gave me his address!" I answered a little too loudly. "What was I supposed to do?"

He turned to Phil. "And you went with her? I thought you might have a little more sense."

Phil was genuinely taken aback. "Why in the world would you think that? I just got out of the looney bin."

"Dr. Waldrop," he said, and it was clear that he was about to deliver a speech.

So I had to stop him.

"Sheriff Sanders," I snapped. "Are you going to help us look for this ridiculously priced first edition or not? Now that you're here."

He was momentarily struck dumb.

Then he said, "I haven't been elected sheriff yet."

"You're running unopposed," Phil reminded him, as if he might have forgotten.

Billy Sanders gave out with the biggest sigh I'd ever heard then, and his entire demeanor collapsed. He stared first at me, then at Dr. Waldrop, then at the floor for what seemed like a long time.

Finally he said, softly, "What's it called again?"

We looked for almost forty-five minutes. The Grimm book wasn't there, at least not on any of the shelves in the library.

"Is there a way to find out who offered the book for sale online?" Phil asked, plunking down onto the red velvet sofa.

"I'm sure there is," I said, taking one of the chairs beside her. "I just don't know what it is."

"I might be able to figure it out," Billy told us, taking the other chair. "You thought it was Bea that was selling it."

"Yes," I said. "Bea got it from Rose, and not that long ago, so I just assumed."

"Maybe Bea already sold it to someone else," Billy suggested, "and now that someone else is trying to sell it."

"Obviously that's a possibility," I admitted.

"And excuse me for asking," he went on, "but how is finding this book going to help you get Gloria Coleman out of jail?"

That put a blanket of silence over everything for a minute. Because he was right. Why had I let myself get distracted by the book? I thought it had something to do with finding out new information about Aunt Rose. It had something to do with how much money was involved. It probably also had to do with my fear that I was getting nowhere in my effort to free Gloria. So a digression took my mind off that problem.

Or it had, momentarily, until Billy reminded me what I was really trying to do.

I stood up. "Thanks, Billy. You're right. To get Gloria out of jail, I need to find who killed Bea. And even though I have a few really great possibilities, I've got no actual idea who did it."

"Well," he said, still slumped down in his chair, "you've been gallivanting. What we try to do in serious police work, is we try to sit still sometimes and just think about the information we've gathered."

"From your *gallivanting*," Phil suggested with the merest hint of a smile.

"Why don't you two go home?" Billy responded. "Sit down, have something to drink, and cogitate until suppertime. I'm telling you: you'd be surprised what comes to the forefront of your mind when you're quiet for a minute. And it is my assumption that you have not remotely tried *that* yet."

He was right again. I'd let action take precedence over meditation, and shame on me for that. The problem was my brain. But Philomena beat me to the punch.

"She can't help it," Phil told Billy. "Her brain is too bossy."

And sure enough, my brain poked me in the eye and made me realize something.

"Hey, Officer," I said to Billy, "you got a call from the security service."

He stared.

"Meaning the power in this house is still on," I continued. "And Bea's been dead for at least six months."

"Yes," he said instantly. "I asked the security company

about that when I had to come up here and chase Marsha away. Apparently, Bea set up automatic payments."

"She did?" I shook my head. "That's interesting."

"No, it's not," Billy insisted. "Now come on, let's clear out, hear? There might be some actual real crime I got to attend to somewhere in town. Go home. Have supper. Sit and *think*."

"Billy," I began in protest.

"Technically," he said, a little louder than he needed to, "I could arrest you both for breaking and entering. Is that what you want?"

"I think I'd like to leave now," Phil said to me.

"Right," I agreed.

We both headed for the front door.

"Wait!" Billy commanded. "Did you close the window where you came in?"

I hadn't. I held up one finger, then dashed for the office. There was a gentle spring breeze coming in through the window, and the scent from a bay laurel momentarily distracted me, but I managed to close the window. That's when I really looked at the desk in the office. There was a typewriter on it, a Remington Home Portable No. 2—the same kind that Agatha Christie used. When she wasn't using her Dictaphone. The point was: no computer. I took a quick look around. There was no computer to be found. And if she didn't have a computer, and she didn't drive, how did she offer the book for sale online, or set up autopay with the power company and the security service?

"Madeline!" Billy bellowed from the other room.

I ran. Billy and Phil were waiting by the door.

"Sorry." I motioned for Phil. "Let's go. Billy's right. I need to think."

Outside the crickets were just beginning to explain something about the night in the deeper shadows of the front porch of Bea Glassie's house, a house that was still alive a half year after Bea was dead. The sun wasn't setting quite yet, but no one would have argued that it wasn't going to eventually. After all, who would have wanted to argue with the inevitable? For example, in the relative silence of that moment, as the three of us left the porch that April evening, I knew, as certainly as I knew that the sun would set, that I was going to find out who killed Bea Glassie.

24

THE INSTANT WE were in the car, I turned to Philomena.

"Someone other than Bea has been taking care of that house," I said, backing the car out of the yard. "And someone other than Bea is trying to sell that Grimm book."

I told her about my typewriter observation as we drove away from Bea's house.

"That's not much to go on, is it?" she asked me.

"Still, someone set up the payments," I said. "Someone is selling the book. And I can't see how Bea could have done that."

"Then who would be doing something like that?" she asked, but it wasn't really a question, it was thinking out loud.

"That's a short list, to me," I said. "Idell might be doing it, or Kell."

"Maybe Bea had a service," Phil objected. "Maybe she had a lawyer who might handle all that."

"Maybe." I drove slowly.

Billy's squad car was almost bumping my bumper, but the road had not been as well maintained as Phil had led me to believe. There were potholes everywhere. And besides, I was distracted. So I was driving a little too slow.

"Damn it!" I shouted suddenly.

Phil jumped. "What's the matter with you? And *language*!"

"I just realized . . . something." I turned to her for a second. "The fireplace screen in Bea's office was set to one side, but if Bea was killed right before I got here, the weather wasn't cool enough to have a fire."

"It wasn't?" Phil tilted her head.

"I got here last October," I assured her, "and it was still quite warm."

"I don't understand what you're saying," she said slowly.

"I'm saying that I wish I had thought to look in the hearth, at the grate," I said.

"Because someone might have burned something in there," she realized. "And it might have been something important."

I glanced in the rearview mirror.

"Do you think Billy would shoot at me if I turned the car around and went back to Bea's place right now?" I wondered out loud.

"Not to kill," she said. "But he might aim for your leg."

"Or shoot out my tire," I agreed. "And Igor's been through enough. Two trips to Hawkinsville and this bumpy road—that's more travel time than he's gotten all this year."

"You can always go back," Phil said, "when the sheriff isn't literally on your tail."

"Billy has been pointing out that he hasn't been elected yet," I told her.

"He's running unopposed," Phil said.

Five more minutes and I was pulling into the Old Juniper's front yard, yellow police tape and all. Billy roared past. He didn't even wave as he would have ordinarily. So he really was mad.

"Come in?" I asked Phil as I switched off the car.

"I just can't," she lamented. "I really shouldn't have gone with you today. I have to get back in the swing of things. I have to grade papers. I have lesson plans. No."

She climbed out of Igor and went straight for her Buick LeSabre.

"Okay," I called to her. "But if I figure all this out by myself, aren't you going to feel left out?"

"Call me," was all she said. She cranked her car, eased it backward, and drove away.

There weren't any lights on in the shop, but it wasn't dark yet and sometimes we didn't turn on the lights until sunset. Maybe Jennifer was still there.

Up the porch and through the front door, I came to a dead stop when I saw someone in a black hoodie, tan shorts, and decorated Crocs sitting at the computer on the business desk in the parlor.

"Hey!" I snapped.

The kid looked up, startled. He had a smattering of whiskers that did nothing to disguise the fact that he was still in his teens. He stood nervously, and with the point of his hoodie straight up over his head he looked like an anemic garden gnome.

Jennifer emerged from the kitchen with two cans of Coke.

"Madeline," she said quickly, "this is Josh. Josh, sit down."

Josh sat.

"Josh is a computer savant from Tifton," Jennifer went on, coming into the parlor and setting one of the Coke cans on a coaster on the desk. "And wait until you hear what he can do!"

"What do you mean?" I stared at Josh.

"Well I was wondering who was trying to sell that Grimm

book, right?" she told me. "I mean, when you click on the 'buy now' button online, you only get kind of a generic 'seller' profile thingy. No real information. So I called Josh. He can do anything on a computer, and he thinks he can find the IP address of the seller, which would, in turn, tell us who the seller is!"

I continued to stare at Josh. "Can you do that? Josh?"

He nodded wordlessly.

"Okay then," I told him, walking toward him. "In that case, can you also find out a couple of other things? Things related to the same . . . situation."

He looked at Jennifer, then back at me. "What situation?"

"I want to find out who set up someone's bills on auto-pay," I said. "Can you find out something like that?"

"Um." He nodded. "Probably."

"Because I think it may be the same person who's trying to sell the book," I went on.

"Oh." He looked at Jennifer.

"It's okay," she told him.

"Are we paying Josh?" I asked Jennifer.

"He's doing me a favor," Jennifer said, and she actually winked at me.

"I see." And I did. I could see that a girl like Jennifer could ask a kid like Josh to do just about anything. "Well, Josh, I would like to make this a professional arrangement. I believe that some kind of remuneration ought to come your way."

"Oh." He looked at Jennifer again.

"How about store credit?" she suggested. "You can have any book in the shop for free. Any book that's not in the rare collectible section, obviously."

"A free book?" He seemed quite enthusiastic.

"If you find out who's selling the Grimm book," I told

him, "and who set up Bea Glassie on autopay, you can have three."

"Three free books?" He squirmed in his seat. "I want the first three Dune books, the trilogy. In hardback. You have them in the science fiction section right now."

"Done," I said.

Without a word, Josh hunched over the computer and his fingers began to move faster than humanly possible. Josh may have been an android.

"So how was your trip to Hawkinsville?" Jennifer asked me.

"The whole trip was odd," I said. "We encountered a ghost at the opera house, and then Marsha at the diner told us about her experience with the same ghost, and *then* we nearly got arrested when we broke into Bea Glassie's house just now."

"Sounds about right," she said, unimpressed. "We had a slow day here at the shop. I had time to study, then I had time to think, which is when I called Josh."

I looked at him. He was oblivious.

"Seems like the right call," I told her. "If he really can do what you think he can do."

"He can." She sipped her Coke.

"So." I just stood there.

"He didn't call," she said softly.

"No," I said. "Of course not."

I headed for the kitchen. Jennifer followed.

"Did you guys have a fight?" she asked.

"Not exactly," I said.

I opened the fridge and stared at the Styrofoam leftover containers and the half-empty jar of mayonnaise.

"So why all the tension about his calling?" she wanted to know.

"I may have inadvertently insulted him," I said. "He misinterpreted something I said about small-town relationships."

"What did you say?"

I closed the refrigerator door. "Doesn't matter. We'll work it out."

"Well, I certainly hope so," she said, taking a seat at the table. "Because he's kind of perfect for you."

I turned her way. "I mean, he kind of *is*."

She leaned back in her chair. "You should tell him that."

I smiled at her. "Yeah, I probably should."

Cannonball wandered in then. Not for any discernible reason, just, really, to make his presence known. He managed to leap up onto the kitchen table and then lay down, looking between Jennifer and me.

"Just want to be included in the conversation?" I asked him.

At which he began to lick his paw and wash his face.

"Did you say you broke into Bea Glassie's house?" Jennifer asked me.

"I did," I assured her. "She didn't seem to have a computer."

"Right." She finished her Coke. "So if that's true, then maybe she's not the one selling the book. And that's why you want to know who set her up with autopay. She could have done that herself over the phone, though, maybe?"

"Sure," I agreed, "but I have in mind a certain image of her. She didn't drive, she didn't own a computer or a cell phone, and she liked to be in charge. Of everything. What I know about her would seem to indicate that she wasn't the kind of person who would relinquish control of something so important to her as her money."

"Should I point out to you that you didn't have a cell phone until recently?"

"No," I told her. "You should not point that out to me."

"Okay." She smiled. "I won't then."

"Found something!" Josh's voice called from the other room.

Jennifer and I were at his side in seconds.

"I don't have, like, anybody's name or address or anything yet," he said, "but I can tell you that the offer to sell that book hasn't been up for long. I mean, it only went up a few days ago. Like, right after they found the dead body here. At this store."

"That is something," I said.

"No, Josh," Jennifer said, a little harshly, "we need to know who's selling it."

"Yeah," he said apologetically. "I'll have that in a minute. I will."

Jennifer shot a look at me then.

"Is it Idell?" she asked softly. "Did Idell get the book from her sister? Is that the reason—look, Idell stole the book from her sister, but then when her sister was found dead, she panicked and decided to get rid of it."

"Except that Idell is as much of a Luddite as Bea was," I said. "Do you really see her as someone who could navigate—wait, what site is the sale on?"

"The top three," Josh said before Jennifer could. "Shopify, eBay, and Etsy."

"Does Idell even know what those are?" I asked.

"Yeah, probably not," Jennifer admitted.

"But," Josh suggested, "she could have hired someone like me."

We both looked at Josh.

"Did she hire you, Josh?" I asked slowly.

"What?" He looked up. "No. I was just thinking."

"Still," Jennifer insisted, "wouldn't it be worth a trip to Idell's house to see if she has the book?"

"I was thinking the same thing," I agreed.

"I could go with you!" Jennifer said a little too enthusiastically.

"No, you could not," I said firmly. "The last thing you need now is to get into trouble right before your international internship."

"No, but I wouldn't get in trouble if I went with you," she whined.

"Are you crazy?" I shook my head. "I just got into *so* much trouble with Sheriff Sanders. I'm the *last* person you want to get next to."

"Shoot," Jennifer demurred. "Billy Sanders would never do anything to you. He still thinks of you as a mother figure."

I turned what I hoped was a withering glance her way.

"In the first place, I am *not* old enough to be anybody's mother figure," I said. "In the second place, you can't apply Dr. Waldrop's Intro to Psych course to every situation in life. And three: shut up."

"Okay." She looked away. "But I'm just saying, he would never arrest you."

"I don't really want to test that theory at the moment," I said. "He was pretty mad at Dr. Waldrop and me for showing up in Bea's house."

"But did he arrest you?"

"Got it!" Josh announced.

We turned his way once again.

"Got *what*?" I asked.

"IP." That's all he said.

"So, who is it?" Jennifer pressed. "Where is it?"

Josh looked up. "Well, see, the IP address can tell you the country and the city, but it can't really tell you any personal information, exactly—not like that. It can, potentially, determine network ownership, but that is going to take a little more digging."

"Okay," I said, "so what is, Josh, the city from which the sale of that book originates?"

Because that would tell me a lot.

"Oh, uh." He glanced back down at the screen. "Hawkinsville, Georgia."

25

BILLY WAS RIGHT. I needed to sit and think. So I did, but sometimes meditation is a wayward thing, and thoughts go wherever they want to, not where you tell them to. For example, I thought about the Brothers Grimm.

They were not creative writers in the strictest sense of the word as far as I was concerned. They were academics who collected folktales and wrote them down, folktales about Cinderella or Hansel and Gretel or Little Red Riding Hood. In nineteenth-century Europe, Romanticism had made traditional stories wildly popular, and, to the Grimms, these stories were the purest form of literature. By the twenty-first century there were more than a hundred translations of the books, and eventually there were plenty of Disney films that diluted the harsher parts of the stories almost beyond recognition.

By all accounts, as Philomena had tried to tell me, the worst of the old stories collected by the Grimms, in terms of the sheer gruesome quotient, was "The Juniper Tree." It included a stepmother murdering a child, cooking him in a pie, and serving the pie to the child's father, unbeknownst. And that's only one of at least ten grotesque elements of the story. None of which would make it into the Disney format.

Although Disney did kill Bambi's mother, for which I, personally, will never forgive them.

So what made the Grimm tales so popular and so enduring? Bruno Bettelheim, in his book *The Uses of Enchantment*, tried to convince us that these stories helped children answer certain important existential questions. He said that he wrote his book as "an educator and therapist of severely disturbed children." This despite the fact that, apparently, he had only ever taken a few introductory courses in psychology, and he was certainly not a therapist. And despite the fact that I couldn't remember posing any real existential questions myself as a child other than the basics: when do I have to go to bed, why do I have to study algebra, does Tommy Gilliam think I'm cute, why are they feeding me broccoli, and when—dearest God—do I get to leave this tiny little town and go to New York?

Still, the thinking remained. The thinking that making children confront very real problems—like the death of a mother—in fanciful stories might just help them deal with death in general when it actually came to visit their homes.

But as I sat in my kitchen just staring at the refrigerator, trying to make it magically be filled with fresh vegetables and barbecue, I had to admit that the Brothers Grimm were doing little to help me face the fact that I was confused about death in general, and about Bea Glassie's death in particular.

Bea was so disliked by the general populace that she'd been gone from the public eye for six months and no one, not a soul, not even her own sister, had questioned her disappearance. Bea was dead, but her house was still alive—electricity, alarm system, all bills apparently still being paid. Bea was companion to Kell Brady, possibly the richest man anywhere around, but she couldn't quite get him to marry her. If that, in fact, was ever an interest of hers. And Bea, dead as she was, had still found a way to get rid of Gloria Coleman, if I didn't do something about it.

Cannonball was stretched languorously on the kitchen table and seemed, if not willing, at least amenable to conversation.

"So," I said to him, "taking the first thought first: why, exactly, didn't Idell go to Billy after her sister disappeared? I kind of get why no one else did. Most people were busy thinking 'good riddance,' I guess. But Idell?"

Cannonball yawned.

"No," I told him, "it's an interesting question. You just don't have an answer so you're trying to pretend it doesn't matter."

I was startled out of my contemplative mood by a sound at the back door.

Then, "I can hear you talking to yourself even with this back door closed. That's the first sign of cognitive decline, you know. Talking to yourself."

I stood up a little too quickly and my chair went scooting.

"What are you doing lurking out there?" I asked him.

"Well," David answered, "I was sitting out in your gazebo for a while, a little hoping you'd notice me and come out."

I went to the door and opened it. There he was, and out of his work clothes, sporting a green T-shirt, black jeans, and fancy gray Taft boots.

"Then I heard Jennifer leave with some other kid," he went on as he came into the kitchen. "And then I heard you talking to yourself, so I thought I should come in and check on you because I was concerned about your mental health."

"I wasn't talking to myself," I said. "I was talking to Cannonball."

He looked down at Cannonball. "Did he answer?"

"Not yet."

"That's something, I guess," he conceded. "At least you're not hallucinating. So do you have a second to talk with someone who can actually respond?"

I knew that he could see the look on my face, I just wasn't certain he could translate it properly.

"Look," I began quickly, "I really think you misinterpreted what I said earlier—"

"Stop," he interrupted. "Before you say anything, let me get out the speech I've been working on all day, okay?"

I nodded. He sat. So did I. Cannonball didn't move.

"Among my many foibles," David said, staring a hole in the tabletop, "is the rare, occasional bout of massive insecurity. It has even been what I would call *debilitating* a couple of times. I've thought about it over the years, and even considered talking with someone about it, but since it only rears its ugly head once a decade or so, I figured it was more or less controllable. The last time it took hold of me was when Faye got married to someone else. The last time, you know, before *this* time. This time I acted like a teenaged boy so you can add embarrassment to the list of things I'm about to apologize for."

"Okay I have to stop you there," I said. "Because I don't need an apology. I just need to tell you something. And here it is. I currently believe that you are perfect for me. I don't know what was wrong with Faye, except that you weren't perfect for her, I guess. But if you were in New York, or Atlanta, or Timbuktu I'd still think that you were perfect for me. And I don't usually speak this forthrightly about my feelings, but it kind of seems like it's important, so, okay?"

He nodded, then he looked up from the table, then he looked into my eyes.

"Have you ever *been* to Timbuktu?"

"My point is—"

"Because I have," he went on. "In 2008, al-Qaeda started kidnapping tourists in the Sahel region. I really can't recommend it. Plus the theatre there is terrible."

"I'm not talking about Timbuktu!"

He smiled. "I know. I was just trying to take a little of the gravity out of the room."

"And by *gravity* do you mean that this is a grave situation," I said, "or are you actually hoping to somehow reduce the earth's gravitational pull?"

"I'm *hoping* to get you to accept my apology for my acting like an adolescent boy," he said.

"And I'm hoping you heard me say that I think you're perfect for me."

He stared. "That's a little hard for me to accept. I can't imagine that I'd be perfect for anybody."

"I mean, I could make you a list," I said. "Would that help?"

"A list?"

"Of all the ways in which I think you and I fit together."

"Oh." He nodded. "A list. That would be impressive."

"Only I can't do it tonight," I said, trying not to take a step closer to him. "Tonight I have to get my thoughts together about—I found out some stuff today. I need to think through some of it. So could you just take it for granted at the moment that I like you better than anybody I ever met, and you like me enough to act crazy and get your feelings hurt over nothing?"

He took in a deep breath. "I have to take all that for *granted*?"

"You do if you want to help me get Gloria out of jail."

"Well," he allowed. "I do want to do that."

"And by the way," I added, softer, "this is the easiest conclusion to an argument I've ever had with anybody."

He touched my shoulder. There was electricity involved.

"Let's try to keep it that way," he told me. "What do you think?"

"I think you should come over to the fridge and help me decide which of the leftovers we're going to eat while we talk over some of the weirder things that happened to me today, just since I saw you last."

He acquiesced without a word. We went to the refrigerator, opened it up, and settled on three containers from Lin's Garden in Tifton. We took them to the kitchen table.

"I don't have any idea how these got here," I told David as we sat down.

"Jennifer?" he suggested.

I opened the first two Styrofoam tops and found them both completely filled with chicken fried rice—and a note from Jennifer.

The note said, "Madeline, I got Josh to bring me some food from Tifton. He brought a lot. Enjoy."

I showed it to David.

He nodded. "That was nice of her. Who's Josh?"

"According to Jennifer he's a computer savant from Tifton," I told him, "if that's not damning with faint praise. But he did find out a couple of interesting things about which I was in the middle of thinking when you came to my back door."

"Such as?" he asked, deftly wielding one of the pairs of chopsticks we'd found in the takeout container.

"Where to begin," I said to myself. "After we had our little misunderstanding and you left, I found out that Bea Glassie bought a book from Rose for, like, eighty thousand dollars."

"What?" He stopped eating. "Was it made out of gold?"

"It was an autographed volume of a first edition Grimm Brothers book," I told him. "And it's worth at least twice that today."

"Amazing." He resumed eating.

"The thing is," I went on, "Jennifer discovered that it was being offered for sale online. Right now."

"The same book?" He shook his head. "How can you be sure it's the same one that Rose sold to Bea?"

"I'll just skip over that question and tell you that the person selling it is Kell Brady!" I couldn't believe what a relief it was to say that out loud, like I'd been keeping a secret that I was really, *really* wanting to tell someone.

He momentarily froze. "Kell Brady is selling a book that Bea Glassie bought from your aunt Rose."

"That's the headline, yes." I was suddenly too excited to eat. "Or at least I think it is. Who else from Hawkinsville would be selling a Grimm book right now?"

"Uh-huh," he conceded, "and what does that tell you?"

"It tells me that Kell somehow got the book from Bea." I took a bite of cold fried rice. "And also this Josh guy found out that Kell set up Bea's expenses on autopay, like, right after Bea went missing."

"Is that when the book went up for sale?"

"No," I said, "that's the thing. The book just went for sale the day after we found Bea's remains. It *just* went up."

"From Kell Brady." He set down his chopsticks and looked me in the eye. "You think you know what that means."

"Yes," I said. "I think Kell Brady killed Bea."

The second I heard myself say those words out loud, the air in the kitchen changed. The light looked different. The food tasted different. Even Cannonball noticed it. He sat up and looked at me like I was about to explode.

"Huh." That's all David said.

"The thing is," I breezed on, "I don't really have any proof."

"It does seem to be what they call 'circumstantial evidence,'" he agreed.

"Right. So the next thing I was thinking was that I had to get Kell to confess." I shook my head. "I have no idea how I would do that."

"Would it do any good to talk with Billy?" David asked. "Or the GBI?"

"Billy's mad at me at the moment," I said, "because I broke into Bea's house."

David laughed out loud. "You did *what*?"

"Yeah," I admitted. "I went into her house through a window and set off some kind of silent alarm system. And Philomena was with me, so at least part of Billy's ire has to do with my getting his favorite college professor in trouble. So."

"And the GBI?"

"They were very clear that they would shoot to kill if they ever discovered that I was investigating Bea's death in any way whatsoever."

"So what are you going to do?" he asked. "I mean, to get Kell to confess."

I stared at him. "You're not questioning my logic or telling me I'm crazy to think that a spooky old rich guy is a murderer?"

"You just told me that you like me better than anybody else," he said. "I would currently agree with you if you told me that the pope killed Bea."

"No," I told him. "I already ruled out the pope. He was in Italy at the time of the murder."

"Well, then." And he resumed eating.

"Okay," I went on, "thanks for being on my side in this foolhardy theoretical prospect."

He nodded. "That was going to be the name of my next string band: Foolhardy Theoretical Prospect."

"You know you've never played me any of your music," I said, trying to make it sound like a challenge. "Or read me any of your poetry out loud. I've read some of it, of course, but I've never heard it in your voice."

"Trying to keep a little mystery in the relationship," he said, resuming his enthusiastic consumption of cold leftover rice.

"Well, I think it's about time to end some of that mystery," I told him. "Lay one on me; give out with some poetry, Mr. Poetry Man."

He shook his head. "I don't think so."

"Come on," I complained. "I just told you my wild and barely coherent theories about a local murder. The least you can do is tell me one poem."

He set down his chopsticks and sat up straight. "All right. I'll give you a new one, something I'm in the middle of working on. Just to see if you can ascertain its immediate inspiration. Ready?"

I set down my chopsticks, turned my chair toward him a little, and folded my hands in my lap.

"Hit me," I said.

He didn't look at me. He just began.

"I was arguing with Icarus. This was before either one of us knew his fate. It's not just a question of wings, I told him. First you'd have to hollow your bones and fill them up with air, and a human being can't live that way. Then there's the question of your brain. You'd have to take out the part that alerts you to the impossible, the part that explains to you all the things you can't do. And it's the only part, my dear Icarus, which is impossible to remove. It's the part of your brain that says to you, 'No matter how much you want to, you *cannot* fly.'"

I sat in silence for, it seemed to me, about a month.

Then I said, "I don't know what I was expecting. Something more horticulturally involved, like how nice roses are in summertime, or something. I didn't expect Greek mythology, existential uncertainty, or the mention of hollow bird bones."

I was just as surprised as David was by what happened next. I leaned close to him, I put my hand on his, I looked into his eyes, and then something very much like a kiss transpired. It wasn't lingering, it was exactly long enough. It wasn't overwrought, it was perfectly passionate and still somehow innocent. It didn't change everything in the entire world—just everything in mine.

And when it was over, we both had a little trouble breathing normally.

"I just started working on it, the poem," he said hoarsely, looking down. "It's not finished."

"And, PS," I went on, still not entirely under control, "I get how it could have been, if not inspired by, at least *caused* by our little misunderstanding yesterday. All in all I'd have to say that I'm not just impressed, I'm intimidated. Maybe you're too great a poet to be involved with an ex-actor who retreated to a small Southern town when the work dried up."

He smiled. "Now who's having a crisis of confidence? I guess we could keep this up for quite a while: I'm not good enough for you, you're not good enough for me."

"I could probably keep it up for years," I agreed.

"Me too," he said, "but how about, for the time being, we just concentrate on how to get Kell Brady to confess to his heinous crime and get our favorite Episcopal priest out of jail?"

"Excellent suggestion," I told him. "Why deal with genuine relationship difficulties when we can deflect to what are most likely made-up suspicions?"

"That's the spirit." He turned back to the chicken fried rice.

"Also," I said, "that was, in my opinion, one of the greatest poems I ever heard out loud."

"You should probably read more poetry, in that case," he suggested.

"I read all the poetry in *The New Yorker* magazine," I said. "I don't usually like it, though. Too depressing. And to be completely honest, I don't actually finish any poem that begins 'as my mother lay dying' or anything that includes the word *betrayal* in the title."

"Which eliminates, like, half the poetry in the magazine, right?"

"Exactly." I picked up my chopsticks. "So. About that kiss."

26

ONE OF MY favorite old English ballads—and who doesn't have at least one?—is called "Rosemary Lane." In it, the singer, a young woman, accepts an invitation from a sailor "to lie in the bed just to keep herself warm." Her confession the next morning is "what was done there I will never disclose, but I wish that short night had been seven long years."

And that's all I'll say about that for the time being.

The next morning David and I heard Jennifer pull up in front of the shop on her little sky-blue Vespa. As soon as she came through the front door, I dragged her into the kitchen and began to tell her the plan. She stared at David while I was plying her with coffee and thanking her for the fried rice before she knew what was happening.

"You told me you have your ID lanyard from the Tate Modern, right?" I tried to sound casual about it.

She blinked. "Yes."

"Okay, great," I said, "go back home, put on some serious business clothes, wear your Tate ID, and get back here as quickly as possible. We're going to bait a trap!"

She looked at me, then at David, before offering her response: "Um . . ."

"Maybe a little bit of background?" David suggested.

So I told her what she already knew, that Kell Brady was selling the Grimm book. Then I told her my plan. She was going to pose as an envoy of the Tate Modern and offer to buy the book from Kell. She had been at the High Museum in Atlanta for some vague reason and happened to see the book for sale online. She was young and ambitious and was trying to impress her bosses by acquiring rare first editions for an upcoming exhibit: Book Art and the Books that Inspired It. Or something. W. W. Denslow's original artwork for Frank Baum first editions of *The Wonderful Wizard of Oz*, Rockwell Kent's *Moby-Dick*, and Arthur Rackham's illustrations for the Grimm fairy-tale book.

Jennifer sat in silence for a little too long before she said, "Would those have been the original illustrations, the Arthur Rackham?"

"Not the point," I told her impatiently. "Are you in or not?"

She looked at David then. "Does this seem a little... half-baked?"

"Oh, it's entirely underdone," he agreed.

"Not to mention," she turned to me, "that if Kell Brady is, in fact, the person who killed Bea Glassie, which I assume is what you're getting at, he's, like, a *killer*. Is poking him the right thing to do? I'm saying, what's to keep him from just giving us, you know, the same treatment?"

"That frail old man doesn't stand a chance against the three of us," I said.

"Is she serious with this?" Jennifer asked David.

He paused. "I think so."

"Well, then, no," she told me. "I'm not *in*. I don't remotely want to be the bait in some half-cocked game of 'trap the killer,' okay?"

"Don't be like that," I said. "Kell Brady is a seventy-seven-year-old man. And if he killed Bea, she was in her seventies too. You've got all the advantage. You're young, you're smart, and you have David and me. I'll be right beside you. And David will be well placed somewhere in the shadows or something. Come on."

"No, Madeline," she insisted. "This is a bad idea. This is a *dangerous* idea."

"Maybe," I admitted, a little giddy. "But what if it ends up catching the person who did in Bea Glassie and we get the Reverend Coleman out of jail?"

"Yeah, I'm all in favor of the good result," she said. "I'm just not in favor of the . . ." She looked to David. "What's the word I'm looking for?"

"Peril?" he suggested.

"You're not helping," I told him. "Look, Jennifer. This is the kind of foolhardy thing you're supposed to do when you're in college. You're supposed to have a story like this to tell the other kids at the Tate Modern this summer. They'll be all 'Of course I vacationed in Mallorca before starting this internship' and you'll be able to say, 'Oh, well, I caught a killer and set an innocent woman free.'"

Again she turned to David for assistance. "You have to tell her that she's crazy."

"Okay." David looked me in the eye. "You're crazy."

I just stared back at him and shook my head.

He turned to Jennifer. "I don't think it's working. She's still crazy."

"Here's the deal," I went on. "You'll tell him that you contacted me because you somehow knew about our rare book collection here in the store. And you decided to meet here, for *his* convenience since our shop is closer to Hawkinsville than Atlanta is. And you wanted to have me here—I don't know . . . to authenticate the book since you're new to the rare book world. Or something."

"You can hear how crazy that sounds, right?" she asked me.

"Yes," I had to admit.

"Then why are you doing it?" she asked, her voice much softer.

"I don't know if I've said this out loud yet," I answered, "but I think the reason he's trying to sell the book is that it belonged to Bea and he has it in his possession and it somehow ties him to the murder. Why else would he suddenly want to sell it as soon as he found out that Bea's remains had been discovered?"

"Why couldn't that just be a coincidence?" she asked. "I mean, do you even know for certain that he did hear about Bea's body right away?"

I looked right into Jennifer's eyes. "Sometimes you have to rely on your intuition. And my intuition is clanging like a five-alarm fire. Kell Brady killed Bea. I just have to get him to admit it."

"Why would he admit it?" she objected.

"For some people," I answered, "guilt is the heaviest substance on the planet. It's impossible to carry around. And Kell had feelings for Bea. Killing her for whatever reason he had would weigh on him like the world on Atlas."

"I don't know what that means," she said, "but Kell Brady is a rich man. It's my observation that rich men don't seem to feel much guilt about anything."

"Good point," David interjected.

"And besides," Jennifer continued, "why me? Why get *me* involved in something so obviously, you know, sketchy?"

"Who else could it be?" I asked. "He knows Dr. Waldrop

and David and even Frank, anyone I might get to do this with me. Plus you have the perfect cover: your gig with the Tate Modern!"

She glared. "Did you just use the word *cover*?"

"I did."

"Do you understand that this is a real thing?" she railed. "It's not a show, it's not theatre. You're asking me to risk my *life* here."

I rolled my eyes. "That old man is not remotely a threat to you or to me."

"Uh-huh," she said, "then why have David lurking in the shadows?"

"Oh." I looked at David. "You know. Just in case."

"You are not instilling me with *any* confidence in this harebrained, ill-conceived, wildly unstable scenario!"

I waited, letting her sentence hang in the air.

"Well." I shrugged. "If you don't want to do it."

"I don't," she assured me.

"Okay." I turned to David. "I guess I'll have to ask Josh. If I get him a nice suit and maybe a shave he could pass for an assistant to someone who wants the book, don't you think?"

"Depends on the suit, I think," David answered.

"Wait a minute," Jennifer objected. "I'm all for taking advantage of Josh when it comes to certain favors but believe me he's not the kind of person who could handle something like this."

"Why not?" I asked innocently.

"He's an adolescent boy!" she snapped. "He does not, currently, think about or act on *anything* because of his brain. His judgment center is a little south of the cranium, if you see what I'm saying."

"Of course I see what you're saying," I told her. "But I can't think of anyone else, and we kind of have to act quickly. Someone else might want the book, someone for real."

"So you admit it," she said. "You're not for real."

"Jennifer," I said, "you've already turned me down, I don't see what this has to do with you anymore."

"I don't want you taking advantage of Josh."

"Like you do?" I suggested.

"Not the same and you know it," she insisted, deadly serious.

"Well, he left me his card," I said. "Why don't I just call him and see what he has to say about it?"

"No! Madeline, do not call Josh." She balled her fists, she thinned her lips, and then she exhaled like she'd been holding her breath for a year. "I'll do it."

I let that sentence hang in the air too, making sure that it sank in.

"You will?" I blinked.

Jennifer went to David for a third time. "She just said that about Josh to get me, right? She just got me, didn't she?"

"Yeah," David said. "I think she did."

"Damn it." She looked down.

"So what kind of business-y clothes do you have that'll work for this thing?" I asked her. "Any ideas?"

She sighed heavily. "My mother bought me a navy business suit when she thought I might intern with a law firm in Atlanta."

"And do something conservative with your hair," I said.

"If I get murdered by that rich old man," she muttered, "my mother is going to be very fussy with you."

"I'm not worried about that," I told her.

"You're not?" she asked.

"God, no," I assured her. "That old man will kill me *way* before he kills you. I'll never have to deal with your mother."

"Once again," she said, "that instills no confidence in me."

"And yet you're still going to do this, right?" I wanted to know.

"Looks like it." She shook her head. "What's the matter with me?"

"There's nothing the matter with you," I said. "*I'm* the one with the problems. This is all my fault, this little bit of theatre we're cooking up here."

"That'll be small comfort to me when I get murdered," she complained.

"This *is* theatre," David chimed in. "I just got that. What you're cooking up here is a scene from a play."

"It is," I agreed.

Jennifer heaved the biggest sigh I'd ever heard outside of the stage. "Okay. When?" Then, with a little smile, "When shall we three meet again?"

"Nice Shakespeare," I told her. "So, can you go home now and get ready and do this today?"

"Sure." She was resigned. "I guess today is as good a day as any to get murdered by a book-collecting psychopath."

"That's the spirit," I told her. "How soon can you be back here?"

"Well, the Vespa doesn't go more than thirty miles an hour," she told me. "Then there are clothing decisions to be made, and I'll need about a half an hour to question my current reality. How about if I'm back here by lunchtime?"

"Sounds reasonable," David said before I could speak.

Jennifer actually wagged a finger at me then.

"You're a bad influence," she scolded. "I thought you were going to be a role model."

"How're things going with that boy?" I asked her, just to change the subject.

She offered a flirty smile. "You'll have to be more specific than that."

"The oddly named Hedge Anderson. From Tennessee," I said.

"Oh, him." She shook her head. "My dreamboat turned out to be a footnote, if I may quote Elvis Costello."

"I *love* that song," I told her enthusiastically. "'Every Day I Write the Book.' How do you know about Elvis Costello? He's not exactly what you kids are listening to these days."

"I have a rich pan-musical knowledge of great songwriters," she said, "that includes, in no particular order, Hoagy Carmichael, Chuck Berry, Terry Callier, HER, Megan Thee Stallion, Burt Bacharach, and the redoubtable Declan MacManus, better known as Elvis Costello."

I laughed. "Well, now I'm sorry that I'm going to get you killed. You *do* have a rich pan-musical knowledge, and that is rare in someone of your age and stature, as far as I can tell."

"Yes," she said, standing up from the kitchen table. "You'll be sorry when I'm gone."

I took her hand for a second. "Hey, Jennifer?"

"What?" She was clearly anxious to leave.

"I really will be sorry when you're gone," I said.

"Yeah." She looked down at my hand. "Let's just hope I've gone to London, not to heaven."

I let go of her wrist. "Okay, then. Hurry back."

And she was gone.

I stood then. "I'm going to close up the shop today, I

think. While Jennifer is at home getting into character, I think I want to pay Idell a little visit."

"Idell?" He kept his seat. "What in the *world* for?"

I closed my eyes. "I'm not sure. But we've got hours before lunchtime and I have a feeling."

"A feeling about what?"

"Maybe I just want to get her take on a couple of things," I said. "For example, does she know that Kell had a book that her sister bought from this shop? Does she know that her sister's household is set up on autopay? Does she still have feelings for Kell? And if she does or if she doesn't, isn't that something I want to be able to say to Kell? And is she still angry with her sister?"

"No, Madeline," David insisted. "This is not a good idea. You only want to do it because you're impatient or nervous or something about baiting Kell."

"And," I continued, ignoring him, "why the hell did she call her relative at the GBI to get Gloria arrested for murder on exactly zero evidence? How did that happen?"

He took a second's reflection, sighed, and answered.

"Well," he said. "There's circumstantial evidence."

"Would we call it evidence if it is comprised almost entirely of gossip and innuendo?"

"Doesn't matter what we'd call it," he said. "It's what the GBI would call it."

"Not the whole GBI." I paced. "It's what Idell would say to what's-his-name at the GBI, the head guy that called me. What *is* his name? Anyway Baxter and Baker don't really think Gloria did it, I'm pretty sure about that."

David looked around the kitchen then as if something in it might help him talk me out of going over to Idell's house. Apparently, he did not find any such assistance.

"Okay." He stood at last. "So we're going over to Idell's house."

"You're going with me?" I smiled. "Don't you have a job?"

"You're going to close up your place of business today," he said. "I can do the same. One phone call."

"I just have to hang a sign on the door. I'm ready to go right now."

"So." He stood very still, avoiding eye contact. "Do we feel a need to discuss . . . last night?"

"Absolutely not," I said firmly. "The more you talk about a miracle, the less miraculous it becomes, in my opinion."

"Miraculous?" His eyebrows raised.

"You heard me." But I blushed. "Make your phone call."

He did. I hung the CLOSED sign on the door. We both got in his truck and drove the seven or eight minutes to Idell's house on the northern outskirts of town, the opposite direction from Bea's.

The mansion was impressive in the bright morning light. I'd only driven past it once or twice; I'd never been inside. It was a brick, two-story Italian Renaissance Revival affair with blindingly white columns on the front porch. All the upstairs windows opened onto narrow balconies. The front door was a double, floor-to-ceiling oak masterpiece of carved wood and stunning brass. The roof was slate, the chimneys were ornate, and the lawn was a spotless green carpet on either side of a grand flagstone walkway.

"Are you sure you want to do this?" David asked me as we parked in front of the house. "I can't see what good will come of it."

"I don't know why," I answered. "But I really feel compelled to talk with Idell now that I'm pretty sure Kell killed Bea."

David grunted, but did not otherwise comment.

We got out of the truck and made our way up the flagstones to the sweeping cement stairway at the front porch.

"Hugh Glassie!" I said suddenly.

"Excuse me?" David stopped in his tracks.

"That's the name of the director of the Sylvester GBI place."

"Glassie?"

"Uh-huh," I said, staring at the front door of the house. "He's related to Idell. Like a cousin or something. Didn't I tell you that?"

But before David could answer, the front door flew open and there stood Idell, dressed head to foot in black lace with a face like a caved-in pumpkin.

"Get off my porch!" she hollered.

"Wait," I said. "I have a message from Kell Brady."

She froze. The three of us stood there for what seemed like a week.

"Can we come in?" I finally asked.

"No!" She took a step backward and nearly closed the door.

"He said you were the love of his life," I told her quickly.

"No, he did not!" She was indignant, for some reason.

"He asked you to marry him, and you turned him down," I went on. "He was heartbroken and he never recovered."

"You don't know anything!" But she didn't close the door.

She was right, I was mostly making things up. On a hunch. But it almost seemed to be working, so I kept it up.

"He turned to your sister for consolation," I continued. "But he couldn't marry her, because he was still in love with you."

"He's spent the rest of his life with *her*! Nearly fifty years!"

I couldn't tell if Idell was angry or grieving, but her face was a mask of pain.

"And now it turns out," I pressed, "that he's selling off her things, one by one."

I watched to see her reaction to that little bit of exaggeration. Her mouth opened and her eyes widened, but she couldn't quite muster a sentence.

"For example, right now he's trying to sell a book that belonged to Bea, a book that Bea bought from my aunt Rose."

Idell's eyes got wider, and so did her mouth. If her hands had been up on her cheeks, she would have been Munch's *Scream*.

Then, at a barely audible whisper, "*That* book?"

I thought it was an opening.

"Yes, can we come in, Idell?" I asked gently. "Let's call a truce, you and I, and just talk, could we do that?"

She took long, silent seconds to make up her mind. Then all she did was open the door a little wider, turn around, and vanish into the darkness of her house.

27

THE INSIDE OF Idell's house looked nothing like Bea's or Kell's. For one thing, it was just shy of being some version of a hoarder's home. There were stacks of newspapers and magazines lining every wall and hallway. There was also the musty smell of a place that hadn't been cleaned in months. Or longer. And despite the lovely springtime sunshine, the whole place was dark as midnight, all curtains closed and not a single light on anywhere.

Idell was walking past the grand staircase toward the back of the downstairs, so we followed silently.

Through a lightless hallway we emerged into the relative welcome of the kitchen. The back door was open, so some light and fresh air came in, but the smell of burnt toast and spoiled fruit still filled the air.

"I'm making tea," Idell mumbled.

"None for me," I said instantly. "I want to talk about Kell Brady."

She whirled around with an energy that startled me.

"Why?" she demanded, full voice.

I looked her right in the eye and decided to use the

sledgehammer approach. "Because I think *he's* the person who killed your sister."

I wanted to see her reaction to such a harsh and wild accusation.

The silence that followed that sentence may have been heard as far as Tokyo. And it lasted a remarkably long, uncomfortable time.

So when Idell didn't move or speak, I went on.

"I think he wanted a certain book that Bea had obtained," I said. "He told me that he likes books better than people, and I've seen his library. He's got some pretty great volumes there."

Idell's tongue finally loosened. "Kell likes to collect things. He has no passion for them, he just likes . . . acquiring. Why are you saying this terrible thing to me, that he killed Bea? It's just to remove that Coleman woman from suspicion. That's all. You're inventing. You're erroneously extrapolating."

"Listen, Idell," I said, softening my approach, "I've always appreciated your patronage at the bookshop. You always seemed like a gentle sort, and a nice person, until all this came up about Bea. And now I've had a couple of illuminating visits with Kell and discover that he really did love you, and probably still does, and couldn't quite get himself to fall in love with Bea because of that."

She looked away. "He spent half a century running around with my sister. They built things. They lived with each other. And they abandoned me. Both of them."

From the pain in her voice I couldn't really tell which abandonment hurt worse, Kell's or her sister's. I slowly realized what it might mean to be the wallflower sister. She had to watch the man who'd proposed marriage roar around with her more gregarious sister. Watch them churning things up. Tearing things down. Living.

"Well," I said quietly, "he told me just . . . I think it was just yesterday or day before, he told me that he was still in love with you."

Okay, that was kind of a lie. He hadn't actually said that out loud. But I was pretty sure I'd correctly intuited his feeling on the subject.

Idell nodded slowly, then looked out the kitchen window.

"I don't think he did tell you that," she said. "But I still want to believe that it's true."

"I really think it is," I told her.

"Well." She turned away from me to attend to the old silver kettle on the right front burner of her equally ancient stovetop. "It doesn't matter now, does it?"

"It matters if he killed your sister."

She just shook her head for a moment, and when she did speak her voice sounded a hundred-years weary. "Why would he do that?"

"To get the Grimm Brothers book," I said, taking one step closer to her. "The book mattered more to him than Bea did."

The kettle started to whistle, but Idell didn't turn off the flame under it, and the piercing screech filled up the kitchen.

After a little too long, David stepped over to the stove and turned the burner off. Idell looked at him as if she hadn't quite realized that he was in the kitchen at all.

"He wouldn't have to kill her to get that book," Idell ventured weakly. "He would have just bought it from her. Bea loved money. More than anything. He would have eventually offered enough money and she would have sold it to him."

"Unless money wasn't her motivation in this particular instance," I improvised. "What if Bea wanted something else."

Idell turned at last to face me. "Such as?"

"What if Bea wanted him to marry her?" I suggested.

"She didn't." Idell almost laughed. "She'd given up on that."

"How would you know?" I asked. "You didn't speak to her for years."

"Why would she want to get married to a man who took her up on the rebound?" Idell asked, a little of the force returning to her voice.

"I don't know why anybody would want to get married at all," I said. "But some people are funny about it, I hear."

David didn't want to laugh, I could tell. But he did.

"What are you doing here?" Idell asked, as if we'd just walked into the house.

"I wanted you to know that I think Kell killed your sister," I repeated. "And also, I wanted to see if you might come back with us to the bookshop to help us prove it."

So, that was a surprise to everyone, me included. I hadn't known I was going to ask her that until the instant I heard myself saying it out loud.

David looked as if he might have swallowed his tongue.

I was never big on the notion of people's auras, but I swear at that moment I saw Idell's change color.

"You wanted me to *what*?" she managed to say, despite her confused surprise.

David started to speak, then exhaled, then stared at me.

"I'm going to get in touch with Kell and tell him that a visiting dignitary to Atlanta from the Tate Modern in London happened to see his online offer," I said. "It's actually

Jennifer, from the shop, you know her. Anyway, I want to get Kell to come to the shop, and then I want to rattle him until a confession or something like it comes rolling out. And I want you there to see it."

"Who," Idell began, then she stopped, looked at David, and slammed an open palm on the stovetop. "Who do you think you are? You don't know anything. This isn't some little mystery novel where the heroine ekes out a confession from some evil murderer. This is *Enigma*, for the love of God! A little do-nothing town in the worst part of the third worst state in the country! You're just as useless as your aunt Rose! Get out of my house!"

It was the loudest and the longest I'd ever heard Idell speak. And the greatest evidence that she was still alive under that black lace and that old-lady perfume and that death mask she used for a face.

"What are the other two states?" David suddenly asked.

Idell turned her fierce gaze his way. "What?"

"If Georgia is the third worst state in the union," he said, "what are the other two?"

"My bet is on Alabama," I said quickly, taking up his air of objective observation. "And then Mississippi."

The changes in topic and attitude seemed to have the effect that David had intended, I thought. Idell was completely confused.

"If you don't believe anything I'm saying," I said to Idell, taking another step closer to her, "then come with us and watch me be wrong. Come with us and see Kell, now that Bea isn't between you and Kell anymore. Come with us, if for no other reason, to see the show."

"The show?" She turned to David for any sort of explanation.

"It appears to me that Madeline has in mind some kind of immersive theatre experience for us all," David said with a straight face. "Starring Kell Brady and the book he's trying to sell."

Idell looked back and forth between me and David at least five times before she asked, "Is it drugs? Are you two children on drugs?"

"No," I said dismissively as I moved toward the stove. "Your kettle is going to get cold. What kind of tea did you want?"

I noticed a single teacup and a kind of tea bag caddy just to the right of the stovetop. Idell danced out of my way, and I examined the various kinds of tea that I might make for her.

"I like Earl Grey," David said.

"Okay." I opened a cabinet hoping for more teacups, but there were only glasses.

"David," Idell said, "you're a gentleman. Would you please leave and take this person with you?"

"Why don't you come with us, Idell?" he asked gently. "You *could* get to see Kell make an idiot out of Madeline."

"Exactly," I confirmed. "Think how much fun that would be. I'm not even sure I have a plan exactly. This is more along the lines of improvisational theatre."

"There really is something wrong with you," Idell mumbled.

"Oh, I think you'd get a lot of people to agree with you on that subject," I said. "And I swear I don't have any conscious plan or agenda or anything. For example, it just occurred to me, like, less than a minute ago, that you might want to be involved in the denouement of the situation."

Idell turned once again to David for help. "I know that a lot of these words she's saying are English but when she puts them all together in a sentence like that, it sounds like she's speaking a foreign language."

He couldn't help but laugh. "It does, doesn't it. And, honestly, I have no idea why she wants you to come to the shop when Kell does, but the thing is, I trust her. No matter what it looks like, she's probably got hold of something important here."

"*Plus* I just got in the new Sofie Kelly book," I enticed. "You love her. And I'll give you the employee discount."

The idea of seeing me humiliated or the idea of seeing Kell Brady or even the idea of finding out who really killed her sister all meant less to Idell, it turned out, than the opportunity of getting two dollars off a twenty-two-dollar hardback.

"All right," she said with only a touch of reticence, "I'll go. But I'm not getting into that *truck* you came here in."

She managed to say the word *truck* in a way that made it sound like a bad part of town.

"Okay, but—" I began slowly.

"I'll be along later this afternoon," she interrupted. "You won't get Kell into your shop before lunch. But I do think he'll come. If he has that Grimm first edition, and he wants to sell it, he'll be there. He doesn't miss many opportunities to make a dollar, I know that."

It sounded like a condemnation, but it was really more along the lines of a takes-one-to-know-one sort of thing.

"Do you want me to come and get you in my car?" I asked.

"I'll walk, thank you," she snapped. "It takes me around forty minutes to get from here to there. So once you've called Kell and set up a time this afternoon for him to visit with you, you'll call me, and I'll set out on my little walk."

It had never occurred to me, all the times I'd seen Idell in the bookshop, that she'd walked there from her home. Which was a little ignorant on my part; I knew she didn't drive. How else would she have gotten there?

"Sounds good," David said when I didn't respond. "We won't take up any more of your time."

He nodded to Idell and turned to exit the kitchen. He gave me a look and a tilt of his head, so I followed him. I was a little disoriented because the entire scene in Idell's house had such an air of unreality. What had made me go to her house at all? What subterranean movement in my psyche had compelled me to follow such a strange whim? But there was David, leaving, so all I could do at that point was follow.

Idell did not say goodbye, she did not follow us to the door, she did not see us out. We just left.

Once we were in David's truck and he was turning around in the street, David leaned forward nearly onto his steering wheel.

"Seriously, Maddy, what the hell?" he began. "Do you have a plan that you're just not saying out loud, or are you actually maybe a little out of your mind?"

I nodded enthusiastically. "I really am maybe a little out of my mind. I don't have a solid conscious reason for this thing with Idell. I just . . . it just feels right. And I don't want to go into a big thing about how I relied on my instincts and my intuitions as an actor, but they stood me in good stead then and I trust them now. I mean, don't you think there might be some fireworks if Kell comes to the shop today and Idell is there?"

He drove in silence for a minute or two, but I could almost hear him thinking.

"Let me see if I've got this right," he said finally. "You

believe that Kell killed Bea because he wanted this book, because he loves books more than people, and now that Bea's body has been found, he wants to get rid of the book because . . . why?"

"He killed her because of the book, because he wanted it and she wouldn't give it to him," I told him. "Or, anyway, the book is something that ties him to Bea's death. And now he has to get rid of it because it's evidence. Plus, he's going to make a tidy profit, he thinks. Which is the main reason he collects first editions and rare books—to make money."

"Not because he loves books?"

"He does love books," I said. "But he loves them more as an investment than as literature, I think."

"Yeah, Jennifer was right." He leaned back and gave the truck a little more gas. "The entire plan, or lack thereof, is *completely* half-baked."

"Yes," I agreed emphatically. "But I have a feeling."

"A feeling about what?"

I looked out the window and watched the little spring scenes of the little Southern town fly by the truck's window: someone was planting coleus, someone else was mowing a lawn, kids rode bikes, other kids walked to school, and there was Mae Etta's diner, filled with breakfast customers.

"When I was a kid," I told David, "Rose and Philomena would tell me, once in a while, about the Mickey Mouse Club. They loved it when they were little. And every once in a while the Mickey Mouse Club would have what they called 'Anything Can Happen Day.' And do you know what happened on those days?"

"Anything?"

"That's right. There might be a ballet dancer or a science

experiment or some big surprise. And do you know what day today is?"

He smiled. "Don't say it."

"That's right," I said as we pulled up in front of the bookshop. "Today is Anything Can Happen Day."

28

THE SHOP SEEMED eerily quiet when we first stepped in. No customers, no Jennifer, and even Cannonball was nowhere in evidence. Like the whole house was waiting to see what was going to happen.

"More coffee, I think," David said, headed for the kitchen.

"Great, I'll have a triple," I said, sitting down at the business desk in the parlor.

"Triple?" David asked.

"Yeah," I turned on the bookshop laptop. "I didn't actually sleep last night."

"At all?"

"Right," I said. "My brain was wide awake. I think this almost entirely accounts for my odd ideas this morning. Including zipping off to Idell's house. And now I'm getting online to make an offer to booklover17 from... what should we call Jennifer?"

"What should we *call* her?" David seemed confused.

"We can't use her real name, can we?" I asked, logging on.

"Won't her credentials from the Tate Modern have her real name on them?" he asked.

"Oh." I looked up. "Right. So we'll just call her Jennifer, then."

"Since that's her name." He disappeared into the kitchen.

I returned my attention to the computer screen. There was a button that read "make an offer" but I was told I had to create an account. I wondered if Rose had created any sort of account, but it didn't seem likely. She'd run the bookshop without computers or even a credit card reader. All business was in person and in cash. Gone are the days. I figured out how to get a message to Kell through the site, but I didn't quite know how to bait him with the offer from the Tate Modern. Then I began to realize just how *many* holes there were in my so-called non-plan. So I amended.

"Hey?" I called out. "I'm having another deranged idea. Can you come in here and talk me out of it?"

"Can I get the coffee first?" he answered.

"Sure." I turned a little so that I could look out the window.

Lack of sleep, too much coffee, and an abundance of anxiety all combined to make me just about as amped up as I could ever remember being. I tried to use that energy as a shield against all the doubts that were circling me like rude carrion birds. It didn't completely succeed.

What if I was just wrong about Kell? How angry was I about to make the richest man within two hundred miles in any direction? What if I was right about Kell? What was to stop him from bashing *me* in the head?

I only fretted about that for ten seconds or so before David delivered my coffee in a mug. He set it down on one of the dozen coasters on the desk and stood silently for a moment.

"All right," he said finally. "What's your newest deranged idea?"

"I want to just call Kell directly," I said quickly. "I want to get him here in person, and that's going to take some persuasion, right? I mean, here he is thinking that he can just sell the book online without any fuss. But he needs to be here, obviously, to confess."

David tossed back his coffee. "What would your story be? What would you say to him?"

"Don't know," I said.

"And you don't even know for absolute certain that he is the person selling the book, do you?" he asked me.

"Who else from Hawkinsville, Georgia, would be selling a rare first edition?" I answered.

And then I picked up the bookshop phone and dialed Kell's number.

David glared. "You're calling him now?"

"Uh-huh." I heard the phone ring on the other end.

"You know his number by heart?" he asked.

"Actor mind," I said, tapping my temple. "I can memorize almost anything just by looking at it once. Almost."

He looked out the window. "That's a superpower."

Then Donna answered the phone in Kell Brady's house.

"Brady residence," she intoned.

"Donna, it's Madeline Brimley, calling on business," I said quickly.

"Business?" Silence.

"Yes." I switched the phone to my other ear. "A representative of the Tate Modern in London contacted me last night about a book that Mr. Brady apparently has for sale. For business reasons, she, this representative, wants to go through the Old Juniper Bookshop to buy the volume that Mr. Brady's selling."

"Yes?" More silence.

"So I'm calling as a kind of intermediary," I told her. "This person from the museum wants to set up a meeting here in the shop, for Mr. Brady's convenience. She wants to examine the book in person, and to meet the seller, so that she can give a full report to her bosses. I think she's a bit green. She sounded young over the phone. But her credentials seem genuine and she has been authorized to meet Mr. Brady's price, if she judges the book to be the genuine article."

"Why would we meet at your store?" Donna asked.

"Well, we've determined that the book was originally purchased through the Old Juniper," I said, trying to sound breezy. "So Miss Davis, that's her name: Jennifer Davis, she wants to... I believe her phrase was 'follow the provenance.'"

"Well, that's ridiculous," Donna complained.

"Be that as it may," I responded. "Would Mr. Brady be amenable to coming to the shop this afternoon, say, just after lunchtime? I've seen the certified check. Two hundred thousand dollars. Miss Davis is serious."

"It does not seem likely that Mr. Brady will want to visit your *shop* today," Donna said, clearly making fun of the word *shop*.

"Miss Davis is going back to London tonight." I hesitated. "She's trying to put together an exhibit they're calling 'Book Art and the Books that Inspired It' and she's already acquired some of the *Oz* books with the original illustrations. But if you don't think Mr. Brady would be interested in being a part of the exhibit..."

I trailed off, hoping Donna would change her attitude. She said nothing.

"Could you at least ask Mr. Brady if he'd be interested?" I asked her. "After all, the Tate Modern is one of the finest galleries in the world. And, if I may, has he had any other two-hundred-thousand-dollar offers for the book?"

She gave me a heavy sigh, and then, "One moment, please."

She set down the phone on her end. After that she was gone for about a decade. David mostly just stared at me and shook his head in disbelief. I finished my coffee, and waited, fidgeting without a single shred of patience.

At last Donna picked up the phone again.

"Mr. Brady and I will be there at precisely one o'clock this afternoon," she said tightly. "Please see to it that Miss Davis is present. With her cashier's check."

And Donna hung up.

I looked up at David. "He's coming."

"I have to say that I'm impressed and a little terrified at your improvisational skills," David said. "That was some *hefty* made-up stuff."

"Yes, *and* . . ." I mumbled.

"You do realize," he continued, "if it turns out that Kell Brady is *not* a stone-cold killer, which seems to me the most likely scenario by far, he will probably sue you and the Old Juniper so hard that you'll go out of business *twice*."

"Twice."

"Once right now," David said, louder, "but his ire will be so long and loud that it will actually reach into the past and also close down Rose's bookshop ten years ago. That's how powerful his lawsuit will be."

"That's a little apocalyptic, don't you think?"

"He's Mr. Great Big Moneybags," David told me, "and you're Little Miss Tiny Shop. You do the math."

I laughed. "Who am I now? 'Little Miss Tiny Shop'?"

"You know what I mean."

"I do." I stood. "So I'd better be right about this. If I lose the shop, Aunt Rose's ghost will never let me hear the end of it. Plus, I'll have no place to live. Homeless in Enigma doesn't seem like the kind of thing I could pull off."

"Not remotely," he agreed.

"So let's just not mention the fact," he said, more softly, "that if you're *right*, he might do something worse than sue you."

I touched his arm. "I may have mentioned that I didn't sleep at all last night. Instead, I did what Billy Sanders suggested, I just sat and thought. More than I already had. And when I did, I put two and two together and came up with theatre."

"I'm going to need a little more," he said patiently.

"*Hamlet*," I said.

He just stood there for a second, and then he said the words that made me like him more than I already did, which was considerable. He quoted Hamlet.

"'The play's the thing, wherein I'll catch the conscience of the king.' You really *do* hope to stage your odd scene and get Kell to confess. Or at the very least you'll watch Kell for signs of guilt as your improvisation plays out, and we'll nail him that way."

I almost cried. "I realize I'm mixing authors here," I told him, "but you make me think of P. G. Wodehouse. Someone in *The Code of the Woosters* calls Jeeves a specific dream-rabbit—and that's you."

He twitched slightly. "I'm a specific dream-rabbit? I don't know if I care for that."

I shook my head and made for the kitchen. "Well, you can't help being what you are. I'm making an omelet. Should I make it big enough for two?"

"What's going to be in this omelet?" He followed me into the kitchen.

"I have dried morels," I said, "and parsley from my garden. If the actual, *real* rabbits haven't eaten it all."

The kitchen was sunnier than usual; the slant of April sunshine made the room momentarily golden. But nothing gold can stay, as the poem says, and after only a few seconds, we stood in clear light and floating dust motes.

I put the dried morels in some warm water and got out four duck eggs, a recent present from Philomena. David volunteered to gather parsley, and seconds later he was in the backyard taking in the morning and gathering what the rabbits had left.

When he came back in, he stopped in the doorway.

"Do you mean to tell me," he said, standing there, "that you spent last night creating the scene we're about to . . . I guess the word is *perform*?"

"Not exactly," I said, cracking eggs into a silver mixing bowl. "I laid out the beats in my head, but the whole thing, in general, was a little impressionistic. I have the *idea* of a scene, not the *outline* of a scene, do you know what I mean?"

"I think so." He came into the kitchen then and set the parsley on the ancient wooden cutting board beside the stovetop. "You have the pieces in place, you just don't quite know how they're going to interact."

"Exactly," I said, delighted that he understood. "Of course I have to call Philomena in a minute, make sure she's here too."

"Not content with risking your life and well-being," he said, getting a knife to mince the parsley, "you want to put your dear old pseudo-aunt in jeopardy too."

"Right." I whisked the eggs and added salt, pepper, and tarragon. "Kell was kind of flirty with her, so I'm hoping that the presence of Philomena plus Idell will have some sort of disconcerting effect on Mr. Brady. Who is simultaneously influenced by and frightened of women in general. In my opinion."

"Okay," he said, glossing over my observation. "Then the players are, in no particular order, you and me, Jennifer playing someone else named Jennifer, Idell, Philomena, and Kell Brady."

"Don't forget Donna," I reminded him.

"She'll be here?"

"Of course," I said. "You don't expect Kell to drive himself. Besides, there's definitely more to her relationship with Kell than immediately meets the eye."

"Fine." He scooped up the minced parsley and sifted it into the bowl with the eggs. "So this motley crew assembles here, Jennifer pretends to buy the book from Kell—if, in fact, he brings it with him—and then what?"

"Idell confronts him, I think," I said. "Or Philomena asks an innocent question that sets off a chain of events."

"Or Kell discovers the truth of this little meeting," David said casually, "and beats us all to death with . . . what's in the shop that he could use to murder us all? Do you have a baseball bat lying around somewhere?"

"No," I said, checking the morels, "but Kell usually walks with a really solid cane."

"Right," he said. "So Mr. Hyde-Kell bops us all with his fancy cane."

"Worst-case scenario," I told him, draining the reconstituted morels, "yes."

"Just a thought," David suggested. "Should Billy Sanders be on hand for this?"

"Don't you think a police presence would have a dampening effect on Kell's enthusiasm for our little drama?"

I reached for the cast-iron skillet, put it over a burner on high, lightly sprinkled it with olive oil, and waited for a wisp of smoke.

"Don't you think," he countered, "that an ounce of prevention is worth a pound of cure? Especially if the cure in this case is Billy Sanders trying to figure out who murdered us all in your bookshop?"

"If you're going to convince me of anything," I told him in no uncertain terms, "you're going to have to do better than a two-dollar cliché."

I poured the eggs into the hot skillet, waited for five seconds, then put the morels all over half of the omelet. It didn't take long for it to set, and I folded it. Moments later we were sitting at the kitchen table.

"Even dried, morels are amazing," David mumbled after his first bite.

"Even dried," I agreed.

A very few moments later, David was clearing and cleaning in the kitchen while I was calling Phil from the parlor desk.

"Good morning," she chirped when she answered her phone.

"Hey, Phil, it's me," I said.

"No," she said instantly.

"What do you mean, no?" I asked. "I haven't even—"

"You're calling to get me to do something with you that I don't want to do and that will take me away from my classes and get me into trouble."

I only paused for a second. "Right."

"Then *that's* what I mean when I say *no*."

"I don't need you until one o'clock and you don't have afternoon classes," I said. "So take a late lunch and come over to the shop."

"Why?" She sounded spectacularly suspicious.

"So you can witness Kell Brady confess to Bea Glassie's murder."

That had a nice solid sound to it, but it struck Philomena momentarily dumb.

"I think I'm hanging up now," she told me after a minute.

"David's here," I said quickly. "We made up. Also Idell, Jennifer, and almost certainly Donna Dukes."

"Oh." She gave out with a little laugh. "The gang's all here."

"Or will be," I said, "if you come too. At one o'clock."

"I don't know," she hedged. "It sounds like it might be an uncomfortable encounter."

"Oh, it will definitely be uncomfortable," I assured her. "Also potentially disastrous and possibly fatal. You *have* to come."

Without missing a beat she said suddenly, "You and David made up?"

"We did." I tried hard not to sound like a high school girl, but I don't think I succeeded.

"What about your poor fireman?" she said in faux lament. "Is he just off your list?"

"Well," I demurred, "I guess I *could* have a backup plan . . ."

"Madeline Brimley!" she chided, but she was laughing.

"So are you coming over here," I asked, "or do I have to come and drag you out of your office?"

"Oh, dear," she said, still laughing a little. "I suppose I *do* have to come, if that's your attitude."

"At one o'clock."

"Stop saying the time," she said. "I'll be there. Now let me go to my first class."

She hung up without saying goodbye.

"Phil's in!" I called out to David. "And I'll phone Idell in a second."

He emerged from the kitchen wiping his hands on his jeans.

"Okay," he said, "what do we have to do to set up for your little extravaganza?"

"All the players are in position," I said. "I just have to keep myself from thinking about it anymore until everyone is here. Because if I think about it I'll either realize what a bad idea this is and call it off, or I'll come up with some sort of ad hoc plan that will just mess up the natural flow of events. So why don't you go to work this morning and just come back here around twelve thirty? I'm going to work in the garden. I have squash plants and jalapeños to put in the ground."

"Oh." He looked around like he'd momentarily lost something. "Okay. Good. Frank and I still have some meadow work to do."

"There you go."

He stood there for a second, and I realized he didn't quite know how to say goodbye.

"David?" I said softly. "I'm really glad we figured some stuff out last night."

He smiled. "Is that what we did?"

I went to him and put my arms around his neck. "I'm pretty sure that's what we did."

Then there was a kiss that made me dizzy and struck me blind. I had no idea how it affected David. By the time I recovered my eyesight, he was gone.

29

WHEN APRIL, WITH sweet showers, pierces the drought of March to the root, some people want to travel. They've been shut up in their houses all winter and they want to get out. But that's a concept that applies more to other parts of the world than it does to the Deep South. I was happy to be at home and garden. Winter had left Enigma by the end of February. We'd already had a day in the nineties. I was close to harvesting my first tomatoes. So on that particular day in April, I sat beside one of the raised beds in my backyard garden smiling and sweating. The direct sun felt like a hundred degrees, but the breeze, still politely vernal, was as cooling as ice water. I was surrounding my yellow squash plants with marjoram, dill, and borage. The marjoram repelled squash bugs, the dill attracted beneficial wasps, and the borage had a nice edible flower. I'd always thought of companion plants as good casting choices for the supporting roles. The star was the squash, which, if properly cooked with slightly caramelized onions and home-made chicken broth, was one of my favorite summer dishes.

In short I was doing what I'd done when I was a child and visiting my aunt Rose at the Old Juniper Bookshop and, upset about something or other in my so-called real life, I was distracting myself with agriculture.

So I was startled out of said distraction by Philomena's voice as she came out of the back door.

"Well, I'm here!" Dripping with exasperation. "What exactly is it you think I can do?"

I smoothed the soil over the last of the borage and stood up.

"It's not just you," I said, walking toward her. "You're going to be one of a quartet of women, besides Donna, who will surround and intimidate Kell Brady until he buckles."

"And by *buckles* you mean *confesses*?"

"That's right," I said.

"And who are the other two women," she asked, "besides you and me?"

"I told you," I said, gathering with her at the back door. "Jennifer, masquerading as a representative of the Tate Modern, and none other than Idell Glassie."

"Idell is really coming?"

"She said she was," I told her as we both went into the kitchen. "Is it one o'clock already?"

"Twelve thirty," she said. "I came early. Why is Idell coming?"

"Because I told her that Kell killed her sister," I said, going for a glass of water.

"She doesn't believe that."

"Probably not," I agreed, running the water for a moment before filling my glass. "She may be coming just to see me embarrassed by my ridiculous accusation."

"Which may well be the actual case," Phil chided.

"Maybe." I downed the entire glass. "It's hot out there in the direct sun."

"Don't be ridiculous," she said. "It's only April. July is hot, not April."

We heard the front door open then, immediately followed by Jennifer calling out, "Hello?"

"In the kitchen," I answered.

Seconds later Jennifer appeared, but if I hadn't known it was her, I would have thought that a stranger had walked into my house, her appearance was so fundamentally different. She was wearing a black business suit with black flats, her hair was pulled back in a bun, and horn-rimmed glasses transformed her face. The perfect finishing touch was her Tate Modern lanyard.

"Perfect costume!" I told her enthusiastically.

"I feel like an adult," she said.

"You look like an adult, sweetheart," Philomena said.

"It's freaking me out." Jennifer fidgeted. "Is there coffee?"

I fetched the French press and set about making some. Phil and Jennifer sat at the kitchen table.

"I've been practicing what I want to say," Jennifer said nervously. "But when I said it out loud in my dorm room, my roommate told me that I sounded like an idiot."

"You're probably thinking too much about it," I said, grinding the coffee beans. "After introductions, all you need to say is 'Let me see the book.' If he's got it with him and he hands it to you, all you have to do is examine it, silently, and then agree to pay him."

"I don't need to talk about my work at the museum?" she asked. "Or why I was in Atlanta, or why I looked online and saw his ad for the book? Or why I drove all the way to Enigma for it?"

"Let him ask those questions before you give him your

answers," I said. "But I don't think he'll ask. He just wants to get rid of the book. And make two hundred thousand dollars."

"I think I have stage fright," Jennifer confessed to Philomena.

"I had that when I was about to go in front of my first class," Phil answered, "after I got out of the looney bin. You know what I did?"

"What?" Jennifer responded.

"I took a diazepam," Phil answered, reaching into the purse she had over one arm. "Do you want one?"

"God, no," Jennifer said. "My roommate asked me if I wanted to get stoned. Now you're offering me . . . what is diazepam?"

"And I was going to see if you wanted tequila," I said.

She glared at me for a second before she realized that I was kidding.

Then I leaned into Jennifer and whispered a very specific instruction in her ear. Jennifer nodded and reached into the inside breast pocket of her coat.

Philomena watched us for a moment and then shrugged, opened her purse, found a prescription bottle, opened it, poured out a little pill, and popped it into her mouth.

"More for me," she said after she swallowed.

We heard the front door again then.

"Hey?" David called out.

"Kitchen," I answered.

"Everybody's early," Phil said to no one.

David appeared. He was in his work clothes—jeans, T-shirt, work boots—but they were relatively clean.

"Coffee?" I asked him.

"At least," he said, coming to the table.

"I'm having diazepam," Phil volunteered cheerfully.

"Your girlfriend offered me tequila," Jennifer said accusingly.

David smiled my way. "Are you my girlfriend?"

"No!" I said firmly. "Because, as I have repeatedly said, in one way or another, I'm not a high school girl."

"Touchy," Jennifer said to Phil.

"I *know*." Phil giggled . . . a little like a high school girl.

David deliberately examined the condition of my clothes. "You put in your squash plants?"

"I should change," I said, realizing that I had dirt on my jeans, my shirt, and my hands.

"I'll finish making the coffee," David volunteered.

I headed upstairs without further small talk.

Sunlight was streaming in through my bedroom window, and the breeze wafted the sheer white curtains. They looked like an angel's wings. I took a second to examine my own preshow jitters. I wasn't nervous exactly. I rarely had anything like stage fright. In fact, I usually depended on the little bump of adrenaline I got from the anticipation of going onstage. I liked it. But this was different.

I'd avoided any real examination of the possible consequences of the scene that was about to be enacted downstairs. I didn't have any idea about the finer legal points involved in offering to buy something that you really had no intention of paying for, but Kell certainly seemed like the kind of person who would sue in the event of such a phenomenon. Sue *hard*. But it seemed unlikely that he would actually kill anyone in the bookshop, even with Donna's help, since it would be two against four—assuming Idell would be on our side.

Then I had a few seconds of realizing what a ridiculous, weird, far-fetched thing I'd set in motion. Why had I done it?

Was it just because I was worried about Gloria? Or because my relationship with David had finally made some progress and I was momentarily out of my mind? Was I out of my mind?

That kind of anxiety made me put on a dress. It was a light cotton, springtime item, pale blue and girlish. But I took it off the second I got it on and went for the charcoal Ann Taylor business suit that made me look like I worked in the same office where Jennifer's imaginary character worked.

I was out of my room and halfway down the stairs when Idell came barreling in through the front door. She was dressed in a black collar-to-floor dress that made her look like one of the maiden aunts in *Arsenic and Old Lace*.

"Well," she announced when she saw me. "I'm here."

The rest of the crew heard and came into the parlor from the kitchen. I finished walking down the stairs in silence, and we all stood there staring for a lot longer than we should have.

Finally Idell said, "I'm not sure *why* I'm here."

I started to answer but Phil took over.

"You are here, Idell, to hear Kell Brady confess to the murder of your sister," Phil told her in no uncertain terms.

And contrary to all my expectations, Idell just nodded.

"I didn't want to think about that," she said very softly. "But it was on my mind from the moment I heard that Bea's bones were dug up."

The way she said "dug up" made me a little sick to my stomach. There was so much packed into those two syllables: rage, regret, loss.

"Kell isn't a human being," Idell went on, "so far as I understand the definition of *human*. He doesn't have regular emotions. He's entirely devoid of empathy or consideration. And what he knows about women wouldn't fill a thimble."

Before anyone could stop her, Phil said, "So you *do* think he killed your sister?"

And once again, I could not have anticipated Idell's response.

"Maybe with Donna's help." She had her eyes closed.

"That Donna is a strange one," Phil said dizzily, the diazepam obviously kicking in sooner than I might have expected.

"Yeah," David joined in, not quite knowing what to say. "What is her deal? Donna's always been a mystery to me."

Idell opened her eyes. "You don't know about Donna?"

We all just stared at her.

"Are you going to offer me a seat?" Idell went on, slightly irritated.

"Oh, my God," I said instantly, "of course. Please come into the parlor."

The bookshop boasted some extremely comfy chairs and sofas and love seats throughout, but the best in my opinion was the antique green sofa in the parlor not far from the business desk. It was sometimes where I did my homework as a child, sometimes where I slept as an adolescent, and seemed to be Rose's favorite.

I guided Idell to the sofa and sat beside her. Everyone else found a chair, dragged it a little closer to the sofa, sat, and waited.

"Do you want coffee?" I asked Idell. "Or tea?"

"No, thank you," she said a little stiffly.

"So about Donna," Phil prompted.

"Donna." Idell clasped her hands in her lap and nodded. "She was married to Kell's younger brother who died in a boating accident, a deep-sea fishing adventure that they were all on. Donna was legally dead too. Drowned. The Coast

Guard revived her, but she never fully recovered. She didn't remember her own name, barely knew where she was, didn't know anything about the accident. This was sometime in the 1980s, if I'm remembering this correctly. And in spite of what I've just said about Kell, he took her in, gave her a place to stay and work to occupy her mind. What there is left of it. She's not quite a real human being either."

Idell sat back, and it slowly dawned on me that she saw her entire world through a strange lens made of loneliness, remorse, and petty ironies, a lens that made most things seem a little unreal. Because she couldn't understand or explain a lot of things that had happened to her over the course of a fairly long lifetime. I found myself having an overwhelming sense of empathy toward her, even though I didn't want to. She was virtually the definition of the *old maid*, that bad old term. She'd been controlled by a distant father, confused by the love of a wealthy man who was probably just like her father, and betrayed by her only ally in the world, a sister who was bolder and more aggressive in five minutes than Idell would ever be in her entire lifetime.

A short fantasy of what had actually happened between her and Kell suddenly assaulted my imagination. She hadn't told Kell no, she'd just told him she needed a little time to process his proposal, because it took her so much by surprise. But by the time she'd figured out that she did, indeed, want to marry him, it was too late. Bea had taken over. Because Bea always took over.

Unfortunately, Phil was full steam ahead. "You just didn't want to come face-to-face with the idea that the man you wanted to marry would kill the sister that *you* wanted to kill. That's why you focused your accusations on Gloria Coleman, even though you know she didn't do it."

That plunged the room into a dark silence, and for a while no one even moved.

Finally Idell looked at me. "While I do not have much respect for her profession, I do have a lot of respect for Dr. Waldrop as a person. She's endured a raft of hardships. But if she continues to speak to me in that manner, I will not stay in this house."

"Phil—" I began.

"Right." Philomena made the zipping-her-lips motion across her face and sat back primly.

"So this Donna is nuts?" Jennifer said, out of nowhere. "And she's coming here today too?"

"I think so," I said. "But she's not *nuts*, exactly."

"Oh, I think she is," Idell said instantly. "I'd never put it that way, but there is something very wrong with her."

At that, we heard a car pull up in front of the shop.

"They're here," Phil whispered excitedly.

"What should we do?" Jennifer asked, looking around at all of us.

David stood. "I should wait in the kitchen. I think Kell might be less inclined to bad behavior if he's dealing with a room full of women. Just a thought."

"You read my mind," I said. "But you're going to keep an ear out."

"If anything goes wrong," he said, "I'll be in like a flash."

He gave me a hug that made me dizzy for a second, then he went to the kitchen.

We heard car doors slam outside. We heard footsteps coming up the stairs. We all watched the door. And when it creaked open, there they were.

Kell was dressed in the most expensive suit in the world. I recognized it from pictures the cast had been shown when

I was in a huge production of *Art* at the Alliance Theatre in Atlanta. It was a Stuart Hughes and Richard Jewels collaboration, a thousand hours in the making, five hundred actual diamonds on the jacket made of cashmere, silk, and wool. And priced north of eight hundred thousand dollars. For one suit.

Donna was similarly decked out in some sort of funereal black suit that looked, foolishly, like silk pajamas. She wore an expensive messenger bag, polished black leather, over one shoulder.

Jennifer, filled with the elation of opening night, launched herself off the sofa, hand outstretched, and raced to greet the couple.

"Jennifer Davis," she said in an extremely ill-advised version of an English accent.

Kell took her hand. "Kellman Brady."

"Thank you for coming." I rushed toward them.

That's when Kell noticed Idell.

Everything stopped for a moment: language, motion, time. Kell and Idell stared at each other in a moment entirely removed from normal reality.

But it was only one moment, and Donna destroyed it almost immediately.

"We would like to see the check, Miss Davis," she said, hard as granite.

Jennifer feigned astonishment and continued in her unfortunate accent. "All in good time, my dear woman. I would never dream of forgoing the proprieties. Please. Let's sit."

It was such a surreal moment—made odder by hearing Jennifer say the phrase "my dear woman" in a voice like Judi Dench.

"And my employers would never allow me to show you the check before I saw the book." Jennifer shot me a glance, and then reached into her coat and produced her cell phone. "You don't mind if I record this transaction for my employers."

She held the phone up, turned on the voice recorder, and waited.

"Of course not, dear," Kell said with an air of demonstrable magnanimity.

"May I see the book then?" Jennifer smiled, putting the phone down on the coffee table in front of the green sofa.

Kell paused for the merest of seconds before he said simply, "Donna?"

Donna didn't move for a moment, then, reluctantly, reached into her messenger bag and produced the book.

"There it is," Idell whispered.

Before anyone knew what was happening, Idell was on her feet. She flew forward with a speed that defied reality, grabbed the book out of Donna's hand, and clutched it to her chest as if it might save her life.

"We loved this book, my sister and I," she said, barely above a whisper. "When we were little we had a copy. Not the first edition, of course—just a book that our mother gave us. Father was displeased. He said that the stories weren't for young ladies. They were filled with too much violence. Too much suggested sexuality. I guess that's why we hid it away. I guess that's why we loved it so much."

She closed her eyes and smiled. I think it was the first time I ever saw Idell smile.

Kell stared in wonder at Idell's face.

But Donna was all business.

"Give the young woman that book, Idell," she said, cold as a glacier. "Don't make me take it away from you."

Idell's eyes opened slowly. "You could never take this book

away from me." She turned a burning look toward Kell. "Or my sister."

"Idell—" Kell began.

"Did you know that Rose already had this book in the shop?" Idell asked me. "I found it one day when Rose was busy and I was drifting. And there it was, the sin of my childhood, the book of books. In the baffling section of books that aren't for sale in this place that sells books. The section Rose always called her 'illegitimate children,' for some reason. The so-called rare and collectible section. No telling how many years it sat there, unrecognized. Did you know that, Kell? Did you know that this book was in this shop all along? I only found it a little more than six months ago."

Kell opened his mouth to speak, but nothing came out. We were all staring at Idell as if her body might have been taken over by a wandering spirit.

"But when I asked Rose about it," Idell went on, almost in a dream, "she said what she always said. 'Those books aren't for sale.' So I told Bea about it. I didn't call her on the telephone. I went to her house. It was the first time we'd spoken in years and years. But I had to tell her that our book was here, didn't I?"

Jennifer nodded silently, as if the question had been addressed to her.

Idell looked at me, and if I hadn't known better, I would have said that there was kindness in her eyes.

"That was after Rose succumbed to her illnesses," she said to me, softly, "and the shop was closed. But that sweet little Tandy Fletcher was here in the shop sometimes. Of course, Tandy didn't stand a chance against Bea. I can imagine Bea charging into this place and bossing that poor girl around like nobody's business. And in the end Bea made her look it up, our book, on the computer, to see how much it was worth. I wasn't with Bea the day that she came here to purchase it, but she told me that she paid eighty thousand dollars for it. She would have paid eight hundred thousand."

"I offered her twice that," Kell said, finally finding his voice.

"Mr. Brady—" Donna began.

But it was too late. Kell was caught up in Idell's dreamy soliloquy.

"When I saw that book," he said, only to Idell, "I couldn't believe it. It completed my Grimm collection. You know what I'm talking about, Idell. You know I have what most collectors believe to be the finest collection of Grimm volumes in the world. I have one that John F. Kennedy wrote in. I have another that Joseph Campbell signed to his wife, Jean. But Bea wouldn't let go of this particular volume, this prize."

"Mr. *Brady*," Donna tried again, "I really have to insist—"

But Idell's voice rose up.

"That was Bea's book!" She held it aloft as if it might be a weapon. "She would never have given it to you. Not for any amount of money. Why do you have it now?"

Kell was up. "She wouldn't give it to me!"

"That's what I know!" Idell's voice was louder than I'd ever heard. "So why are you here trying to sell this book, Kell? Especially if it actually completed your Grimm collection?"

Kell turned to Jennifer for some reason. Maybe it was because she was the only stranger in the room.

"You have to understand—Miss Davis, was it?" He was clearly making a serious effort to sound reasonable. "*I* came here with Bea that day, the day she purchased this book, because I was going to make a counteroffer. But that stupid little girl wouldn't hear me out. She said she'd promised to sell it to Bea and that was that. And Bea was, well, quite upset with me for trying to usurp her . . . her bid."

Kell's logic or diction or memory seemed to be abandoning him, and there was a small but noticeable bit of sweat at his hairline.

"We began to argue, you see," he kept going. "Bea and I began to argue. It made the little girl uncomfortable. She took Bea's check and told us that the transaction was complete. That it was the end of the day. That she was closing the shop. That we were to exit the premises. She ushered us out in such a rude manner—I had a few choice words for her, I can tell you."

Donna stood then and took Kell's elbow.

"I think we're going home now, Mr. Brady," she said, tugging his arm.

He raised his elbow and sidestepped. "Before I sell the book? Not really. Now, Idell, give the book to Miss Davis."

Idell clutched the book tighter. "Why do you have this book, Kell?"

"Well, that stupid little girl, as I was saying, herded us out and locked the door behind us," Kell answered, his voice higher. "She told us we weren't really supposed to be there. And anyway it was getting dark and she wanted to leave. And then we saw her leave across the back field out there. I guess she'd gone out the back door, hadn't she? So, anyway, there we were, Bea and I, out on the porch here—Donna was sitting in the car, that Mercedes limousine that Dr. Waldrop seems to like so well, in fact, and one thing led to another. That's all."

He stopped talking. He seemed to think that his story was complete. Donna took his arm again.

"Let's *go*, Kell!" she said, almost commanding him.

"You fought," I said to Kell.

I could see it clear as day, but I wanted Kell to say it out loud, especially for Idell to hear.

"We did." He was still trying to sound reasonable. "We stood out there on that very porch, and she was clutching the book in more or less the same way as Idell is now. So I grabbed it. Did I mention that we'd been drinking? Bea and I, of course. Not Donna. But Bea and I were quite replete with gin martinis. The secret of my martinis is that they're half and half: half gin, half sweet vermouth, with extra bitters, so they go down without a fight. Bea preferred them that way."

"You fought," I said again. It had worked the first time.

"I grabbed the book," he said, "she grabbed it back, it was like some ridiculous tango for a moment there. Until."

"Kell!" Donna had both hands on his upper arm and she was trying to drag him away from the conversation. From *his* conversation.

"Until what, Kell?" I asked, but it sounded more like an accusation than a question.

"Bea fell." He exhaled the words as if he'd been holding his breath for six months.

"Bea fell?" I repeated.

"She took a tumble backward, yes," he said as if it had been a harmless toppling of some sort. "I had the book in my hands. And there she was at the bottom of the porch steps, her head positioned at a decidedly improper angle."

"We're going!" Donna tugged hard and Kell nearly fell, but it was clear that Donna was just about to take Kell away—far away.

I moved. "You're not going anywhere."

"Oh," Donna assured me, "yes, we are."

She dragged Kell a few feet closer to the exit. Philomena made a squeaking sound; Jennifer's breathing was louder.

You can learn a lot about real fighting from stage combat instructions, and with Donna it was easy because she was already off balance trying to pull Kell.

All I did was put my foot behind her left ankle and pop the flat of my hand against her chest. She fell backward like a saw-cut pine. She landed on the floor with a thud that knocked the breath out of her, and she was momentarily incapacitated.

"Bea didn't just fall," I snarled. "You hit her with your cane."

"I may have hit her." He looked down at Donna. "Then pushed her a bit, as you just did to Donna."

"No, it was an accident," Donna managed to say from her place on the floor. "He didn't mean it."

"You hit her," I said through my teeth. "And then she was dead."

"She was dead," he agreed, still showing no sign of any emotion.

"Why did you bury her here in the yard?" Phil whispered.

"Oh. Well." Kell actually smiled. "This front yard had always been a mess, as you know. That particular day it had been raining and the yard was deep in mud. Bea was filthy with it, you understand, so there was never a question of putting her in the Mercedes. It was actually Donna's suggestion that we give her a final resting place here."

"No." But Donna still couldn't quite manage to get up.

"I had some things in the trunk of the limo," Kell went on, "that I had planned to take over to the opera house: a couple of shovels and a few bags of QUIKRETE. It was Donna's idea that the ground was too muddy to just leave it alone because the body would be exposed in the next rain. So QUIKRETE it was. Dug, buried, packed and solid in under an hour, can you imagine?"

Donna managed to sit up. "This doesn't mean anything. If you tell anyone about this, it's your word against ours. The richest man in Georgia against a gaggle of ridiculous women. I like our chances."

She steadied herself, about to stand.

Jennifer stepped forward then, her poorly realized accent gone. "You could say that, I guess. Except for the fact that my phone has been recording us ever since you got here, if you recall. Just like Madeline asked me to."

She reached down to the top of the coffee table and produced exhibit A, her phone.

"In fact," she said, "it's *still* recording. Do you have anything else to say?"

Before Donna—or Kell—could answer, David emerged from the kitchen.

"I've just called Officer Sanders," he said calmly. "He's on his way now."

30

EVERYTHING AFTER THAT was a blur of activity; it seemed entirely unconnected with any sort of reality.

Billy showed up first, I guess, then Baxter and Baker, and then two plainclothes policemen from Hawkinsville whom Billy had called.

Kell didn't quite understand what was happening, but he seemed happy to be the center of attention, swanning on, answering questions and telling stale jokes.

Donna, on the other hand, just kept saying "Wait" over and over again, and a lot of light had gone out of her eyes.

In the end, Kell left with Baxter and Baker, Donna was taken away by the policemen from Hawkinsville, and Idell sat down on my favorite sofa to look at her favorite book.

Billy ended up at the kitchen table with the rest of us.

"There's paperwork to do," Billy told us, sipping coffee, "but they said that Reverend Coleman *will* be ready for pickup by noon."

"I'll go get her," I snapped.

"Well," he said slowly, "I'm going to go get her, but you can come with me if you want to."

"You do realize," Jennifer said to him, clearly amped up

from her performance, "that *Madeline* is the one who figured all of this out. And she's the one who suggested that I record everything, so you have solid evidence."

"Uh-huh," he said, "tell me one more time that you absolutely asked Kell if it was okay to record him *before* anything happened."

"Oh, my Lord, Billy," Philomena chided, "how many times do we have to tell you that?"

"I just don't want anything to go wrong with this," he said patiently, "and sometimes a lawyer will get a recording thrown out of court if there was no consent to record."

"You have at least four witnesses," David said. "And even Idell might testify."

Philomena lowered her voice. "Did you see the way Idell looked when she sat down to read the Grimm Brothers?"

I nodded. "I've *never* seen that look on her face. Nothing like it."

"And I'm worried about Donna," Phil fretted. "I'm afraid she might need a little help now."

"Your sort of help, you mean?" I asked. "Psychological."

"Don't you think?" Phil asked.

Jennifer stood up suddenly. "I'm going home to write this in my journal! All of this!"

"Jennifer," I said, "I want to say how proud of you I am, if that doesn't sound condescending or something. You were just great in all of this."

"It was so cool!" She was close to jumping up and down. "Thank you so much for getting me into this."

Phil, clearly a little concerned about Jennifer's heightened state, stood up too.

"Would you like a ride back to the dorm, sweetheart?" she asked Jennifer. "I have to get back to the college."

"I have my Vespa." Jennifer looked around the table. "Wasn't this amazing, everything that happened?"

"It was," I said. "You can take the rest of the day off, obviously."

"Not a chance!" she roared. "I'm going to change, write some stuff in my journal, and I'll be back. When people find out what happened here, we're going to have a *ton* of business!"

"All right, dear," Phil said, using a tone of voice that might ordinarily have been saved for a child.

They left side by side, Jennifer still talking and Philomena still offering calm replies.

"I'll be surprised if Jennifer comes back today," I said to Billy and David. "When she gets to her room and sits down on her bed to change her clothes, the adrenaline will start to wear off, and she'll just fall asleep."

They both laughed, but the laughter was mostly perfunctory.

David stood then. "I guess I'll get to work, then. You're both going to pick up Gloria pretty soon?"

"If we leave now," Billy said, "we can be there when she comes out of the holding cell. Soon as I finish my coffee. I'm still not quite awake."

"I'm ready now," I said.

"Walk me to the door first?" David suggested.

I was up and by his side before he cleared the corner of the table.

In the parlor, Idell looked up.

"I love this book," she said to me as we approached her.

"Do you want to keep it?" I ventured. "Your sister paid for it fair and square. I guess that makes it yours now, right?"

"Oh, no," Idell told me, closing the book and bringing herself to her feet. "I know just where this book belongs."

With that she headed for the dining room and the smaller room beyond it where all the not-for-sale volumes slept.

"I'm going to put this back right where I found it," she told me over her shoulder. "That way I'll know where it is when I need it. You've seen my house. It's a bit . . . overwhelmed."

Remembering the hoarder atmosphere of her place, I just nodded.

"And then I'm on my way," Idell continued, trundling toward the back bookcases in the other room. "You can tell that Coleman woman I'm sorry, I suppose. But I'll be around at her church on Sunday to tell her myself. I owe her that."

She didn't sound sorry. She sounded irritated that she'd have to *say* she was sorry. Still, it was something.

Idell vanished into the shadows; David and I stood at the front door.

"Well," he said, not looking at me. "This has been a packed couple of days."

"Yes it has," I agreed. "But my favorite part is that people in this town are going to begin referring to us as 'an item.'"

"They are?" He smiled.

"They are if I have any say about it," I assured him.

"Okay," he said, "I'm leaning in for a kiss, then."

And he did. And I did. And we did.

And then he was gone.

"He's a lovely young man," Idell said from the shadows.

"Isn't he?" I asked, deliberately keeping myself from sounding too . . . dreamy.

She emerged from the darkness, shuffling through the dining room toward me.

"You said you had the new Sofie Kelly book," she said, more or less back to her usual self. "At a discount."

At a discount. All the money in the world and probably

about to get a lot more from her sister's estate, and she still wanted a two-dollar discount.

"I set it aside for you especially," I told her, going to the desk. "Put it on your account?"

"With the discount," she asserted.

"Yes."

I opened a lower drawer and produced the volume. Idell took it without looking at me or saying a word, and then she wheeled away, out the door, down the stairs, across the bitter lawn, and away.

Billy appeared seconds later.

"Okay," he said, his jaw set. "Let's go get your friend out of jail."

I patted my pocket to make sure I had my wallet, got my keys, and made for the front door.

"If I had a nickel for every time someone said *that* to me," I told him.

"Theatre people," he harrumphed. "You're just this side of carny folk."

"And proud of it," I told him. "Are you taking your car or mine?"

AND so it was that, next Sunday afternoon, Gloria Coleman and I were sitting on my front porch looking out over the ruins of my front yard, sans, at last, the yellow police tape.

"Nice sermon today," I mumbled, mimosa in hand.

"Nice crowd too," she agreed, hoisting her mimosa into the air. "Everybody loves a jailbird priest."

"Were you surprised to see Idell there?"

"You know she spoke with me afterward," Gloria said, sipping.

"She told me that she would. She apologized?"

"Not in the traditional sense." Gloria laughed. "She handed me a check, a donation to the church."

"Oh." I turned her way. "How much, do you mind my asking?"

"Eighty thousand dollars," Gloria said.

I almost choked. "What?"

Gloria finished her mimosa. "That's right, the exact amount her sister paid for a certain book from this shop."

"That's quite an apology," I said, still trying to get my mind around the dollar amount.

"Yes, it is." Gloria laughed. "She didn't really say much about it. But I think it was a perfect example of putting her money where her mouth was."

"I would say so, yes." I looked at her empty glass. "Another one of those?"

"At least."

We both reluctantly left our front porch chairs, made it inside, and steered for the kitchen.

As I pulled the pitcher of mimosas out of the fridge, Gloria cleared her throat.

"I'm eventually going to find a way to thank you, by the way," she said quietly. "I knew you would figure this all out and get me sprung."

"You could help me plant the roses in front of the house like you were going to," I suggested.

"Not on your life," she said cheerfully. "Hire a service. I'll give you the number for the guys who are going to take care of the church grounds from now on, thanks to a recent, generous donation."

"I thought you did that kind of work yourself," I said, pouring into her glass.

"I *did*," she said, "but after this experience, I'm not going to be digging anything up for a while. Not even for roses."

I poured the last of the pitcher into my glass. "Fair enough."

MY aunt's roses, Ophelia's Last Laugh, were planted—by a service, thanks to another generous donation, this one from Gloria—on April 26th, Shakespeare's alleged birthday. There was a ceremony. It was Gloria's idea. I was surprised by the number of people who showed up. There must have been thirty people there, most of whom had never been in the shop.

Jennifer was in attendance even though I hadn't required her to be. And her date was not the flirty dreamboat Hedge Anderson. It was the computer elf, Josh. Which made me happy for some reason.

Baxter and Baker were also there; don't ask me why. They only said hello and then stood quietly beside Billy, who was dressed in a suit, for the entire ceremony.

And Idell came with Mae Etta—two sides of an odd, small-town coin, both dressed in black and silent as the grave.

David stood beside me. He also wore a suit. Shaved, hair combed, dress shoes—Phil later told me that she thought he looked like James Bond. But he didn't. He looked just like David.

Phil stood beside me too, dabbing her eyes and sniffing a little because of what was being said.

I had on a spring dress that Aunt Rose had sent me for the opening night of my first play in New York. It was a Michael Kors little black dress. She said I'd need it for all sorts of occasions. This seemed like one.

"We're here today," Gloria began, full voiced, "to dedicate these lovely roses to three women. First to Rose Brimley, the founder of this bookshop and the creator of this hybrid. Second to Dr. Philomena Waldrop, who inspired Rose to create these beautiful things. And third, to Beatrice Glassie, in whose loving memory her sister, Idell, has donated the plaque which we have just attached to the porch."

Here Gloria's voice dropped down to a confidential volume.

"Frankly," she said, "it's *got* to be the strangest dedication of flowers I've ever seen. It says, 'My sister Marlene gathered all my bones, tied them in a silken scarf, and laid them beneath the juniper tree.'"

Some laughed. I didn't.

When the ceremony was over, almost everyone came into the shop for lemonade and cookies; it filled up the place with a soothing chamber music of small talk and laughter. Cannonball presided benignly.

As the day slowly drew to a close, most of the attendees drifted away. David, Phil, Gloria, and I found ourselves in the gazebo sipping lemonade and silently watching the night come on.

"I still don't understand," Phil said suddenly, shifting uneasily on the bench.

"Understand what?" I asked her.

"I see how Kell and Bea could have argued so irresponsibly," she mused, "because they'd been drinking. But it's hard to figure what happened next. How could they have done what they did, Kell and Donna? Why didn't they call Billy or someone and just say what happened? Why bury poor Bea in the ground right there and then? And why use *concrete*, for heaven's sake?"

"When I was drinking," Gloria said, "and I mean *really*

drinking, I would often look back on the morning after the night before and think to myself, 'What did I *do*?' And then, in the cold light of day, it was too late. I'd already done something monumentally stupid with little or no way to rectify it."

"I think it has more to do with a rich man's entitlement," David said. "Especially a narcissist like Kell. He might not even have considered that he did anything wrong. And then Donna, who is clearly some kind of sociopath, enabled or supported that feeling, right?"

"Here's what I think," I announced. "I think that asking *why* something happened is almost always folly. I believe in *is*. *Is* has a lot more reality to it than *why*."

David started to sip his lemonade, then lowered his glass and said, "I think you might have to explain that a little more."

"Ask anybody who ever dealt with a two-year-old for very long," I told him. "*Why* is a never-ending question. Why is the sky blue? Sure, you can go into a long scientific explanation of Rayleigh scattering, but when you're done a two-year-old will still ask why."

"What's Rayleigh scattering?" Phil asked.

"Sunlight is scattered in every direction," David said, "by all the gases and particles in the air. Blue light is in shorter waves, so it's scattered more than the other colors."

"Where did you learn that?" Gloria asked.

"All my life I've tried to learn more about the poetry of science and physics," he said, grinning, "just so I can say something like that in a conversation and sound smart."

"You do sound smart," Gloria admitted.

"And it is poetry," I said. "Scattered particles of light making my sky blue—that's poetry. But my point is that you tell a two-year-old, 'It just *is* blue, that's all.' Nine times out of ten the kid will be satisfied with that as an answer. I'm not going to think too much about why Kell did what he did."

"I'm more worried about Idell," Gloria said then. "My heart goes out to her."

"She almost had you pay dearly," Phil said, "for a crime which you did not commit. Why would your heart go out to her?"

"Well, first of all, I'm a priest," said Gloria, "so I'm *supposed* to be that way. But also, there she is in that big old lonely house, sister's dead, boyfriend's a monster, and now people in her hometown think of her as that crazy lady who accused an innocent priest of murder. That has to be tough, don't you think? Don't you kind of feel for her a little?"

Phil shrugged. "I don't think I would feel sorry for her if she'd put me in jail."

Gloria sat back and smiled. "Jail's not so bad."

"Yes," I said. "I found out just how much you know about that particular subject from Father Davis. Hey! I just realized that Jennifer's last name is Davis too!"

"They're not related," Gloria assured me.

"Yeah," I said, "but it's an interesting coincidence, considering how much they both did to help in our effort to liberate you."

"I should call Father Davis," Gloria reflected, more to herself than to us. "Let him know I'm okay."

"From my conversation with him," I said, "I think he'd like that."

"I'm always a little melancholy in the spring," Phil said, apropos of nothing. "I know you're supposed to be jolly, but I always have a gentle or almost loving sadness."

Gloria sat up a little. "Why do you think that is?"

"That's easy," Phil told her. "At my age, with all the things

I've seen and done, I see the autumnal end of every new leaf or rosebud or robin's egg. All the newborn things that are so glorious in their April youth, they'll all come to fallen leaves and broken petals and pieces of shell on the ground. Life's only goal, it often seems to me, is to constantly remind us of death."

David laughed. "That's it, Philomena," he said. "I'm turning over all my philological credentials to you right now."

"Your *what*?" she asked him.

"My poetic license," he said.

Gloria turned to me. "You have to get a *license* for that?"

"That was beautiful, what you just said," David told Phil, ignoring Gloria's sad attempt at humor, "about spring melancholy. Just beautiful."

There was a sudden rustle from a darker part of the yard, and then, one by one, seven rabbits emerged from the thicket at the back of the lawn. They began to make their slow way toward my parsley plants. We all watched as they drew near. Then, just when they hit the last amber beam of light from the waning sun, three of them stood up on their hind legs for a moment and sniffed.

"'To feel that the light is a rabbit-light,'" David said softly and to the rabbits, "'in which everything is meant for you and nothing need be explained.'"

"What's that?" Gloria asked a little too loudly. "Is that your poetry?"

"God, no," he said. "That's Wallace Stevens. When I was younger I did everything I could to imitate his work."

"Not now?" Phil asked.

"No." Then David turned to me, put his hand on my shoulder, and smiled. "No. Now my poetry just . . . *is*."

We sat there after that, all four of us, without saying

anything. We watched the rabbits eat their fill of parsley, and then they went for some sort of grass that was growing wild in the yard. Daylight crept away slowly, and the rabbits—maybe because they were content with what they'd eaten or maybe because they heard an owl in the pine tree next door—retreated into the thicket.

The breeze picked up suddenly then, and it was so filled with the scent of the newly planted roses in the front yard that all four of us sat up, breathed deeply, and sighed, smiling.

Because it was spring.

ACKNOWLEDGMENTS

Grateful acknowledgment is made to Keith Kahla not just for editing this book but for all the books we've worked on together; to the late Janet Reid; to the current Jennifer Weltz. Acknowledgment is also made to the Georgia Council for the Arts, which placed the author in dozens of small towns all over Georgia as a writer in residence. During those residences, the author met and fell in love with most of the people in this book.

ABOUT THE AUTHOR

P. J. Nelson is the pseudonym of an award-winning actor, dramatist, professor, and novelist (among many other professions) who has done just about everything except run a bookstore. He lives in Decatur, Georgia.